THE ROAD TO SCANDAL IS PAVED WITH WICKED INTENTIONS

MERRY FARMER

THE ROAD TO SCANDAL IS PAVED WITH WICKED INTENTIONS

Cover design by Erin Dameron-Hill (the miracle-worker)

ASIN: B086H3K6Y5

Paperback ISBN: 9798685351968

Click here for a complete list of other works by Merry Farmer.

If you'd like to be the first to learn about when the next books in the series come out and more, please sign up for my newsletter here: http://eepurl.com/RQ-KX

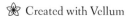 Created with Vellum

CHAPTER 1

London – June, 1887

LADY PHOEBE DARLINGTON HAD ALWAYS HAD AN exquisite eye for fashion. Even as a young girl, she had pored over *La Mode* and all of the other fashion magazines coming out of Paris, London, and even New York. She'd done her very best to dress impeccably and carry herself with grace, even when her family's fortunes began to slip. The less money her profligate father gave to her and her mother, the harder Phoebe worked to make the best of what few pieces of clothing they had. She'd learned to make gloves last for months beyond their standard lifetime, hats look refreshed and new, even though they were years old, and faded, old dresses seem straight off the modiste's mannequin.

Phoebe knew fashion, which was why it was no surprise to her that she found herself standing behind a counter at Harrods department store instead of in front of it, selling gloves to the women she had once counted as her peers instead of purchasing them for herself.

"We've just received this shipment from Paris," she informed Lady Eastleigh in a sophisticated yet humble voice as she took a box of fresh, white, kid gloves from the wide shelf behind her. As she set the display box on the counter, she peeked at Lady Eastleigh. "As you can see, the workmanship is second to none."

"Yes, I can see that," Lady Eastleigh said without looking at Phoebe. She picked through the gloves with an almost careless air, caressing a few of the ones with embroidered cuffs with a hand sheathed in a glove that Phoebe could have made use of for months more. Lady Eastleigh didn't need new things, but making purchases was a symbol of wealth and status.

Phoebe knew that as definitively as she knew how reduced her own circumstances were, and she knew how to make the most of it.

"I think you would find these silk gloves particularly interesting, my lady," she said, bending to take a special tray of ridiculously expensive gloves from a compartment under the counter. She set the tray on the table and peeked at Lady Eastleigh again. "As I understand it, Lady Germaine will be hosting a ball next Friday, and I can say with absolute certainty that none of the people I expect to be on her guest list have so much as looked at these gloves."

"Oh?" Lady Eastleigh glanced directly at her for the first time.

"You would be an original," Phoebe added with a modest tilt of her head.

Lady Eastleigh studied her for a moment with a mixture of calculation and pity in her eyes. Phoebe knew the look well. It was the way that almost all of her former acquaintances looked at her—as though she were an embarrassment to their class, and yet someone who still spoke their language and could be of use. Indeed, even though Phoebe had never once in her entire life felt as though she belonged in the upper echelons of society, ever since her fall a year before, she had made a point of keeping abreast of the gossip and social life of high society. The information wasn't accessible to any of the other shop girls at Harrods, and it had served her well.

"I'll take these," Lady Eastleigh said, selecting a pair of lavender silk gloves decorated with silver embroidery. "And these and these as well." She selected two more pairs from the white kid gloves.

"Excellent choices, my lady," Phoebe told the woman with a smile she hoped was pleasant. "One moment while I ring them up for you."

In a flash, Lady Eastleigh's expression was veiled once more, as though the gilt of Phoebe's former life had flaked off, leaving her as nothing more than a lowly shop girl. Any hint of recognition disappeared from Lady East-leigh's eyes, and she turned away from the counter, as though it were beneath her to be seen conversing with the girl behind the counter. Even if that girl was the daughter of a marquess and had once attended parties at Eastleigh House.

It still stung. A year after taking up the position at Harrods and bidding goodbye to her old life, it still hurt to be snubbed. Not that she hadn't been snubbed wher-ever she went before the money ran out. Phoebe's father, Lord Darlington, had been as bad as they came. He'd rung up debts all over England and the continent, alien-ated all of his peers of good taste and good standing, and generally made a nuisance of himself through bad debts, worse wine, and loose women. His decline had been such that society began turning their backs on Phoebe and her mother long before her father's death. And once he had finally expired—dead of a heart attack in the bed of a prostitute he'd engaged at Piccadilly Circus, a prostitute who wore a dress but allegedly was not a woman—society had washed their hands of Phoebe and her mother and hadn't looked back. All that was left of the Darlington fortune were debts and an estate that was entailed away to some fourth cousin no one had been able to find yet. Phoebe and her mother had been forced to fend for themselves.

Which meant Phoebe had been forced to fend for both of them, since all her mother could manage to do was squander what little money they had left, wring her hands, and complain about her lot in life. Harrods and a second-rate boarding house in Marylebone were the only options left to them.

"Here you go, my lady." Phoebe handed Lady Eastleigh her wrapped purchases after payment was exchanged. She managed to keep her smile, even as Lady Eastleigh took her parcel and walked away without so much as a grin.

Phoebe's smile dropped into a wistful sigh.

She snapped straight a moment later at the sound of her manager, Mr. Waters, clearing his throat. He frowned at her and shook his head, warning her to keep the proper demeanor. Phoebe plastered on a pleasant smile for him, in spite of the melancholy in her heart, and turned to face the new customers approaching her counter.

"May I help—"

She stopped dead and her heart sank at the sight of Lady Jane Hocksley and Lady Maude Carmichael. Her two former acquaintances approached the counter with sly, demeaning grins. They exchanged a look that said they were looking forward to the cruel sport they were about to engage in.

"I'd like to purchase some gloves," Jane said with a sneer, tilting her nose up. "Show me your latest styles."

"Yes," Maude echoed imperiously. "Show us."

Phoebe shot a covert glance to Mr. Waters—who was watching the exchange intently—before dipping into a slight curtsy and turning to the shelves behind her.

"It's perfectly scandalous," Lady Jane said once

Phoebe's back was turned. "I've never seen anything like it before."

Phoebe's heart sank, and she let herself take longer to select a tray of gloves than she normally would have.

"I would be too embarrassed to show my face out of doors again if it'd happened to me," Lady Maude agreed.

"As would I," Lady Jane sniffed. "But I am certain that every word of the story is true. Millicent always was like that."

Phoebe frowned, choosing a tray and turning to set it on the counter. As she did, she noticed Lady Maude leafing through a newspaper of some sort that was tinted pink.

"Don't let your mama see you with that," Lady Jane warned her. "She would expire of an attack of the vapors."

"Everyone is reading *Nocturne*," Lady Maude said, folding the paper and tucking it under her arm.

"*Nocturne?*" Phoebe asked.

Lady Jane and Lady Maude reacted to her simple question as though Phoebe had asked them to show their knickers. Mr. Waters cleared his throat, causing Phoebe's cheeks to flare red.

"How dare you engage us in conversation?" Lady Jane said.

"Yes," Lady Maude agreed. "Do your job." She sniffed, then added, "I doubt that a shop girl like you would be able to find or afford the sort of shocking literary sensation that has all of high society buzzing."

"Yes, my ladies," Phoebe said, her voice hoarse. She glanced to Mr. Waters, but there was nothing more she could do except pretend her former acquaintances weren't trying to deliberately goad her. "As it happens, my ladies, this fine selection of kid gloves has just arrived from Paris." She gestured to the box she'd taken off the shelf, and then to the one Lady Eastleigh had looked through. "These as well."

"I don't want those," Jane snapped. "They look as though every cheap working-class girl has rifled through them." Her mouth twitched into a grin as she directed her insult toward Phoebe. "Show me something new."

"These are our latest acquisitions," Phoebe said, her voice going hoarse and her face hot.

"She said she doesn't want those," Maude snapped.

Mr. Waters cleared his throat yet again—Phoebe was growing to hate the sound—adding humiliation to the pile already pressing down on Phoebe. She nodded silently to Jane and Maude, then turned to take a second box down from the shelves. With three trays of merchandise already on the counter, Phoebe had to shuffle what was in her hands and maneuver the tray of silk gloves back under the counter. Jane and Maude seemed to find her work amusing. They snorted to each other and giggled behind their hands.

"As you can see," Phoebe told them, face burning, "what we have here are some of the most delicate and fresh styles the season has to offer."

"I don't like them," Jane said with a sniff. "They look cheap to me." She stared straight at Phoebe as she spoke.

There was no denying the game her former acquaintances were playing. They hadn't come to purchase gloves, they'd come to gawk at her and tweak her about *Nocturne*, whatever the journal was. Not a week went by when fine ladies of society didn't come by to stare at the daughter of a marquess who had been forced into common employment to survive. Phoebe supposed she could have taken a more traditional route and retired with her mother to a country cottage to live out the rest of her days in genteel poverty. Or she could have married whatever loathsome lord wanted a bride, as her mother kept insisting she do. But Phoebe had far too much pride to marry the sort of men who were still interested in her, now that she didn't have a penny to her name, and she was much too stubborn to starve. She had other talents that she'd only discovered when push came to shove.

"I'm so sorry these gloves don't meet with your approval," she told Jane and Maude, her eyes downcast. "Only, Lady Eastleigh just purchased two pairs of these kid gloves and one of the silk. And earlier, Lady Clerkenwell expressed an interest in this pair with the crewel work on the cuff." She glanced up and met Jane's eyes. "I hinted that I would save this pair for Lady Clerkenwell, but—"

Jane made a disgusted noise. "I would sooner see something this fine on swine's feet." She sniffed. "It's only a matter of time before Lady Clerkenwell shows up in the pages of *Nocturne*." She peeked at Phoebe as if to judge whether her comment had the desired effect of making Phoebe jealous over being left out. Phoebe pretended she hadn't noticed at all. Disappointed, Lady Jane went on. "I'll take them." She paused. "And this pair as well."

"And I like these. And these," Maude added.

"As you wish," Phoebe said, eyes still downcast. She knew Jane well enough to know that if Lady Clerkenwell, formerly Bianca Marlowe, her sworn enemy, wanted something, Jane would snatch it up. Knowing the rivalries of the upper class as well as their social goings on had helped Phoebe to make enough commission from selling gloves to pay the rent on the respectable boarding house where she and her mother lived.

"I must wear these to the May Flowers meeting next Thursday," Jane said with a vicious grin. "Lady Clerkenwell will be green with envy."

"I hear Lady Clerkenwell is green with illness from a particular condition yet again," Maude sneered in return. "Honestly, the woman is obscene with her fecundity."

Phoebe kept her expression neutral at the news. She's always liked Bianca Marlowe, and if she were honest, she was envious of the happiness Bianca had found in her marriage, as unconventional as it was. Her own chances for a marriage that wasn't a complete humiliation had evaporated along with her father's money.

"I do wish Claudia would get on with things and make a full break with the rest of the May Flowers,"

Maude said with a sigh. "She keeps threatening to break entirely, then going back on that decision and dragging us all back into odious company."

"Claudia enjoys conflict," Jane said with a knowing look, seeming to forget Phoebe was still listening and knew whom they were speaking about. "Honestly, how she can even show her face in society, after the debacle with her brother is—"

"Phoebe!"

Jane and Maude's gossip, as well as Phoebe's work wrapping their purchases, was sharply interrupted as Phoebe's mother charged down the aisle, drawing attention as she went. Phoebe winced as not only Mr. Waters, but Hilda—who worked the counter across from Phoebe's, selling handkerchiefs—and Imogen—who stood behind the counter next to Phoebe's, selling stockings—glanced up from their customers to see what was going on.

"Phoebe, look who I've found," her mother fluttered on, far too loud, pushing her way through a few ladies studying the wares for sale. "You remember Lord Cosgrove."

Phoebe blanched and shot a quick look to Jane and Maude. The two women lit with amusement, exchanging laughing looks and covering their mouths with their hands. But the true source of her horror was the man walking through the aisle of ladies' finery with her mother.

"Lord Cosgrove," she said shakily as her mother brought the man to a stop at the end of her counter.

"My dear Lady Phoebe. What a pleasure it is to see you again," Lord Cosgrove said with a wolfish smile. He was a friend of her father's, inasmuch as her father had had friends. His grey hair was slick with something that looked like boot-black and parted in a fashion popular with men half his age. In fact, everything from the way the old roué was dressed to the way he carried himself suggested a man far past his prime who was attempting to present himself as still in the flush of youth, which he most certainly wasn't.

Jane and Maude could hardly contain their amusement. Phoebe swallowed hard and rang up their purchases, eager to get rid of them before her mother diminished her even more in their eyes. But even after their gloves were paid for, they lingered by the edge of the counter to watch the show.

"You cannot imagine how overjoyed I was to see our old friend again," Phoebe's mother went on in a rush. "I was thrilled to encounter Lord Cosgrove in Green Park just now."

"It was a fortuitous meeting," Lord Cosgrove said, sending a smile to Phoebe's mother before turning a more appraising look on Phoebe. The look made her skin crawl.

"When Lord Cosgrove asked about you, I had to bring him to see you right away," her mother went on. "Can you believe that he paid our cab fare to come all this way? I haven't ridden in a cab in ages," she sighed wistfully.

Phoebe's face heated even more than it already was. To admit in front of acquaintances like Jane and Maude, and Lord Cosgrove, that they couldn't afford cab fare was as good as admitting the extent of their poverty.

"I'm glad to see you looking so well, Lady Phoebe," Lord Cosgrove said, raking her with a look that left Phoebe repulsed. "The summer sun agrees with you."

It was as though he'd shot another arrow into her already wounded body. Yes, Phoebe was well aware that she'd lost the porcelain complexion of a lady of means, thanks to being forced to walk from Marylebone to Kensington for work nearly every day. "Thank you," she mumbled, not knowing what else to say.

"I told Lord Cosgrove that you'd be happy to see him," her mother went on, evidently not seeing how ragingly uncomfortable Phoebe was. "And see, I was right." She giggled and glanced to Lord Cosgrove.

Phoebe prayed for sudden death. It would have been less embarrassing than the attention she was getting. "It is good to see you again, my lord," she said, the same way she would speak to a customer. She darted a glance to Mr. Waters, who was only barely tolerating the conversation.

"I also told Lord Cosgrove that you would be delighted to walk out with him," her mother said.

Phoebe's eyes snapped wide. "Mama," she hissed. There was no way to dress her mother down the way she wanted to, though. She could only smile vacantly at Lord Cosgrove and say, "I'm afraid I am at work at the moment."

Jane and Maude, who were still watching, giggled.

"Perfectly understandable," Lord Cosgrove said. "Perhaps some other time." He glanced to Phoebe's mother. "Now that I have made your mother's acquaintance again, I'm certain we will have ample opportunity for further encounters."

Phoebe wanted to groan at the words. What had her mother done?

"This nonsense about working is unimportant," her mother balked. "Surely there is someone else who can fiddle with gloves while you engage in more important matters." She glanced sideways at Lord Cosgrove with a look of urgency. Phoebe knew exactly what her mother had in mind and rebelled at the idea.

"I'm afraid leaving work is entirely out of the question, Mama," she said. She gambled on glancing in Mr. Waters's direction.

Blessedly, the man stepped forward from his position. He cleared his throat and addressed her mother and Lord Cosgrove. "I'm terribly sorry to be a nuisance, my lord, but I must ask that you either make a purchase or kindly leave my staff alone to tend to other customers." He nodded to a pair of ladies hovering near the counter.

"Yes, yes, of course," Lord Cosgrove said, nodding to the man, then turning a wide smile on Phoebe. "We will speak again soon."

"I'm certain you will," Phoebe's mother said.

It took a few more, threatening looks from Mr. Waters to get the pair to leave. Once they departed, Jane and Maude left as well, seeing as the show was over. Phoebe was relieved to be able to turn her attention to the waiting customers, but before they approached the counter, Mr. Waters tapped her arm and dragged her aside.

"I'm so sorry, sir," Phoebe said before the man could chastise her. "I did not expect my mother to arrive like that."

Mr. Waters pursed his lips, clearly annoyed, but perhaps a tiny bit sympathetic. "I understand your circumstances, Miss Darlington. Truly, I do. But need I remind you, yet again, that this is a place of business and not a social club?"

"No, Mr. Waters. I understand, sir." Phoebe kept her head lowered. She'd asked to be called Miss Darlington instead of Lady Phoebe when she was hired, but there was still something soul-crushing in hearing herself addressed as such by a man whom her former self would hardly have noticed. That woman was long gone now.

Mr. Waters let out an impatient breath. "You are far and away our best sales girl," he said. "I've never seen anyone as adept at selling sundries as you are, Miss Darlington."

"Thank you, sir?" Phoebe glanced up at him, not certain if he meant his words as a compliment or not.

Mr. Water's expression was tight with impatience. "If

you were not as skilled at sales as you are, Miss Darlington, I would have sacked you months ago."

Phoebe's spirits sank all over again. It was a harsh reality that her position in life, such as it was, now depended on the whims of a man as surely as it had when her father frittered away his money and his reputation.

"I will do better, sir," she said, because it was the only thing she could say.

Mr. Waters nodded and returned to his position. Phoebe dragged herself back to her counter and put on a smile to serve her next customers. Inwardly, she wanted to weep. Nothing had gone right in her life since long before her father died. Every which way she turned, misery and misfortune seemed to befall her. But she'd pushed through so far. She was determined to keep pushing through as well.

That thought stayed with her for the remaining hour of her shift. It bolstered her as she gathered her things from the employee dressing room reserved for Harrods' female staff. It even stayed with her as she headed out into a dreary afternoon. Thick, grey clouds hung low over London, giving the entire city a depressed air. The streets of Mayfair and the greens of Hyde Park might have been cheery and beautiful, but once she passed on to the narrow passageways between Brook Street and Oxford Street, the pragmatic, commercial side of London became more pronounced, giving it a dirty, dreary, and utilitarian quality.

To make matters worse, as she hurried up Oxford

Street, a commotion due to a collision between several carriages forced her to make a long and arduous detour up toward Fitzrovia just as the skies opened and rain poured down.

"Blast," Phoebe muttered, clapping a hand to her already battered hat, wishing she had an umbrella. Her only umbrella had broken the week before, though, and she had yet to save up enough to purchase a new one.

The rain quickly shifted from a light patter to a full downpour, threatening to soak Phoebe to the bone. All she could do was dash for the nearest shelter, a pub with a shingle over the door that read The Watchman. She only barely managed to avoid getting soaked enough to look like a drowned rat before leaping into the pub, though her threadbare coat and her hat dripped all over the pub's floor. That wasn't what caused her to gasp and question her wisdom in ducking into a pub to stay out of the rain, though. Instead, it was the man who glanced up at her from one of the tables near the front of the pub.

CHAPTER 2

"The shipping investments are coming along well. The stake you purchased in Riverton Shipping Enterprise is paying off nicely. But as I've said several times before, your portfolio's strength is and always has been your family's real estate investments."

Daniel Long nodded as his man of business, Oswald Tuttle, ran through the piles of reports and ledgers strewn across one of the tables in the pub. Everything was in order as far as Danny could see, though he liked hearing Tuttle explain it all during their weekly meetings.

"How are the properties in Belgravia doing?" he asked, focusing on the list of costs and income generated by the investment he'd made in the area a year ago.

Tuttle shuffled through the papers on the table until he found the report he was looking for. "Very well, all things considered," he said with a smile. "I must admire your acumen, once again, in knowing exactly where to

17

purchase land, when to purchase it, and what to build on it, Mr. Long."

Danny shrugged. "There's a housing crisis. People need to live somewhere. Anyone who pays attention can see where the next big market for houses will be."

He was playing down his knack for investment and he knew it. Tuttle knew it as well. Danny was the third generation of Longs to invest in real estate and come out on top. The family legacy had started when his great-grandfather and namesake had won the deed to a small property on Oxford Street in a mad-capped card game. Rumor had it that he'd won a woman in the process, but Great-Granddad had only been a green lad at the time, and since another man was in love with the woman in question, he'd gladly handed her over.

Great-Granddad had taken over the running of the Oxford Street pub, reinvesting the profits in the building adjacent to the pub. Danny's grandfather had purchased the buildings on either side of those two and expanded the family holdings. His father had reinvested those profits in bits and pieces of land around the outskirts of the burgeoning city, growing the family fortune exponentially. But Danny was the first of the family to be sent to university on the profits. And though he hadn't gone anywhere as grand as Oxford or Cambridge, and while his snooty classmates had snubbed him for his lower-class accent and habits, he'd learned more about investing, financial markets, and compound interest than any of his forbearers.

Danny was the one who had turned a comfortable portfolio of London properties into a real estate empire. He was the one who bought up half of what was now West London before any other investor had an inkling that the property would be worth anything. Danny had the Midas touch, and unbeknownst to just about anyone, other than Tuttle and a few of his closest friends, he was in the running for the wealthiest man in London.

Lower-class accent, rough demeanor, ribald sense of humor, and all.

And he still conducted all of his business out of his beloved pub in humble Fitzrovia.

But something was missing. He'd felt it for a while, but couldn't quite put his finger on it.

"What's next?" he asked Tuttle, glancing across the neat ledgers and carefully compiled information spread on the table in front of him. "What hill are we going to climb now?"

Maybe if he could find a new investment to master or a new project to excite him, he wouldn't feel the gaping hole in his chest. There had to be more than investments and money. He had more of that than he needed. It wasn't even fun to spend it anymore.

"There's always Earl's Court," Tuttle said with a shrug, sifting through the papers in front of him and taking out a clipping from *The Times*. "By all reports, Earl's Court is a veritable gold mine right now. They can't build those terraced houses fast enough down there."

"So we should jump into those waters," Danny said, taking the clipping from Tuttle and reading through it with lightning speed. That was another trick he'd mastered. He could read faster than anyone else he knew and recall whatever he'd read at a moment's notice. Him, a man who most of the toffs who danced in and out of his pub, thinking they'd have a laugh by slumming it for a night, assumed couldn't read at all. Then again, Danny had always loved being underestimated by the high and mighty, and anyone with a stick up their arses, the way most noblemen had.

"That's what I recommend," Tuttle said. "There is a particular parcel of land I think you'd be interested in. Parliament will be holding a hearing soon to decide which company to grant the building contracts to. It's here, relatively close to the new Earl's Court Exhibition Centre."

Danny's brow shot up. "That is valuable property."

"And you could easily win the contracts to develop it," Tuttle said. "If you ask me, the area needs a man with a vision like yours to make something of it."

A vision like his. Danny grinned at the idea, but it was hard to keep his grin in place. He kept buying properties, building on them, and selling the houses for a profit. Over and over. It was lucrative, but it was growing repetitive. There had to be something else to do with his life besides making money. He'd made it, now he wanted to enjoy it. He wanted acknowledgement too, if he were honest with himself. Secret wealth was no fun at all. But the idea of breaking into society left him cold. Why? What was the point? Those people would never accept a man like him, no matter how much cash he had. He was and always would be inferior in their eyes, a dressed-up dog that they could kick whenever they wanted to. There had to be something else he could do, some other way he could—

His thoughts were cut short as the door to his pub flew open, bringing with it the sound of rain pounding on the street and buildings outside. The rush of sound lasted only a moment before the door shut again. And there she was, framed against the dark wood, soggy and bedraggled, but strikingly beautiful. Her blond hair was damp under the ugliest hat Danny had ever seen, but the rain that soaked her lightweight coat only served to highlight her glorious shape.

And then she glanced up at him, her green eyes sparkling with shock to find him staring at her. Her cheeks were pink from walking and her lips were parted just enough to be tempting as she flinched under his gaze.

"Hello," Danny said, standing abruptly and abandoning the table, his business, and Tuttle. He stepped around an empty table, feeling like he couldn't reach her side fast enough. "What brings a bird like you into a rough and tumble place like this in the middle of a Wednesday afternoon, love?" he asked, his accent sharp with cockney drawl.

"I…er…that is…it's raining," she said in a soft, refined

voice, twisting to point out the window in the pub's front door. "I don't have an umbrella."

"Well, come inside and sit by the fire then," Danny said, moving closer to her than he should and gesturing toward the small, crackling fire on one side of his mostly-empty pub. It was too early in the day for the crowds that thronged the place in the evening to be there yet, which was why he and Tuttle were conducting business out in the open instead of in his cramped back office, but the few patrons who were there glanced up from their pints and pies to take a look at the unusual newcomer.

"I shouldn't stay long," she said, seeming to shrink in on herself as Danny shuffled her over to the table closest to the fireplace. "Only until the rain stops." She unbuttoned her long overcoat.

"You can stay as long as you'd like, Lady Darlington," Danny said, breaking into a wide, sly smile.

As he expected, Lady Phoebe Darlington started as he called her by name, pausing in the act of removing her coat. "It's actually Lady Phoebe, not—" She blinked. "You...you know who I am?"

"Of course I do, love." He winked. "We met last year, at Lady Clerkenwell's benefit for orphans. Don't you remember?"

He would never forget. It had been a fleeting encounter. He'd been bellowing away at anyone who passed by, bullying them into donating as much money as they could, and then some, to Bianca's cause. Lady Phoebe had happened by with her mother. He'd been struck by her beauty in an instant. Admittedly, he had teased her in an attempt to get her to donate to the cause before being informed that she and her mother were, in fact, as poor as church mice. The brief encounter had driven home the point to him that it didn't matter what class someone was born into these days, how much money and security they had was more about effort than birth.

Phoebe blinked at him in confusion before sudden understanding dawned in her eyes. "Oh." Her already pink cheeks flushed deeper, stirring purely male appreciation deep in Danny's gut. "Oh, I do remember. Mr. Long, is it?" She finished removing her coat.

"You can call me Danny, love," he said in an overly friendly tone, taking her coat and draping it over an empty chair before pulling out a seat at the table by the fire for her. He leaned far closer than he should have to her as she sat. "All my friends do."

"I couldn't possibly do that," she said, flustered.

"Course you can." Danny nudged her chair in, then sat on the edge of the table facing her. Perhaps it made him a lout, but he rather liked the difference their positions made in their height. She had to crane her neck to look up at him. "How does it go in your circles? We've already been formally introduced," he affected an upper-class accent and attitude. "So you're free to call me by a more familiar name and talk to me like we're friends."

Phoebe blinked again, probably startled by his change in accent. Everyone was when he talked proper. He loved shocking the sunshine out of the nobs by presenting himself like one of them now and then.

Just as he was beginning to enjoy Phoebe's surprise, her whole countenance sagged. "They're not my circle anymore."

An uncomfortable twist hit Danny's gut. Come to think of it, he had heard some of his upper-class friends mention something about Darlington at some point. He shifted to sit in the chair beside her, gesturing for Bess, one of his bar maids, to fetch them some refreshments.

"What happened, then, love?" he asked, back to his rough and tumble self.

Phoebe eyed him suspiciously, but she didn't shy away or get up and leave. "I wouldn't want to bother you with my problems."

Danny didn't like the way she looked down. Lady Phoebe Darlington wasn't meant to be downcast, not at all. "It's no trouble," he said, his desire to tease her giving way to a genuine need to hear her story. "And it's not like you've got much else to do until this rain ends."

She glanced up, looking out the nearest window. "It doesn't seem to be letting up," she said in a somewhat distant voice. "It doesn't ever seem to want to let up."

Alarm bells sounded in Danny's chest. He didn't need his university degree to see sadness in the poor woman's eyes. "Tell me," he said, reaching out to cover her tiny, gloved hands with one of his own.

Phoebe's eyes went wide for a moment and her hands

tensed under his. She stole a furtive look at him. A moment later, she let out a breath.

"I don't suppose it could do any harm," she said, clearly speaking to herself. She swallowed, then glanced to Danny. "If you know my name, I would assume you know my circumstances as well."

Danny shrugged. "Father died, leaving you and your mum with nothing but debts. No family to come to your rescue. Not exactly the darling of high society. Did I get that right?"

Her shoulders sagged and she glanced down at her hands, which she'd pulled away from his and into her lap. "Yes, I'm afraid you did," she said, barely above a whisper. "Mama and I currently reside at a boarding house in Marylebone. I pay our rent by working at Harrods."

Danny was impressed and let it show in his expression. "That's a damn sight more than most women in your position would be able to say."

She glanced suddenly up at him. "That's not the reaction I get from most people when I confess how low I've sunk."

"How low you've sunk?" Danny laughed. "Love, you could be selling yourself instead of, what, ladies' knickers?"

She flushed a deep shade of scarlet and looked away.

"Sorry," he said, no idea why he felt such a need to apologize. "I'm no better than a street urchin, I know." He slouched back in his chair, shaping his posture and his expression to exactly what she must have thought he was

—a lewd, crass bounder. He didn't mind playing that part. It was far more fun than playing the stuffed gentleman.

"Apparently, I'm no better than a street urchin now as well," she said, barely above a whisper.

"Come now, sweetheart. You're much better than that." He shouldn't have, but he leered at her just a little to prove his point. In his experience, a woman liked feeling appreciated by a man, no matter how high-born they were. "You've got gainful employment," he pointed out. "You look as though you take care of yourself. And if you're living in one of those places in Marylebone, you've obviously maintained your respectability. I'd say you're quite a catch."

He held his breath, waiting to see if she'd be soothed or offended.

She smiled weakly, sending him a shy look that had his trousers tightening in the best possible way. "Thank you. I think you're the first person to see all of my efforts as a good thing instead of an embarrassment to my former class and standing."

Her words and the sadness with which they were spoken made Danny want to punch someone. He hated the upper classes and their stodgy rules and prejudices. Poor Phoebe had obviously been cast off by that set, but aside from the handful of gentlemen he knew and welcomed into his pub with open arms whenever they came to visit, she was the finest example of that barmy class that he'd ever seen.

"Here you are," Bess said, sidling over to the table with a tray laden with treats. She set the tray down and proceeded to unload two delicious-looking sausage pies and two pints of beer for him and Phoebe. "Have a care with the pies. They've just come out of the oven."

"Oh, I couldn't possibly—" Phoebe reached up to refuse the refreshments just as Bess moved the pint in front of her. Their hands collided, and a generous splash of beer spilled across Phoebe's skirt.

"Oh, dear," Danny said, leaning suddenly forward. "We can't have that."

He snagged the towel tucked into Bess's apron and proceeded to dab at the wet spot on Phoebe's skirt. Bess grinned knowingly and hurried away from the table.

"I'm sorry," Phoebe said, distressed, but not at the way Danny more or less manhandled her. "I'm so sorry. I don't know how I've become so clumsy of late. Nothing seems to go my way anymore."

She was near tears, which tugged at something deep within Danny. Something beyond lust or teasing. Something that seemed to fit right into that emptiness inside of him.

"It's nothing to worry about, love," he said, finishing cleaning her skirt and tossing the towel on the empty table next to them. "Here. Eat up. Drink some beer. It'll make you feel much better."

"I'm afraid I don't consume alcohol," she said, too embarrassed to meet his eyes.

"Whyever not?" he laughed, sliding her pint in front

of her, then picking up his own and taking a swig. "This is the good stuff."

She peeked mournfully up at him. "I'm afraid the boarding house where Mama and I live has a strict temperance policy."

"Bloody hell," Danny growled, then downed a large swig of beer. "That's no way to live."

"I'm afraid it's the best we can do right now," Phoebe sighed.

The sound and the sight of her looking so defeated made him want to wrap her in his arms and never let her go. "Where did you say you work again?" he asked, the light of an idea in his eyes.

"Harrods," she said. "Selling gloves, not knickers." The ghost of a grin flitted across her face. It was the most beautiful thing Danny had seen all day.

"Harrods," he repeated. "Well, if you can't drink this very fine beer, at least you can eat some of this delicious pie." He picked up one of the forks Bess had brought along with the food and handed it to her.

Phoebe's beautiful face turned red all over again. "I'm afraid I cannot pay for it."

Danny snorted. "There's no money between friends, and we've established that we're friends. Consider this my treat. Now eat up. You look famished, and I won't have any of my friends looking famished."

Phoebe smiled and took the fork from him. The simple expression and gesture did amazing things to his heart and to his cock. He wasn't too proud to admit that he wanted her. A man would be a fool not to want a woman as magnificent as Lady Phoebe Darlington. But he wasn't a brute, in spite of his background. He would look, but he wouldn't dare to touch.

"You really are too kind, Mr. Long," she said, cracking the crust of her pie with the side of her fork.

"It's Danny, remember?" he told her, taking up his own fork and breaking into the pie Bess had set in front of him. He'd need to put something in his mouth in order to stop himself from leaning into her and stealing a kiss. Phoebe deserved more than a bounder like him taking liberties.

Truthfully, he suspected that what she probably deserved was a long night of thorough love-making that left her breathless and floating on a cloud of satisfaction. If she'd been any other woman, he'd have offered it all to her right then and there. But there was something more about Phoebe, something he would have to investigate as carefully as he did any of his new investments. He had a feeling that she was as precious as any land and just as ripe for development. But she was a lady, and if he wanted her, he would have to woo her.

He loved the idea.

CHAPTER 3

*I*t was nearly dark by the time Phoebe left The Watchman pub and the kindness of Mr. Long to scurry home. The very last thing she'd expected when taking shelter in a pub was to have the owner offer her food and drink, a place to dry off by the fire, and a shoulder to cry on. Even though she didn't actually cry. It embarrassed her to think about it as she ducked and dodged her way through foot traffic made up of businessmen returning home from The City for the night, but she had spilled out more of her tragic story to Mr. Long than she'd intended to. In spite of his rough ways, too-wide smiles, and clear lack of breeding, he'd exhibited more kindness toward her than anyone had for years.

Thoughts of Mr. Long's kindness—as well as his mischievous, blue eyes, dark hair that curled wildly in a startlingly unfashionable way, and expressive mouth—

were at the forefront of her mind as she stepped into the foyer of Mrs. Jones's boarding house only to find Mrs. Jones herself standing with her arms crossed, a deep frown creasing her brow.

"I'm terribly sorry, Mrs. Jones," Phoebe said in a rush. "There was an accident on Oxford Street that necessitated a detour, and then the rain began to pour down."

"It is after six o'clock, Miss Darlington," Mrs. Jones snapped. In spite of her mother's protests, Phoebe had insisted that Mrs. Jones address her as "Miss" instead of "Lady", the same as she had with Mr. Waters. And like Mr. Waters, Phoebe cringed every time the fussy old matron referred to her that way. But that was the price she paid to give herself the mental distance from her old, dead life that she needed to carry on. "You know the rules about curfew," Mrs. Jones continued.

"Yes, madam, I do, and again, I am so sorry," Phoebe said in a rush, unbuttoning her long coat and shaking the last of the rain from it.

Mrs. Jones wrinkled her nose and sniffed. "What is that horrid smell?"

"It's—" Phoebe paused, her mouth open. It was beer from where the barmaid had spilled on her skirt, and likely cigar smoke as well, as a few of the patrons who had come into The Watchman as she finished her complimentary supper had been smoking.

Understanding dawned in Mrs. Jones's eyes. She pulled herself up to her full height and tilted her head so that she could look down her nose at Phoebe. "You smell like a pub," she said through clenched teeth.

"As I said," Phoebe began in a wary voice, "the rain began to pour before I could reach home. I was forced to wait out the storm in a pub."

"Miss Darlington," Mrs. Jones snapped. "You know my rules about illicit entertainment."

"I only took shelter in the pub for an hour or so, madam."

"Consumption of alcohol of any sort by my boarders is strictly prohibited."

"I didn't consume anything. I had beer spilled on my skirt." Phoebe turned to show Mrs. Jones the stain on her skirt—a stain she would have to figure out how to wash out, as she only had three skirts total to her name.

"Carousing with rough crowds, such as the sort of men who frequent pubs, is expressly forbidden as well," Mrs. Jones went on, crossing her arms.

"I know, Mrs. Jones, and believe me, if there had been any other options—"

"I do *not* allow loose women to board with me, Miss Darlington."

Phoebe could see the writing on the wall and gave up the fight. Her shoulders sagged and she lowered her head and said, "Yes, Mrs. Jones."

"Profligate manners and low morals have no place under my roof," Mrs. Jones said with a sniff.

"Yes, madam." Phoebe lowered her head farther,

knowing only absolute humility would get her out of the situation.

"I would expect more from a daughter of the aristocracy," Mrs. Jones said in her most superior tone, her lip curling into a self-righteous sneer.

"Yes, madam."

"Or perhaps not," Mrs. Jones went on. "You nobs think you're so much better than the rest of us, but my, how the mighty have fallen."

Phoebe could do nothing but bow her head and clench her jaw. If the associates of her former life only knew how much the middle classes resented them—even as they tried to emulate them in every way—they might think twice about their lofty attitudes and dismissive ways.

"I will let this pass," Mrs. Jones continued. "But only this once. If I catch you misbehaving again, there will be consequences."

A flutter of desperation in Phoebe's stomach made her wish she hadn't eaten the entire pie Mr. Long had offered her, or that she'd had some of the beer after all. "I understand, madam," she said. "It won't happen again."

"Good." Mrs. Jones nodded sharply. "You've missed supper."

She said nothing else before turning and marching off to the back part of the house.

Phoebe let out a shaky breath, rubbing her temples for a moment before removing her hat. Aside from her interlude at The Watchman, the day had been about as miserable as could be. All she wanted to do was go up to her room, remove her boots, and—

"Phoebe! Oh, Phoebe, there you are." Her mother slid open the door to a small side parlor and stepped into the hall. She peeked toward the back of the house, the way Mrs. Jones had gone, then gestured to Phoebe to follow her into the side parlor. "I've a surprise for you, my dear."

Dread pooled in Phoebe's stomach as she stepped toward the parlor. "Mama, why on earth do you have the door closed? What could you possibly have in here that you don't want Mrs. Jones to—"

Her question died on her lips as she entered the parlor only to find Lord Cosgrove standing by the fireplace. The odious man wore a victorious grin, as though he'd accomplished a feat Phoebe should be proud of.

"Lady Phoebe," he said with a toothy grin. "I told you we would meet again soon."

Phoebe rounded on her mother. "Mama! What have you done? You know we are not allowed to have male guests."

"Lord Cosgrove couldn't possibly be seen as an indiscretion," her mother said, waving away Phoebe's protest. "He's a viscount, for pity's sake."

"He's still a man, Mama." Phoebe shot Lord Cosgrove a disapproving look, then stared hard at her mother. "The boarding house has rules. You cannot break them."

"Rules are for the middle class," her mother sniffed.

For a moment, she looked imperious. Then her expression changed to mischief and delight. "I'll just leave the two of you alone." She grabbed Phoebe's overcoat and hat from her arms.

"Mama!" Phoebe called after her in alarm as her mother fled the room. "You cannot leave me alone in here with him."

Her mother ignored her, giggling as she slid the parlor door shut.

Phoebe whipped back to face Lord Cosgrove.

"Your mother is right," he said with a predatory sort of grace, striding away from the fireplace. "The mistress of the boarding house couldn't possibly object to a man of my status speaking with you, especially as I have come to speak about a particularly delicate matter."

Phoebe thought she might be sick. She moved around the perimeter of the room, deliberately putting a settee and end table between her and Lord Cosgrove. "I will not pretend to be ignorant of your mission here, Lord Cosgrove," she began. "But I can tell you before you ask, my answer is no."

Rather than being put off, Lord Cosgrove chuckled as though she couldn't possibly be serious. "You haven't heard what I have to offer yet, my dear."

"Forgive me, my lord, but there is little you could offer that would entice me." Phoebe continued to move around the room, keeping as much furniture between her and Lord Cosgrove as possible.

"I was friends with your father, my dear," Lord Cosgrove pushed on.

"That is not a piece of information that would endear you to me," Phoebe muttered, likely too softly for Lord Cosgrove to hear.

"He used to speak fondly of you to me," he went on.

"I highly doubt that," Phoebe continued to mutter.

"I believe it was his wish that I take care of you in his absence."

"I have done an adequate job of taking care of myself and Mama," Phoebe said, tilting her chin up proudly. And she was proud of everything she'd managed to do to keep herself afloat.

"You cannot possibly enjoy living this sort of diminished life," Lord Cosgrove went on.

"It is good enough for me," Phoebe insisted, skirting an overstuffed chair as Lord Cosgrove circled closer to her.

"But I could offer you so much more, my dear," he said. "I have an estate of my own in Hampshire. Wouldn't it be much nicer to live there, or in my London townhouse, than in a place like this?"

"I would say it depends greatly on the conditions under which I would live there," Phoebe said, voice hoarse, face heating. She wasn't so much of an innocent that she didn't know the way of things between men and women. In fact, with her father's proclivities constantly thrown in her face as a reason why not a soul in society would raise a finger to help her or her mother, she knew a great deal more about relations between men and women than most ladies of her former station.

"True," Lord Cosgrove said as though it were inconsequential. "I would expect you to give me an heir or two, as well as keeping me happy."

Phoebe tried not to look physically repulsed by the suggestion.

"But I would make it worth your while," Lord Cosgrove went on. "In fact, I could offer you a life of luxury and ease, as soon as my investments pay off."

"Investments?" Phoebe arched one eyebrow and continued to move away from him. Any noblemen who spoke of investments was more or less admitting that his traditional means of income were failing. Which meant he could be lying about the lifestyle he promised.

"I have begun engaging in land development speculations," he said. "London has a terrible housing shortage these days. Men are making fortunes building houses on what was once farmland west of the city."

"Yes, I have heard."

"Have you?" Lord Cosgrove looked surprised, as if Phoebe didn't do things as simple as reading the newspaper or engaging her customers at Harrods in conversation. "Then you must know that I stand to make some woman very happy," he went on.

"That woman will not be me, my lord," she insisted.

Lord Cosgrove chuckled. The sound chilled Phoebe's blood. "I think you might be made to see reason," he said, his tone turning threatening.

Twin feelings of fear and helplessness gripped Phoebe as she darted around a chair to avoid Lord Cosgrove's continued pursuit. The sudden comparison between Lord Cosgrove and Mr. Long shot to her mind. Lord Cosgrove was well-born, titled, and accepted by society. Mr. Long was rough, crude, and owned a pub. Yet, Mr. Long had showed her utmost kindness and consideration. Not once had she felt threatened or in danger in his presence, in spite of the fact that he was a well-formed man who likely could have bent her to his will with ease. Kindness shone in his eyes, whereas nothing but malice and greed shone in Lord Cosgrove's. And Lord Cosgrove was the one that acquaintances of her former life would have considered the better man. It was madness.

"Lord Cosgrove." Phoebe stopped dodging him, moving to stand in the center of the parlor and putting her foot down, proverbially, if not actually. "I will not marry you. I simply am not interested. Please go."

"I am not inclined to take no for an answer." Lord Cosgrove made a sudden move toward her. "There are other ways to secure a favorable answer to a proposal. Ways favored by the Vikings and other marauders."

"You couldn't possibly—oh!" Phoebe shouted before she could stop herself as Lord Cosgrove grabbed her around the waist and pulled her flush against him. "Let me go, let me go!" She pushed against him.

"Never," Lord Cosgrove said, leaning into her and attempting to kiss her. "You are mine."

"Oh, stop, stop!" Phoebe shoved against his shoulders as hard as he could, but the man was surprisingly strong. He brought his lips closer to hers, but she twisted her head this way and that to avoid his kiss.

"What is the meaning of this?" Mrs. Jones's voice boomed from the doorway.

Instantly, Lord Cosgrove let Phoebe go. Phoebe leapt to the side, gasping for breath and shaking with fear.

"Do we have an answer yet?" her mother said cheerfully, skipping into the parlor to stand by Mrs. Jones's side.

Phoebe was so overcome with terror that she could only shake her head and move as far away from Lord Cosgrove as possible.

"That is it," Mrs. Jones shouted, glaring at Phoebe as though she were the one in the wrong. "You know the rules about gentlemen callers. And what did I say to you not fifteen minutes before?"

"Believe me, Mrs. Jones, this is not what you think it is," Phoebe said, gasping for air.

"I shall go," Lord Cosgrove said, back stiff and head tilted up as though he were the wronged party. "But this is not the end of my suit, Lady Phoebe." He marched past Mrs. Jones and Phoebe's mother, leaving the parlor and the boarding house.

Phoebe wasn't relieved, though. Not by a long shot.

"This is intolerable," Mrs. Jones said, practically shaking with fury. "I will not stand for this sort of misbehavior under my roof."

"But Lord Cosgrove is a viscount," Phoebe's mother said, as though Mrs. Jones were dense.

Mrs. Jones rounded on her, eyes wide. "You, madam, have been a thorn in my side from the moment you and your daughter arrived on my doorstep."

"I have not," Phoebe's mother protested, clapping a hand to her chest in offense.

"You give yourself airs, madam," Mrs. Jones said.

"That's 'my lady' to you. I am a dowager marchioness."

"A dowager marchioness who does nothing of any use to anyone, who steals food from the kitchens, and who vexes the poor girls working for me as though they are your own personal staff."

"I have a right to be treated with the respect due my position," Phoebe's mother said imperiously.

"Your position is that of beggar, madam," Mrs. Jones shouted. "And by the end of this week, it will be that of vagrant." She turned to Phoebe. "I want you and your mother out of this house by the end of day on Friday."

"But Mrs. Jones." Phoebe started toward her, gut churning with anxiety.

"No buts about it. You have broken my rules and you are out." She turned to go.

"But we have nowhere else to go," Phoebe started after her. She had investigated several boarding houses before finding Mrs. Jones, and none of them would accept her and her mother without a more substantial deposit than she was able to manage on her income from Harrods.

"Then you will go to the street," Mrs. Jones snapped. She didn't even turn to look at Phoebe as she marched off to whatever other task she had to do.

Phoebe stopped in the foyer, clasping a hand to her mouth, fighting her tears. She hadn't let herself bemoan her fate or feel sorry for herself so far, and she would be damned if she did now. But it was hard, so terribly hard, to be cast off by fortune, tossed from one threatening shore to another without any hope of a port in the storm.

"There, there, dear," her mother said, coming up behind her and patting Phoebe's shoulder. "I'm sure Lord Cosgrove will take us in once you go to him and apologize."

"Apologize?" Phoebe whipped around to face her mother, eyes blazing with indignation. "He assaulted me, Mama."

"He was simply being overzealous," her mother said with a shrug. "Marrying Lord Cosgrove would be a boon," she went on, beaming at the prospect. "He is a viscount, and he holds a respectable place in society."

"He isn't well-liked, Mama," Phoebe growled, balling her hands into fists at her sides. "Just as father was not well-liked."

"That is inconsequential, as we both know from experience." Her mother lost her smile.

"And where was he when Father died and left us penniless?" Phoebe went on. "Why did he not come to our aid right away? Why did he wait until now to make himself known?"

"Who knows why men do the things they do?" her mother said with a nervous laugh. "The important thing is that he wishes to marry you. That means a home for us, a return to our former life."

"Our former life was not the sort of thing anyone would want to return to," Phoebe said with a frown, marching past her toward the stairs and up to their pitifully small room.

"Yes, but it is a life in society," her mother argued, following.

"A society that turned its back on us," Phoebe reminded her. She shook her head as she pushed open the door to their room. She would have to pack their things, and the sooner the better. Mrs. Jones had given them a few days to find another situation and to move out, but there was no telling if the woman would change her mind and toss them out sometime sooner.

"If you would just consider Lord Cosgrove's suit," her mother pressed her case.

Phoebe turned to face her. "I will never marry a man like Lord Cosgrove," she said. "I would sooner take up a position as a match girl than lower myself to that level."

"You don't mean that."

"I do, Mama," Phoebe insisted. "Now, if you will excuse me, I need to puzzle out how I am going to put a roof over your head after Friday."

"Lord Cosgrove—" her mother tried one last time.

Phoebe held up a hand to stop her. "I never want to hear the man's name again. I will figure a way out of this situation, as I have figured a way out of every situation you and Father have thrown me into in this curse of a life. I will do whatever it takes."

She only shuddered to think what that might end up being.

CHAPTER 4

*L*ady Phoebe Darlington. Danny couldn't get the delectable thing out of his mind for days after their meeting at the pub. Not that he wanted to. Phoebe was as darling as her name implied. He caught himself thinking about her sweet smile and her self-effacing manner as he went about his business, both at the pub and while inspecting the site in Earl's Court that he was thinking of investing in. He couldn't concentrate on the figures and reports Tuttle spewed off to him through any of their business meetings, which was as unusual as an ostrich in Piccadilly.

He most certainly couldn't banish her from his thoughts—and didn't want to—as he lay in bed each night, pondering her beauty. And imagining what she would feel like under him, of course. And over him, for that matter. His imagination had conjured up more than a few tantalizing images as he'd relieved himself from the tension of wanting her, and he wasn't at all ashamed about it.

But thoughts and fantasy had never been enough for Danny. He'd only gotten where he was in life by acting, not dreaming. And for him, action began with research. He'd spoken to his friends, Rupert Marlowe, Jack Craig, and Reese Howsden, about Phoebe and her situation. In the process, he'd learned all about her profligate father, the way society had turned its back on Phoebe and her mother, the extent of the debt Lord Darlington had left behind, and the mess that had happened in Ireland the year before with Lady Maude Darlington and Linus Townsend's father. Every new bit of information Danny learned made him as mad as a hornet. It also made him want to do something to change Phoebe's fate.

Which was how he found himself wandering the aisles of Harrods on a Thursday afternoon instead of inspecting housing designs or investigating the members of parliament who would be voting on which company to grant the contract for the Earl's Court development to. He needed a new suit if he was going to meet with those members of parliament, after all, and as long as he was at Harrods....

Danny's heart gave an uncharacteristic leap in his chest as he turned a corner and started down the aisle of counters containing every bit of women's frippery he couldn't have cared less about, unless it was while in the process of removing it from a willing partner. There she was, standing behind a pristine glass and wood counter, surrounded by boxes and trays of women's gloves in every shade of the rainbow. She was a vision of loveliness, even though she only wore a simple, grey skirt, fashionable white blouse, and some sort of uniform pinafore covering the ensemble. Her golden hair was caught up in a tight and serviceable bun at the back of her head, and a slight flush painted her porcelain cheeks as she straightened and folded gloves in the wake of a customer who had just departed.

But it was the sorrow in her expression, the way her shoulders hunched and her face seemed drawn, that made Danny pick up his pace as he strolled down the aisle toward her. There were slight, dark circles under her eyes, which were downcast as she worked.

"Excuse me, miss," he said in his lowest accent as he leaned one elbow against her counter and rested his chin in his hand. "Can you tell a bloke where he might find a pretty pair of gloves to give to his sweety?"

A slight pinch came to Lady Phoebe's brow as she turned to him. Danny was beyond gratified when her frown turned into a look of delight at the sight of him.

"Mr. Long," she said, her shoulders relaxing and her smile turning genuine. "What a pleasant surprise to see you here."

"I could say the same about you," he said, standing straight.

Out of the corner of his eye, he noticed the shop girl

at the counter beside Phoebe's break into a wide, knowing grin. She glanced across to the girl at the counter across the aisle, tilting her head as if to point out the conversation.

"Have you come to purchase gloves for your...your sweetheart?" Lady Phoebe asked, flushing pinker, her eyes fluttering down for a moment.

It tickled Danny to his core to think she might be jealous of some imaginary lover. "Yes," he said seriously, glancing over the trays of gloves. "Which are your favorite?"

She drew in a breath, transitioning into a stern, businesslike demeanor. "Are they for day wear or for a special occasion?"

Danny tilted his head to the side, studying her. "Day wear," he said, remembering how worn and scuffed the gloves she'd been wearing at the pub the other day were.

"And are you looking for kid or something simpler?" she asked on.

"Which is the best?" He tried not to smile.

"Kid are finer, and they tend to last longer if cared for properly," she answered.

"And which do you like best?" he asked.

She shifted to a tray of dazzlingly white gloves, some plain, some with embroidery. "These are our new arrivals from Paris," she said, smiling fondly at the gloves.

"Which are the most expensive?" His mouth twitched into a grin.

Lady Phoebe studied the tray. "I would recommend

anything with embroidery if you're trying to impress a sweetheart," she said. Her lithe fingers flittered over the gloves for a moment. Danny sucked in a breath, wondering what those fingers would feel like brushing over his skin. "These are my favorite," she said.

The pair she selected were elegant, with vines and roses embroidered around the cuffs. Lady Phoebe Darlington had exquisite tastes. Danny caught himself wondering what she might be able to do if he gave her free reign over his purse.

"I'll take them," he said in a loud clip, earning a disapproving frown from a passing pair of middle-aged biddies in clothes too fine for their sour faces.

"Very good, sir," Phoebe said with a happy smile.

She took the gloves to the register and rang up the purchase. After Danny paid, she wrapped the gloves carefully in tissue and brown paper and handed them to him.

"I'm sure these will be greatly appreciated," he said with a wink, then handed the parcel back to her.

Phoebe blinked but didn't take the parcel. "Is something wrong?" she asked, suddenly nervous.

"No, not at all," Danny said, shaking the extended parcel at her.

She stared at it, then at him. Understanding dawned in her eyes, which went wide. "You didn't buy those for me, did you?" she asked.

"Of course I did." Danny beamed, more pleased with

his little trick than any grown man should have been. "Who else would I buy them for?"

"You said you were purchasing them for your sweetheart," Phoebe said warily.

Warning flags went up in Danny's mind. He rethought his teasing tactics. The last thing he wanted to do was frighten her. Especially since she had the look of a woman who'd learned to be wary of men.

"I don't have a sweetheart," he said with genial good humor. "I just thought you could use some cheering up. You looked so glum when I turned down the aisle just now and caught sight of you."

Phoebe flushed, her expression flashing through a wealth of emotions before settling on bashful gratitude. "I couldn't possibly accept," she said, lowering her eyes.

Danny decided then and there that he didn't like the way she looked down at the very moment she should smile and be proud. "I've already paid for them," he said with a shrug, setting the parcel on the counter. "It would be too much of a hassle to refund my money. And since I've no one else to give them to, they'd only go to waste if you don't take them." He risked a wicked grin. "And you said they were your favorite, so it would be a bloody shame to waste them."

She glanced up at him through her lowered eyes. On second thought, maybe he didn't mind the way she looked down, because when she glanced up like that, all coy-like, her long eyelashes brushing her cheeks, it fired

Danny's blood in a way that was entirely inappropriate for Harrods.

He returned to his earlier tactic of familiarity, leaning against the counter like a bounder. "Come on, love. You wanna tell me why the long face just now?"

He was a rascal and he knew it, but his methods got results. Phoebe sent a quick, covert glance around the shop—looking for her boss, no doubt—then moved closer to him. Her sadness returned.

"My mother and I stand on the verge of being dismissed from our boarding house," she confided in him.

"No!" He straightened, pulling back in horror. It didn't seem right to be so far away from her, so he stepped back into the counter. "What happened?"

She shrugged. "When I returned to the boarding house after spending time in your pub the other day, Mrs. Jones, the owner, smelled beer and smoke on me. She believed I had been carousing at a pub, which is strictly against her rules. And then my mother...." She lowered her eyes again, guilt accompanying the flush that came to her cheeks. Danny instantly boiled with curiosity. She went on with, "My mother had a gentleman guest over, which is also expressly against the rules." She glanced up to meet his eyes again. "With two offenses in one day, Mrs. Jones had had enough. Besides, my mother isn't exactly the easiest person to live with."

"She's not?" Danny asked, though in his research into Phoebe's situation and through inquiries of his nob friends, he'd learned that Lady Maude Darlington was an absolute pill and a blight on the nation.

Phoebe shook her head and sighed. "She's had a difficult life."

Danny thought the estimation was beautifully generous of Phoebe.

"And now things are about to get even more difficult," she went on, looking sadder than ever. "We have until tomorrow night to pack our things and move out of the boarding house, but I've been unable to find suitable accommodations that can accept us on short notice and without much in the way of means to make a deposit."

A thrill of victory ricocheted through Danny's chest. "That is unfortunate," he said, standing straight again and willing himself not to smile for joy. "But it's not a problem."

She pursed her lips, staring incredulously at him. "It is, in fact, a major problem, sir. You may think it easy to find a place in a boarding house as a man, but I can assure you, it is infinitely more complicated for single women without means to find a respectable place on short notice."

"Is it?" Danny made a considering face. He'd never stopped to think that it might be more difficult for some than for others to find respectable housing. Then again, that was what the entire housing crisis that had plagued London for the last decade was all about.

"It is," Phoebe said. "In fact—"

"Lady Phoebe, we meet again," a nasal, male voice said from somewhere behind Danny's back.

"Bloody Christ," Phoebe hissed, causing Danny to burst into an amused, snorting laugh. He spun to see whom she was looking at and cursing so effectively.

A ridiculous-looking older nob in a suit that was too tight for his paunchy frame and too youthfully cut for his advanced years approached Phoebe's counter. He had something that looked like soot in his hair to give it a younger appearance, but bits of it were smeared down the sides of his neck with sweat. He ignored Danny entirely, which was perfect, as far as Danny was concerned.

"Lady Phoebe, I am pleased to see you looking so well," the nob said, nudging Danny out of the way as though he were a used piece of newspaper.

Danny took a large step back, grinning from ear to ear, eager to see what sort of madness was about to unfold.

Phoebe shot him the briefest of looks before turning her wary and depressed attention to the man. "Lord Cosgrove. To what do I owe the...this visit."

Danny arched one eyebrow. So it wasn't a pleasure for her to meet this Lord Cosgrove, was it?

"My dear, I believe you know why I am here," Lord Cosgrove said. "We were interrupted so rudely the other night. I have not finished pressing my suit."

"Oy, there's a laundress over in menswear who'll press your suit for you," Danny cut in with as garish a Cockney accent as he could manage, pointing rudely.

Lord Cosgrove turned to glare at him. Phoebe stared at him with wide eyes and, if Danny wasn't mistaken, lips that twitched in her effort not to grin.

"Excuse me," Lord Cosgrove said, turning his back on Danny.

Danny stayed where he was, stifling a laugh, but let the fool prattle on.

"As I was saying, we have unfinished business, you and I."

"No, Lord Cosgrove, we do not," Phoebe said. She busied herself tidying up her gloves, folding some, and tucking a few of the trays back onto the shelf behind her.

"You cannot possibly wish to be a shop girl for the rest of your life," Lord Cosgrove went on, as if being a shop girl were worse than being a whore. "I am offering you a return to the glory of your old life."

Danny's jaw hardened. From what he had been able to uncover, her old life wasn't much to talk about. Judging by the looks of Cosgrove, anything he offered her wouldn't be much to talk about either.

"Please, my lord," Phoebe said with a sigh. "As I informed you the other night, I am not interested, nor will I ever be."

Danny grinned, proud of Phoebe's backbone. He had considered interfering on her behalf, but she seemed to have the situation well in hand. All the same, he would stay right where he was until the bastard left.

"I could make you wealthy beyond anything you've ever experienced before," Lord Cosgrove went on. "Do you not remember the land speculation I am about to be part of?"

"I am not interested, my lord." Phoebe continued to work. Most notably, she picked up the parcel with the gloves Danny had purchased for her and tucked them into her pinafore. Danny tried not to grin, especially when she shot him a brief look.

"I think you will want to reconsider when I share with you the profits I am about to make on the Earl's Court development," Lord Cosgrove said.

In a flash, all teasing and all amusement flew out of Danny's mind, leaving only business in its wake.

"Hang on," he said, cleaning up his accent a little and stepping forward. "You're putting in a bid for the Earl's Court development?"

Lord Cosgrove turned to look at him as though he were a cockroach. "Not that it is any concern of yours, but yes, I am." He turned back to Phoebe, dismissing Danny entirely. "Wouldn't you like to be the wife of a wealthy and important man?"

Danny might have asked her the question himself on any other day. He still hadn't made it past Cosgrove's statement, though.

"You think you're going to be awarded the parliamentary contract?" he asked, making his accent posher still.

Lord Cosgrove huffed out a breath and turned fully

to face him. "Who are you, sir, and why do you persist in bothering me and this fine woman?"

Danny put on his most charming smile and extended a hand. "Daniel Long. Property developer." It was the closest he cared to come to the truth. Experience had taught him never to reveal the extent of his business dealings to anyone he didn't fully trust, and he wouldn't trust Lord Cosgrove as far as he could spit.

Lord Cosgrove evidently felt the same way about him. "You're a lying fool," he said, raking Danny with a sneer. "Stop accosting me and leave this shop at once or I will have you expelled."

Danny's brow shot up. "Expelled, is it? When I am a paying customer?"

"I highly doubt you are," Lord Cosgrove snorted, turning back to Phoebe. "You're nothing more than a low-born confidence man, I'd wager."

It wasn't the first time Danny had been accused of being a confidence man—based solely on his accent and mannerisms, combined with dressing more expensively than a man of his station was supposed to, while being in a place frequented by nobs. He'd always found the accusation amusing, particularly as he could probably purchase Lord Cosgrove a dozen times over.

"Let's just find ourselves a copper and see who they toss out on their ear first, shall we?" he asked, grinning at Lord Cosgrove. He stood at his full height, glancing around for someone who looked as though they fit the bill of manager or protection against thieves.

"Will you stop drawing attention to yourself, you blackguard," Lord Cosgrove hissed, glancing around anxiously.

Danny made a face as though he found Cosgrove's reaction terribly interesting. And indeed, what nob would shy away from the possibility of intervention by the law? Danny made a mental note to research Cosgrove a bit to find out what the man was really up to.

"I can see that this is neither the time nor the place to pursue the matter between us further," Lord Cosgrove said to Phoebe. "I shall call on you at Mrs. Jones's as soon as possible to resolve things."

"Any time after tomorrow night," Phoebe said with a straight face and a tight jaw.

Lord Cosgrove evidently thought he'd won his point. He grinned proudly and rapped the countertop before sauntering off. Danny watched him go, seething internally at the man's audacity, but also calculating just how big of a problem the man would be in his bid to win the Earl's Court contract.

"What a sodding prick," he said, sliding closer to Phoebe and shaking his head.

Phoebe merely hummed in response, glancing warily in the direction in which Lord Cosgrove had disappeared. Danny noted that she neither blanched at his rough speech nor chastised him for it. God, but he liked her.

Which led him to say, "And now we should discuss that other problem of yours."

She'd busied herself straightening her counter and putting away gloves all through the confrontation, but now she froze and stared at him. "My other problem?"

"Your problem of accommodation," he said, breaking into a wide grin. "It's a problem no more," he went on.

"It isn't?" She glanced up at him with those big, gorgeous, green eyes of hers.

"No," he said, buzzing with triumph. "Because I've got just the place for you to live."

CHAPTER 5

$\mathcal{T}$win thrills of excitement and wariness sliced through Phoebe as she blinked at Mr. Long's offer.

"You...you have a place where I can live?" she asked, her voice cracking. His offer sounded a great deal like Lord Cosgrove's promise that she would be able to live in a grand country house if she married him.

And yet, Mr. Long's way of delivering his offer couldn't have been further from Lord Cosgrove's loathsome proposal. Whereas every instinct she had told her to run from Lord Cosgrove, something about Mr. Long inspired trust.

Mr. Long shrugged, tracing his fingertip along the edge of her counter. "I own more properties than just the pub," he said modestly. "I don't just ply damsels in distress with beer and sausage pie. I'm a landlord of sorts as well."

Hope zipped through Phoebe before she could be suspicious of it. "You have flats to let?"

"Tons of 'em," Mr. Long said, falling back into a teasing grin. "I've got just the place for you among 'em."

Phoebe's mouth dropped, but she couldn't think of a thing to say. She could forgive Mr. Long his crass accent and rough manners, and a great many other things, for the offer he appeared to be making her. His kindness shone above his breeding a thousand times over.

But within seconds, her hopes flattened. "I doubt I could afford an entire flat on my income from the shop," she said, lowering her eyes.

"Hey." His clipped response snapped her head up again. Mr. Long wore a deeply concerned look. "Don't droop on me like that. You haven't seen the place yet."

Phoebe tilted her head to the side in consideration. "True." Perhaps he was offering her a cramped, attic room with little ventilation and no light. She could afford something like that.

But the twinkle in his eyes and the way he stared at her expectantly gave Phoebe the feeling he was offering her more than cheap accommodations.

"What do you say?" he asked with a rakish wink. "Will you come see the place? When do you get off of work here?" He glanced around as if looking for Mr. Waters to tell him her shift ended immediately.

Phoebe glanced at the watch brooch pinned to her blouse. "I have one more hour until I am dismissed," she said.

"Good," Mr. Long said, knocking on the counter. "I'll be back in one hour to escort you to your new home."

He grinned cheekily, then turned to leave. Phoebe watched him as he strolled to the end of the aisle. As he turned the corner, he raised an eyebrow at her and winked once more before disappearing.

"Laws, Miss Darlington," Imogen said, slipping through the space that separated their two counters to come close enough to Phoebe to whisper. "I've never seen a man so finely formed."

Hilda skipped out from behind her counter, coming to lean in over Phoebe's counter with a bright-eyed look. "My heart fluttered all over just looking at him."

"Is he your beau?" Imogen asked, cheeks pink and eyes shining.

"Mr. Long? No!" Phoebe felt flutters of her own as she denied it, though. Her hand moved automatically to the parcel of expensive gloves in her apron pocket. "We've only just met."

"He's the kind you like to meet over and over again," Hilda said dreamily.

"He can meet me any day he likes," Imogen agreed, one eyebrow raised lasciviously.

Phoebe giggled in spite of herself, her face heating. "I can assure you, ladies, it's nothing of that sort at all." Though she would be lying if she said she hadn't had a natural reaction to Mr. Long's manly presence. "My mother and I are in need of new living arrangements, and Mr. Long has just offered to show me a flat he manages."

"I hope he shows you more than just a flat," Imogen giggled.

"I'd go flat for him any day," Hilda sighed.

It was shocking and base, but Phoebe found herself giggling along with her coworkers all the same. Both Hilda and Imogen had been born in East London and worked their way into enough respectability to be given positions at Harrods, but in that moment, Phoebe felt friendlier with them than she ever had with the likes of Lady Jane Hocksley or Lady Maude Carmichael.

"Ladies!" Mr. Waters's tight scolding shocked the three of them out of their girlish giggling. Hilda and Imogen immediately leapt back to their counters. "That's better," Mr. Waters said as he walked down the aisle between the counters, hands clasped behind him.

Phoebe was grateful for the timid young woman who stepped up to her counter in search of gloves. It gave her the opportunity to busy herself and avoid Mr. Waters's scrutiny. She wasn't sure what would have happened to her if Mr. Waters had caught her talking to Mr. Long. It reminded her a bit too much of the way Mrs. Jones had caught her with Lord Cosgrove. Although, once again, when Phoebe compared the situation with Mr. Long and the one with Lord Cosgrove in her mind, they felt as different as chalk and cheese. Both men had offered to help her, but only one offer felt like real help.

Those thoughts occupied her mind during the last hour of her shift. It was, blessedly, an uneventful hour, but as she was relieved by her replacement and went to the ladies' dressing room to change out of her apron, carefully tucking the parcel with the gloves into the pocket of her skirt when no one was looking on the off chance someone would think she stole them, her pulse picked up.

She was almost dizzy with anticipation as she donned her hat and overcoat and made her way down to Harrods' main entrance. A burst of inexplicable joy struck her as she spotted Mr. Long standing in the afternoon sunlight on the busy street, waiting for her.

"Took you long enough," he said with a wide smile the moment he saw her.

She knew he was teasing, which only made the fluttering in her insides increase. "I'm so sorry to have kept you waiting, Mr. Long," she replied with what she hoped was a coy smile.

Something warm and enticing flashed through Mr. Long's eyes. "How many times am I going to have to tell you to call me Danny?" he asked, his tone irritated, but his smile delighted. He offered her his elbow.

"It is highly improper for me to call you by your given name," Phoebe said, slipping her hand into the crook of his arm. The fact that he would want to escort her through the city streets was endearing. The blossom of pride she felt walking by his side was unexpected and heartening.

He made a crude, snorting sound, waving her objection away. "I don't give a rip about proper," he said. "Especially not if I'm to be your landlord."

Phoebe laughed lightly. "Whether you become my landlord or not has yet to be determined," she said. "But if you absolutely insist I throw my manners and propriety to the wind…."

"I absolutely insist," he said with false gravity and a finer accent.

Phoebe peeked sideways at him. His accent didn't seem to be fixed. She'd heard him speak in Cockney, but also in more refined tones. He seemed to be able to switch between demeanors with ease, which left Phoebe wondering who or what he really was.

"So you own a pub and you also rent out flats," she said, unsure how to frame the question she wanted to ask.

"You're right, I do," he said, grinning and giving her no other information.

A slow smile spread across Phoebe's lips. He was going to make her pry it out of him for sport. She was up for the challenge.

"And I suppose the flats you rent are in the same building as your pub? Are we heading to Fitzrovia?" she asked.

"I do rent out the rooms above the pub, and we are headed to Fitzrovia," he said with a nod. "But the flat I have in mind for you is not in the pub."

"I see," Phoebe said, nodding and taking in the information. "So you own more than one building then?"

"Correct." His smile grew wider and more mysterious.

"More than two?" she asked, enjoying the banter.

"Possibly." She could see in the way his eyes glittered that there was quite a bit he wasn't telling her.

She bit her lip to keep from giggling at the pure enjoyment of their silly conversation as they walked on. "You told Lord Cosgrove that you were a property developer," she said, hoping he would see the statement as a question.

"Do you know, I did." He peeked at her with a downright devilish grin.

Phoebe laughed outright. "So you are a pub owner, a landlord, and a property developer."

"I am all of those things," he agreed, laughing himself.

There was more, much more, to Mr. Danny Long than met the eye. Phoebe didn't have the first idea about how to pry it all out of him, though. Their conversation was cut short as he hailed a handsome cab, then helped her inside.

"I suppose it is a long way to walk to Fitzrovia," she admitted as she settled into the forward-facing seat.

"Much too long for a tired shop girl who has been on her feet all day," Danny agreed, sitting on the seat facing her. His face held so much amusement over the situation that Phoebe could hardly keep herself from beaming from ear to ear. It had been so long since she had felt so truly happy and at ease that she could hardly recall the last time.

"Perhaps I should search for lodgings for Mama and I that are closer to Harrods," she said once they were in motion again, hoping he would give her more clues as to his real estate holdings.

"Nah." He sniffed at the suggestion. "You don't want to live down this way. Too many toffs and nobs who think they're better than the rest of us." He sent her a downright wicked smile that said he knew she'd come from that same set of people.

"Oh yes," she agreed, rolling her eyes. "Lord help the poor, unfortunate souls who are trapped in the upper classes. They live like birds in gilded cages." She was joking, but part of her wondered if she meant it.

"No one should live in a cage," he said, seeming to agree with her. "It's far better to live free."

"I couldn't agree more," she said with a nod.

Their silly banter and Phoebe's unsuccessful attempts to pry more personal information out of Danny continued through their journey around Belgravia and Mayfair and along Oxford Street. The scenery was familiar to Phoebe from her daily walks to and from work, and even from her detour to The Watchman pub earlier in the week. In fact, when the cab stopped in front of The Watchman, she began to wonder if Danny had been lying to her when he said the room he had for her wasn't above the pub.

"Here we are, home at last," he said once the cab stopped and he opened the door to hand her down.

"It looks very much like your pub to me," she told him with a teasing look as he paid the cabbie.

When the cab drove on, she attempted to cross the street to the pub, but Danny grabbed her elbow.

"Not that one, love. This one."

He turned her to look at the building they stood in front of, directly across the street from the pub. It was a surprisingly fine-looking building with a brick façade and boxes of flowers in the downstairs windows. It was four stories tall and had a cheery air to it. Everything about the building put Phoebe at ease.

"Come along," Danny said, grabbing her hand—a gesture Phoebe noted as being far more intimate then offering his arm, as he'd done outside of Harrods. As soon as they stepped into the building, he hollered, "Oy! Umbridge! Keys!"

The door nearest to the building's entrance was open, and after a thump inside that room, a middle-aged man dashed out into the hall with a ring of keys. "Here you are, sir," the man said, handing the ring over to Danny.

"I'll return them in a trice," Danny told him without breaking stride, heading on to a staircase near the back of the ground floor. "I'm just going to show Miss Darlington here the vacancy."

"Very good, sir." Mr. Umbridge bowed and nodded as though Danny were the king, then slipped back into his room.

"He seems delightful," Phoebe said as they headed upstairs, all the way to the second floor.

"He's a corking property manager," Danny said with a delighted grin, taking her to a door halfway down the wide hall. He fit the key in the lock and turned it. "Now, tell me this isn't exactly what you've been hoping and praying for each night."

A tremor of expectation filled Phoebe as he pushed open the door and shooed her inside. The moment Phoebe stepped into the flat's large front room, her breath caught in her chest. The front room was wide and airy, with windows all along one side that let in plenty of light. Through one doorway, she could see a cozy kitchen and dining area. Through another, a small bedroom, and through another still, a second bedroom. It was modest by any measure, but with two bedrooms and enough light to bring joy to her heart, the flat was everything she could ever have asked for and more.

"It's perfect," she sighed, stepping farther into the room and spinning in a circle to take in the details. There were no furnishings, but her heart refused to see that as a problem.

"Told you," Danny said, shutting the door and following her into the center of the room. "Nice view of the pub too," he teased her, pointing to one of the windows.

Phoebe sent him a smiling glance before heading to one of the windows to look out. The view was as lovely as a view of a pub and the surrounding street could be. The area was clean and well-kept. There were even children playing farther down the street.

As Phoebe straightened and turned back to Danny, her heart twisted and sank. "It's perfect," she sighed, lowering her head. "But there's no possible way I could afford this."

He crossed the room in a few strides, coming to stand immediately in front of her and placing a hand under her chin. "Hey," he said, the twinkle in his eyes turning to more of a spark as he nudged her to look at him. "Don't worry about rent. We'll work something out."

She opened her mouth to protest, but before a single word made it past her lips, his mouth was on hers. She gasped as he slipped an arm around her, molding his lips to hers in a kiss that spun her head and took her breath away. He nibbled on her lower lip for a moment before increasing the ardor of his kiss and sliding his tongue against hers. Phoebe made a sound deep in her throat, but it wasn't one of protest. Her arms circled his sides, but not to push him away.

She'd gone completely mad. Sense screamed at her to back away at once. She wasn't fool enough not to realize what working something out as rent payment meant. But that didn't stop her heart from banging against her ribs or her sex from throbbing as he caressed her back and held her closer while devouring her with the most powerful kiss she'd ever received.

"This might be a good time for me to admit that I live upstairs," he whispered against her lips, loosening his hold on her.

Yes, there was no doubt whatsoever what he intended her to pay for the privilege of staying in this beautiful flat.

"Is that so?" she asked breathlessly.

He nodded, grinning as though he'd discovered a treasure, letting her go, but taking only a half-step back. "So what do you think? Is this the home for you?" Hope that was almost tender shone in his eyes.

"I—" Phoebe pressed a hand to her stomach.

Could she really do it? Could she offer herself to a man she barely knew in exchange for a roof over her head? Every silly, teasing thing Imogen and Hilda said came back to her. Women were probably lining up to share Danny's bed. And yet, he'd told her he didn't have a sweetheart. That could be a lie. Though as far as she knew, he hadn't lied to her once in their short acquaintance.

"I have to think about it," she said, her voice cracking. She cleared her throat and went on. "I have to consult with Mama."

"Then by all means, consult away." He took a larger step back, his voice booming again and his smile crassly broad.

Phoebe sucked in a breath, marveling at Danny. He was loud and boisterous, he'd taken an astounding liberty with her person, but mad as it felt, she still felt safe with him. Far safer than she had with Lord Cosgrove.

"I should go," she said, heading for the door.

"Let me walk you down," Danny said, following her. "And I'll call you another cab."

"You don't have to," she said over her shoulder, trying not to feel as though she were fleeing as she headed down the stairs. "The boarding house is only a handful of blocks from here. And I need the walk to think."

"Understood," Danny said. She caught a peek at his expression as they reached the ground floor. He *did* understand. Far more than she might have wanted him to. His gaze as he watched her walk down the hall to the outside door was as good as a caress. "You know where to find me with your answer," he called after her as she stepped out to the street.

"I know," she said over her shoulder. "And thank you," she hesitated, then added, "Danny."

The smile he sent her was a delicious reward for using his given name. It sent all sorts of dangerous swirls swooping through her gut and lower.

She hurried along to the cross street, turning towards Mrs. Jones's boarding house, pressing a hand to her stomach and feeling as though she'd gotten in over her head. She must have lost her mind entirely to even consider the offer Danny had made. No woman of respect and dignity would trade her body for a place to live. But the more she thought about the possibility, the more she ached to do just that. It didn't feel like a wicked compromise at all. Phoebe was filled with the mad feeling that she would have gone to bed with Danny for the price of another pie, or perhaps for nothing at all. She might actually be looking forward to it. And what kind of a woman did that make her?

CHAPTER 6

$\mathcal{T}$wo days later, Phoebe was back at the Fitzrovia flat, up to her eyeballs in chaos.

"That bureau goes in the front bedroom," she told the pair of removers who were carrying the borrowed furniture up two flights of stairs. "Thank you," she added as she hurried past them to where Natalia Townsend was attempting to unroll a large, Persian carpet in the center of the main room while balancing her infant son in her arms. "Natalia, you don't have to do that."

"Nonsense," Natalia said, waving away Phoebe's attempts to stop her and shuffling young master Dennis in her arms. "I was the one who convinced Henrietta and Fergus to loan you all of their unused furniture, so I should be the one to help you place it."

"At least let me hold the baby," Phoebe insisted, reaching for Dennis.

Baby Dennis fussed and squirmed and wriggled in his mother's arms. "He really doesn't like anyone other than me holding him," Natalia said, still trying to push the rolled-up carpet with her foot while simultaneously trying to soothe Dennis.

"I'll handle the carpet then," Phoebe said, shaking her head.

She couldn't believe the turn her life had taken in the last two days. On Thursday morning, she was convinced her life had reached the direst crossroads possible. She and her mother had been on the verge of being homeless, and they were most certainly friendless. Two days later, and she was moving into a beautiful, safe flat and had been granted the free use of more furniture than she could possibly have used. All because Natalia Townsend had dropped by Mrs. Jones's boarding house unexpectedly on Thursday evening, just as Phoebe had returned from viewing the flat. Natalia, Phoebe's one remaining friend in society, had listened to Phoebe's story of woe and immediately rallied her own forces to come to Phoebe's aid.

"Henrietta and Fergus are in Ireland at the moment, of course," Natalia chattered as Dennis fussed, Phoebe unrolled the carpet, and the removers continued to tramp in and out of the flat, bringing in more borrowed furniture. "Fergus's sisters are causing him no end of grief. I found them to be perfectly delightful, didn't you?"

"They were spritely," Phoebe said, puffing as she finished with the carpet and dragged it to exactly the position she wanted it in the center of the room. The O'Shea sisters were some of the most outlandish and unconventional women Phoebe had ever met. They had made her miserable mission to Ireland the summer before even more colorful than it could have been.

"Fergus is determined to marry them all off now to get them to settle," Natalia went on. "But I don't think they'll ever truly behave the way everyone seems to want them to. And why should they? Women who behave are terribly dull."

Phoebe glanced up at her friend with a wary look. No one knew better than Natalia how to be unconventional. She was the daughter of one of London's most powerful and notorious women, Lady Katya Campbell, and she had married a humble doctor, Dr. Linus Townsend, after being caught in a compromising position with him on an island in the middle of the Irish Sea the summer before. Natalia had the last laugh in the end, though. Dr. Townsend was the talk of London with his efforts to bring medical aid to poorer neighborhoods in the city. He'd spoken before Parliament three times in the last year and was lauded as a social visionary. And while he and Natalia continued to live under Henrietta and Fergus's roof so that Linus could serve as Fergus's personal physician, they more or less had the entire townhouse to themselves whenever Henrietta and Fergus were in Ireland.

"Oh!" Natalia gasped, seemingly out of the blue. "I have to tell you all the latest about the May Flowers."

Phoebe turned to her from where she was directing the removers to place the various sofas, chairs, and decorative cabinets in the main room. "Do I want to know what the May Flowers are up to?" Ever since Henrietta had stepped down as head of the women's political organization—after the failed vote over Irish Home Rule, really—the May Flowers had been split down the middle and rife with conflict.

"Lady Claudia and her cabal still won't leave outright," Natalia said with a longsuffering sigh. "Everyone wishes they would simply shove off and create their own organization. Lenore believes they're hanging on simply to disrupt things."

Phoebe hummed and began moving crates of dishes, utensils, and other kitchen items that Natalia had secured for her from Henrietta's house into the kitchen. "Lenore Garrett is American," she called over her shoulder to Natalia, who had managed to quiet Dennis by bouncing him against her shoulder. "She comes from the wild American West. She's likely to see conflict anywhere."

"Lenore is an absolute dream," Natalia said, meeting Phoebe at the kitchen door as she headed back into the main room. "I'm so glad Freddy decided to marry her. London has never seen anything like her. Not even from the other dollar princesses stealing our titled gentlemen."

Phoebe shot Natalia a wary look as she went to move another box. She didn't know much about Lenore Garrett, but she thought she knew a little something about Lord Frederick Herrington. Specifically, that he was particular friends with Lord Reese Howsden in a way that would preclude him from engaging himself to a woman at all.

"Have they set a date for the wedding?" she asked Natalia, wondering if her friend knew the open secret.

"Of course not," Natalia said, laughing. "But, oh! You should have been there to see the way she took on Lady Jane at the last May Flowers meeting."

Phoebe grinned as she passed Natalia on her way into the kitchen once more. Just like that, they'd moved on to a subject other than the odd engagement between Lenore Garrett and Frederick Harrington.

"Apparently everyone is up in arms about this land development deal in Earl's Court," Natalia said.

Phoebe nearly dropped the box she'd been carrying. "Earl's Court?" It was the deal Lord Cosgrove had dangled over her, like a carrot before a donkey, to get her to accept his proposal.

"Yes," Natalia followed Phoebe as she crossed back into the main room to fetch the last of the crates. "Apparently, whoever wins that parliamentary contract will be in a position to make a killing building and selling houses."

"Is that so?" Phoebe crossed her again on her last trip into the kitchen. Perhaps Lord Cosgrove was right about his prospects after all. If he won the contract.

As she set the last crate down in the kitchen, the thought crossed her mind that Danny claimed to be a real estate developer too. She wondered if he was aware of Earl's Court.

"Linus told me that there are two major contenders for the contract," Natalia went on as Phoebe paused to pour herself a glass of water and dab the sweat of working hard off her brow. "He doesn't know who they are, but he hinted that competition to win the contract could turn fierce."

"And this is something that concerns the May Flowers?" Phoebe asked between sips of water.

"You cannot possibly imagine," Natalia said, making her eyes large with wariness, as though remembering some sort of argument. "Now that the Irish Question is no longer as interesting as it once was, and considering that the May Flowers are divided on the topic of women's suffrage, it's as though everyone is grasping at whatever issue they think might make a splash. Of course, Cece wants the May Flowers to champion the cause of affordable housing for all to solve the current housing crisis. But Lady Claudia and her cabal are more interested in supporting the interests of the upper classes."

Phoebe finished her water, set her glass on the small kitchen counter, and started back into the main room. "What does that have to do with the price of bread?"

"Well, as I understand it," Natalia said, trailing her back into the main room, "one of the companies bidding for the development contract is owned by a peer."

"Lord Cosgrove," Phoebe said. "Or so he told me."

"And the other is owned by a commoner," Natalia

said with a renewed spark of interest in her eyes. "Isn't it exciting?"

"As exciting as land development could be," Phoebe said with a wry grin. Politics must have been dreary and dull indeed if Natalia was exciting herself over the housing crisis and parliamentary contracts.

The conversation was cut short as Phoebe's mother shrieked from the larger of the two bedrooms, "No, no, you cannot put that there. It doesn't belong there." A moment later, she scurried into the main room and locked eyes with her daughter. "Phoebe! Come tell these horrible men not to manhandle my wardrobe as they are."

Phoebe sighed and approached her mother. "They are doing the best they can, Mama." She stepped into the doorway of the bedroom only to find everything exactly as it should have been.

Her mother crept up to her back and peeked over her shoulder, as if using Phoebe as a shield against rough men who would importune her character. "Well, they've done it right now."

"Mama," Phoebe scolded, pushing her mother back toward the center of the flat. "Leave the removers to do their job. You can fuss and fiddle over the flat as soon as they've brought all of the furniture in and placed it."

"It's just so horrible," her mother squealed. "To have so many men crawling all over our flat like this." She gave an overdramatic shudder to prove her point. "It's bad enough that we have to live in *Fitzrovia*." She spoke the name as though it were a sewer.

"It's a perfectly beautiful flat, Mama," Phoebe said, shaking her head and moving to adjust the placement of a chair near the empty fireplace.

"But it's not Mayfair," her mother whined. "Oh, how our circumstances had been reduced."

"You like the flat," Phoebe reminded her mother. "You said as much yesterday when you toured it."

"I said I liked it enough for a flat in *Fitzrovia*." Her mother sniffed. "And it lies across the street from a *pub*."

"A right nice pub too." The comment was made in a booming voice by Danny as he barged through the flat's open door.

Phoebe's mother let out a dramatic cry and scurried to hide behind Phoebe, shaking her hands as though the world were about to come to an end. Phoebe's gut filled with butterflies at the sight of Danny. He was tall and broad and loud in every way. His blue eyes glittered, and his dark hair curled wildly. The sheer breadth of his smile as he approached Phoebe and her mother made him look half mad, but Phoebe suspected that was on purpose to tease her mother.

"Hello, Mrs. Darlington, Phoebe," he all but roared in greeting.

Phoebe sent him a sardonic grin, trying not to laugh at his antics. Her look hid the lingering temptation and uncertainty of the moment that had passed between them when he offered her the flat, though. They still hadn't discussed the deal in explicit terms, and not

THE ROAD TO SCANDAL IS PAVED WITH WICKED INTEN…

knowing how or when so-called payment would be exchanged had Phoebe on tenterhooks.

"It's Lady Darlington to you, sir," Phoebe's mother sniffed, standing straighter.

"Sorry." Danny winked at Phoebe. "Lady Darlington."

"No, *I'm* Lady Darlington," Phoebe's mother said, her fear melting into indignation.

Danny put on a look of exaggerated confusion. "Isn't she Darlington too?"

"Yes, but—"

"And she's a lady." Danny sent Phoebe a wildly inappropriate look, dropping his voice to an improper purr as he spoke. It made Phoebe burn, inside and out.

"She is Lady Phoebe," Phoebe's mother said with an impatient cluck, blessedly missing the flirtation entirely. "I am Lady Darlington."

"It's all the same to me," Danny said with a shrug and a sniff that made him seem as ill-mannered as a street urchin. Which Phoebe believed was the point. "I came to see how things were getting along here," he went on. He made a show of noticing Natalia, then smiled and greeted her with, "Hello, Mrs. Dr. Townsend."

"Heavens! Where are my smelling salts," Phoebe's mother said, staggering to grip the back of the sofa that the removers had just placed in the center of the room. "I never thought I'd see the day when a man like that addressed the daughter of an earl in such a low manner."

"Mr. Long is friends with my husband, Lady

Darlington," Natalia said with a laugh that shook Dennis out of the slumber he'd fallen into. "He's friends with Lord Marlowe, Lord Clerkenwell, and Lord Howsden as well."

Phoebe's brow raised. She'd forgotten Danny was so well-connected. It left her wondering how Danny had fallen into company with the likes of Rupert Marlowe and Reese Howsden to begin with.

"He could be friends with the devil, for all I care," Phoebe's mother said, fanning herself with one hand. "A man like him simply does not speak to a woman of refinement in such a way."

"I beg your pardon, my lady," Danny said in perfect imitation of an upper-class accent. "Do forgive me, Mrs. Townsend. Terribly sorry."

Natalia laughed. "You're forgiven, Mr. Long." She shot Phoebe a bright look.

"The removers are almost finished bringing in the furniture," Phoebe said, taking a few steps closer to Danny. "All that's left to do is arrange things the way we want them and to unpack sundries."

"Unpacking sundries." Danny's smile filled with mischief. "Let me know if you need any help with that."

Phoebe sucked in a breath in spite of herself. She absolutely should not, in any way, shape, or form, react in such a visceral way to Danny's lascivious teasing. But everything about the man excited her in ways that her mother absolutely would not approve of.

"I think we can manage on our own," she said, her

lips twitching with the need to smile and flirt as blatantly as he was.

For a moment, she could have sworn Danny would swoop forward, gather her in his arms the way he had when he first showed her the flat, and kiss her senseless. But with her mother, Natalia, and half a dozen removers wandering in and out, there was no way even someone as wicked as Danny would attempt such a thing.

"Right," he said, taking a step back. "If you need me, I'll be down in the pub. Some friends have just arrived, and we're going to talk business." He sent her a significant look, making Phoebe wonder if they truly would be discussing business or if they were there to drink and chatter about whatever wildly inappropriate topics men discussed at a pub.

"Thank you, Mr. Long," Phoebe said as he turned to go.

"My pleasure, my lady," he said in a fine accent before rounding the corner. The sound of him whistling a bawdy tune as he headed for the stairs echoed in the hall.

Phoebe fought the urge to laugh, but she couldn't stop herself from blushing.

"Really," her mother scoffed behind her. "If that's what we have to put up with to enjoy this flat, I'm not sure it's worth the price."

"Mr. Long has been extremely generous with us, Mama," Phoebe said, turning back to the mountain of work that needed to be done. "And he's renting this flat to us at a greatly reduced rate." How much of a reduced rate she had yet to determine. Whatever it was, she certainly wouldn't discuss it with her mother.

Her mother sniffed and sat dramatically on the sofa. "You should have married Lord Cosgrove," she said. "Then we wouldn't have had to stoop to this level."

Phoebe couldn't stop herself from rolling her eyes and exchanging a look with Natalia. "I would never marry Lord Cosgrove, Mama. We are in exactly the sort of situation we need to be in."

Though how she would manage that situation when the rent came due was another story.

Giving the flat to Phoebe and her mother was a stroke of genius, as far as Danny was concerned. He kept a smile on his face and a spring in his step as he headed downstairs and crossed the street to enter The Watchman. Not only was he doing a good deed by helping someone who had been cruelly shunted aside by the very people who should have stepped up to help her, he now had a beautiful, intelligent, and formidable woman living in the same building as him. A woman who had kissed like she wanted to. A woman he would be daft if he didn't make some sort of play for.

But there were a thousand other things pressing for Danny's attention. He wanted Phoebe and he intended to have her, but all in good time.

The regular Saturday evening crowd was already beginning to fill the pub as he strode in. Several of the regulars and friends of his called to him and waved in greeting as he crossed through the front room. He waved back and called out greetings to a few of them, but it was the table in the back corner that had his full attention.

"Reese," he shouted, deliberately louder than he should have been as he greeted his friends. "Freddy. Rupert. How is life treating you on this fine summer day?"

The three men—all of them noblemen of considerable rank, and all of them men Danny would have given his life for—stood to shake his hand and thump him on the back in greeting. They were among the few nobs he actually liked, mostly because they were young and cut from a different cloth than the pricks that had sired them.

"Danny. You're looking well as usual," Reese said, then gestured to a fourth man with them, a man Danny didn't know. "I'd like you to meet a friend of mine, Mr. John Dandie."

Danny put on his friendliest smile and extended a hand to the unknown man. He was tall and blond with a mien that suggested intelligence and competence. And he didn't have a "Lord" attached to his title. "Mr. Dandie," he said boisterously. "Any friend of this lot is a friend of mine."

"I'm glad to hear it," Dandie said. "Particularly since I hear you are in the running for a certain parliamentary building contract."

Danny's brow shot up. He glanced to his friends.

"Don't tell me that you lot brought me business instead of fun this evening."

They all took seats around the table. Reese grinned knowingly. "John has a proposal that I think you'll be interested in."

"Since it sounds like you are most likely to be granted the parliamentary contract," Freddy added.

A stirring of hope filled Danny's chest, and he glanced to Rupert. "Is that so?"

Rupert held up his hands. "I may be on the committee to make the decision, but I have no information that I'm able to share." He paused, then said, "But I do think you should hear Mr. Dandie out."

Danny turned to the newcomer with an expectant look. "What do you propose, sir?"

"Well." Dandie inched his chair closer to the table, glancing around to see if they would be overheard before continuing. "I have been given to understand that you are sympathetic to certain, shall we say, unusual causes."

In an instant, Danny was intrigued. "I am."

Dandie glanced around again. "I represent a certain organization here in London." He paused, but gave no further details. "As you may know, it is difficult for certain men to find safe housing in protected areas. Not for anything untoward or illegal, mind you," he was quick to add. "But discrimination in this time of housing shortage is a real problem for some of my friends."

The pieces clicked together. Reese and Freddy seemed particularly interested in the conversation. They were "certain men" of the sort Danny was beginning to think John Dandie was speaking of. Their sort certainly did have difficulty finding safe places to live, as he'd discovered through his real estate dealings of the past.

"I understand your meaning," Danny said. His mind jumped ahead to what Dandie might be asking him. And frankly, he relished the idea of thumbing his nose at the right and proper channels of society by getting involved with a project of the sort he thought Dandie might be talking about.

"This Earl's Court development," Dandie went on, lowering his voice. "If parliament does grant you this contract, you could be in a position to help a lot of men whom society would otherwise turn its back on."

"I take your meaning," Danny said. "You want me to build a community within a community for friends of yours."

"Yes," Dandie said, seemingly relieved that he didn't have to explain further.

"What an intriguing idea." Danny leaned back in his chair, stroking his chin. "People would hate it." His smile grew.

"If they ever became aware of it," Dandie said. "Nothing needs to be said aloud and no promises need to be made, but if friends I know who are desperately in need of a place to live got wind that there was, shall we say, a garden square where they knew they would be welcome...."

Danny liked the idea. He'd seen far too many people

of all sorts kicked around and treated terribly by the moralizing middle-class. And the upper classes did nothing to help them. Class, situation, status, he abhorred all of it. John Dandie was offering him a chance to be part of a much-needed solution to an ages old social problem.

But before he could give the man an answer, the pub door slammed open, and none other than Lord bloody Cosgrove marched in.

"I should have known it was you," the man growled, stomping straight through the center of the pub to where Danny sat with his friends near the back. "You lying blackguard."

"Lord Cosgrove. We meet again." Danny stood, smiling at the fun he was about to have. "Welcome to The Watchman. Pull up a chair and I'll have Nora bring you a pint." He waved to one of the barmaids.

The entire pub was instantly on the alert. The regulars turned to stare at Lord Cosgrove, wondering what the man was doing there and likely waiting for Danny to run circles around him.

"How dare you put yourself forward for the Earl's Court development contract," Lord Cosgrove said, standing with his chest puffed out like an indignant peacock.

"What business is it of yours how I conduct my affairs?" Danny asked with a laugh designed to make the man feel snubbed.

Lord Cosgrove balled his hands into fists at his sides, practically quivering with rage. "You only approached

Parliament after hearing me say that I was on the verge of winning that contract the other day," he said.

"Is that what you think?" Danny glanced around at his friends and customers, as though they were part of a stage show and the audience was encouraged to react to the drama.

"It's what I know." Lord Cosgrove narrowed his eyes. "I saw the way you dared to look at Lady Phoebe the other day. It was disgusting, sir, and I will not stand for the mistreatment of a woman such as her."

Danny laughed. "Then you would do well to leave her alone yourself, since she made it clear she wants nothing to do with you."

Lord Cosgrove bristled. "Lady Phoebe needs some convincing is all. She will see the value in marrying me."

"I highly doubt that." Danny turned away. He didn't want to waste his time with Cosgrove anymore.

"You will withdraw your name from consideration for the Earl's Court development." Lord Cosgrove said as though it were a foregone conclusion.

"I will do no such thing," Danny laughed.

Cosgrove started to protest, but he was interrupted as the pub's door banged open once again and Lady Darlington charged in, followed by Phoebe and her friend, Mrs. Townsend.

"I will not stand for this, sir. Not for another moment," Lady Darlington roared. "That man, Mr. Umbridge cannot—"

She stopped short at the sight of Lord Cosgrove.

Phoebe nearly barreled right into her back. Her face lost all of its color at the sight of Cosgrove. Worse still, Cosgrove's expression darkened as he stared at her.

"Lady Phoebe," he said, tilting his head up as though offended. "You lied to me."

CHAPTER 7

The moment Phoebe clapped eyes on Lord Cosgrove, her stomach sank. She knew she would have to account for telling the man to call on her at Mrs. Jones's boarding house after Friday, but she hadn't realized that reckoning would come so soon.

She thought fast, saying, "'Lie' is a very strong word, my lord." Her voice came out wispy, in spite of her determination to be bold.

"Imagine my shock when I arrived at that second-rate boarding house, only to be told you and Lady Darlington had vacated," Lord Cosgrove said, glowering as he moved closer to her, proving her suspicion about his reason for being upset to be right. "What is the meaning of this subterfuge?"

"The meaning is that she doesn't want to see you, just like I told you." Danny stepped into the argument, moving to stand slightly in front of Phoebe, as though he would block Lord Cosgrove from interfering with her.

That action prompted Phoebe's mother to push herself forward to face Danny. "What right do you have to involve yourself in my daughter's disagreement with her suitor, sir?" she demanded.

Phoebe was tempted to hide her face in her hands. "Mama, Mr. Long is a friend."

"Oh, a friend, is he?" Lord Cosgrove bristled like an indignant turkey.

"He is renting Lady Darlington and Phoebe a flat in the building across the street," Natalia said, joining the fray with a spark of excitement in her eyes as little Dennis began to fuss and wail.

Phoebe rather felt like fussing and wailing herself. "It's true," she sighed, rubbing her forehead and wishing the entire situation would go away. Particularly as Lord Howsden, Lord Marlowe, Lord Harrington, and a man Phoebe didn't recognize seemed to be losing their battle not to chuckle at the entire confrontation from the table where they sat in the corner. "Mrs. Jones demanded that Mama and I leave her establishment."

"Which was your fault," Natalia added with a glare for Lord Cosgrove, "because you called without permission when callers were forbidden."

"He's a viscount," Phoebe's mother argued indignantly. "The rules of a third-rate boarding house do not apply to him."

"Mama." Phoebe pursed her lips and gave her mother a sideways look.

"Whether the rules of a fourth-rate boarding house apply to a viscount or not," Danny boomed, mirth dancing in his eyes as he degraded Mrs. Jones's establishment even further, "Lady Darlington and her mother are now tenants of mine."

Phoebe's mother snorted and shook her head. "No, no, I am Lady Darlington. My daughter is Lady Phoebe."

"And I'm the bloody Queen of Siam," Danny said, mouth pulling into a grin.

The gentlemen at the table hid their laughter behind their hands, their shoulders shaking. Phoebe was inclined to be furious with them for making sport of her plight, but the fact that they were so amused gave her the paradoxical feeling that the situation couldn't be too serious.

"This is outrageous," Lord Cosgrove blustered on, sideburns quivering as he snapped straight in indignation. "For such fine ladies to be reduced to this?" He sneered at Danny.

"Actually, their new flat is quite large and comfortable," Natalia interjected, grinning as broadly as the gentlemen at the table. "I wouldn't mind if Dr. Townsend and I lived there ourselves."

"If you're truly in the market for a flat, I've got several vacant units I could show you," Danny said in what Phoebe felt was a deliberately off-hand way, ignoring Lord Cosgrove completely.

Lord Cosgrove would not be ignored, though. "I will not stand to be made fun of like this," he said, appearing to assume that Danny's offer was meant as a slight to him. "It is a disgrace that a *pub owner*," he spoke the words with venom, "could be so audacious as to think he has the right to challenge a peer over a land deal that is far, far above his station."

Lord Marlowe cleared his throat. "My lord, Mr. Long is more than just a pub owner."

Lord Cosgrove ignored him. "He is a villain who is seeking to rise above his station," he said, tilting his nose up into the air. "And if he does not cease his arrogant activities, I shall have the authorities brought to this establishment to make him stop."

"Authorities?" Danny crossed his arms, looking as though he were barely able to contain his humor. "Like Lord Clerkenwell?"

"If necessary," Lord Cosgrove sniffed.

Danny shrugged. "Good. I'll have his usual table prepared for him before he gets here."

Lord Cosgrove lost some of his swagger, his shoulders dropping. He hissed in annoyance. "What has become of the world when any street urchin thinks they can challenge establishment and breeding?"

"You think establishment and breeding makes a man competent in business and land development?" Danny asked, one eyebrow raised.

"Yes," Lord Cosgrove said, gaping as though it were obvious. "It is a well-known fact that the lower classes are mentally deficient, that their brains are malformed, and that they are incapable of even the meanest tasks without supervision and instruction."

Phoebe expected Danny to laugh the comment off, as he'd laughed the rest of Lord Cosgrove's nonsense off. Instead, all teasing vanished from his expression, leaving him the very picture of dangerous determination.

"You think that where I was born and who my parents are is a determining factor in whether I am as much of a man as you are?" he asked in a threatening voice, stepping closer to Lord Cosgrove.

Lord Cosgrove pulled back, seeming to shrink before Phoebe's eyes. "Well, yes," he admitted.

Danny continued to close the space between them. "You think that because I speak in a certain way that I am incapable of thinking circles around you or acting propitiously to advance my business concerns?" His accent shifted to one as fine as any gentleman would use.

Phoebe raised a hand to her stomach to still the butterflies there. Her heart raced at the way Danny arched an eyebrow at Lord Cosgrove, demanding an answer.

All Lord Cosgrove could manage was, "The contract should go to me."

Lord Marlowe stood at the table. "The contract will go to whichever firm offers the best proposal and makes the most convincing case in parliamentary hearings."

"Ah!" Lord Cosgrove jumped back, pointing to Lord Marlowe as though his statement won him the argument. "You see? The contract will go to the best candidate. And we all know what that means when it comes to Parliament."

Phoebe thought the argument was nonsense, but Danny's face fell into a frown.

"This isn't over yet, Cosgrove," he said in a growl that sent shivers down Phoebe's spine. "I advise you to leave my pub immediately."

"I shall, sir." Lord Cosgrove tilted his chin up and marched past Danny. Before he reached the door, he turned to Phoebe. "Will you accompany me, Lady Phoebe? I am quite certain I can find better accommodations for you than anything this bounder has offered."

"I am quite satisfied with the flat Mr. Long is renting to us," Phoebe said, pressing her hand to her stomach harder as the butterflies switched to some more sinister kind of fluttering.

"Phoebe," her mother hissed. "Lord Cosgrove is making an offer you cannot refuse."

"And yet, I do refuse it, Mama," Phoebe said with a long-suffering sigh. "Please do not ask me again, Lord Cosgrove." She met Lord Cosgrove's eyes with what she hoped was a firm stare.

"I can see I will need to sweeten the pot a bit," Lord Cosgrove said with a sniff. He glanced past Phoebe to Danny. "But rest assured, I know how to convince Parliament to grant the development contract to the correct party." He looked to Phoebe again. "You will see all I have to offer you in time."

Phoebe opened her mouth to protest, but Lord Cosgrove turned abruptly and marched out to the street.

"Well. Isn't this a fine kettle of fish?" Phoebe's mother snapped. "Turning down the best proposal you're ever likely to get out of sheer stubbornness." She clucked her tongue and turned to Danny with a glare. "And you, sir. Attempting to rise above your betters. You should be ashamed of yourself."

"Shame is a wasted emotion, my lady," Danny said with a shrug. "I never had much use for it."

"I can see that," Phoebe's mother said tightly. "And your manager, Mr. Umbridge, apparently sees that too. You will tell the man that he is not to barge into our flat whenever he feels the need. He is a loathsome oaf who cannot keep his smiles to himself."

"He was fitting the door for a new lock, Lady Darlington," Natalia said, bouncing Dennis in her arms.

"Yes, a lock which he no doubt holds the key for and will creep into our flat in the dead of night to murder us in our beds," Phoebe's mother said with almost theatrical levels of drama.

"Umbridge doesn't even like swatting flies," Danny laughed, his humor returning. "But I'll tell him to have a care, if you'd like."

"Very good." Phoebe's mother squared her shoulders and tried to look like the marchioness she once was. "Now, come along, Phoebe. We have decorating to do."

"Yes, Mama," Phoebe sighed and started out of the pub with her mother.

"Hang on a minute." Danny jumped after her. "I need Lady Darlington's help with something."

"It's Lady *Phoebe*," Phoebe's mother sighed in irritation. "And you cannot have her."

Phoebe glanced between Danny and her mother. "I really do owe it to Mr. Long to help out with whatever concern he has, Mama, seeing as he's giving us the flat at a greatly reduced rate."

"I'll help you decorate, Lady Darlington," Natalia said with a broad smile.

Phoebe's mother sighed as though the weight of the world were on her shoulders. "Very well, then."

The two of them left the pub, Phoebe's mother muttering and Natalia giggling. Phoebe watched until they were gone, then turned to Danny.

"What can I do for you?" Her gut quivered in expectation. Then again, surely Danny wouldn't spell out the illicit terms of their rental agreement in the middle of an increasingly crowded pub with a table full of noblemen who knew them both mere feet away.

She was right. Danny motioned for Phoebe to join him with the others at the table. He even pulled out a chair so she could be seated.

"How do we beat him?" he asked.

Phoebe blinked a few times, baffled at the turn of events. She wasn't sure she entirely grasped the situation until Lord Howsden said, "He'll play dirty. It's likely he'll seek out the names of the men serving on the land development committee."

"He'll find a way to woo them," Lord Harrington agreed, nodding to Lord Howsden. Not for the first time, Phoebe was struck by the sweetness between the two men.

Before she could think more of it, Danny went on with, "If Cosgrove thinks he can charm the land committee, then we need to charm them first."

Phoebe raised her eyebrows at him. "I'm not sure that's entirely above board."

"Of course it isn't above board," Danny said with a teasing grin. "Nothing is ever truly above board in business."

"You can say that again," the man Phoebe didn't know said with a half-laugh.

"So we have to find a way to beat him at his game," Danny went on. "You lot know nobs far better than I do. What sort of thing would sway the opinion of a bunch of peers parceling out development deals?" He glanced around the table at the men, then stared square at Phoebe.

Phoebe's mouth dropped open, and she blinked rapidly for a moment as she thought. "I suppose gentlemen in Parliament would want to see that the man they are granting the contract to speaks their same language."

"Very true," Lord Howsden said. The others nodded and hummed in agreement.

"Cosgrove is right about the peerage not breaking ranks if they can possibly avoid it," Lord Harrington agreed.

"So, what?" Danny shrugged. "How do I convince a bunch of toffs that I'm as much of a toff as they are?"

"You could try speaking in a more refined way," Lord Marlowe said, looking sheepish as he made the suggestion.

"You dress well enough, but you could always try to outmatch those members of Parliament with the latest fashions," the man Phoebe didn't know said.

Lord Marlowe grunted and shook his head. "I'm not sure that would be a good idea. Class is defined by dress, and the quickest way to offend the nobility is for someone to dress above their station."

"Stations are for trains," Danny growled, sitting back in his chair and crossing his arms. "Have we made no progress at all as a society? Is rank and birth still more important than ability and cleverness?"

"Yes," All three of the gentlemen at the table answered in unison.

The man Phoebe didn't know merely winced and glanced warily at the others. The simple reaction told Phoebe he wasn't a member of the aristocracy.

"You could host a ball," she said quietly, not entirely comfortable with speaking out at a table filled with men. Class wasn't the only determining factor in leadership. Women were looked down on as much as men like Danny. Which inspired a wave of sympathy for Danny's plight that Phoebe hadn't expected.

"A ball," Danny said, his smile returning. "That

might just do the trick." He stroked his chin, leaning back farther in his chair. "Ply them all with food and drink. Show them a good time. Offer a few parting gifts as they say their goodbyes for the evening."

"You cannot bribe members of Parliament," Phoebe said, astonished that Danny would even think as much.

The others seemed entirely nonplussed. "You might be on to something there," Lord Harrington said.

"I wouldn't put it past Cosgrove to try something similar," Lord Marlowe said with a shrug.

Danny swayed suddenly forward, thumping his hands on the table. "It's settled, then. We'll throw a ball to woo parliamentary nobs into rewarding me the contract. Then you and I can discuss your plans for a safe settlement, Mr. Dandie," he said to the man Phoebe didn't know.

"I look forward to it," Mr. Dandie said, rising. "Now if you will excuse me, gentlemen. I have a business to run. My partner, Mr. Wirth, and I are interviewing candidates for an open office manager position today."

The other gentlemen stood to shake Mr. Dandie's hand and wish him goodbye. Whatever business they'd come for seemed to be concluded, and the rest of them said their goodbyes and gathered their things to leave as well.

Phoebe smiled and nodded to the men, then turned to leave herself.

"Wait one moment," Danny whispered to her, catching the fabric of her sleeve and tugging her toward the bar at the back of the increasingly noisy common room. "We have one other thing to discuss."

Butterflies filled Phoebe's stomach anew as she followed Danny around the bar to what appeared to be an office at the back of the pub. The small room contained a desk piled with ledgers, shelves lined with more ledgers and what looked to be samples of mugs, plates, and cutlery, as well as other thing that might be used for service in a pub. She could barely catch her breath as Danny shut the door, sealing the two of them alone in the room.

"I'd like you to do something for me," Danny said, a spark of cunning in his eyes as he turned to face her.

Phoebe gulped and pressed a hand to her stomach. This was it. This was the moment when she had to decide just how far she'd go to put a roof over her and her mother's heads. "What would you like me to do?" she asked, her voice cracking.

The corner of Danny's mouth twitched as he stepped closer to her. His presence was overpowering to the point where Phoebe knew beyond a shadow of a doubt that she wouldn't be able to resist whatever he had in mind.

"I want you," he began slowly, "to plan this ball for me." He stopped only a few feet in front of her.

Phoebe held her breath, then blinked. "You want me to plan a ball for you?" She dropped her hand to her side.

"I don't know the first thing about nob balls," he said, then burst into a sudden grin. "Though I suspect Reese and Freddy do." He chuckled.

Phoebe had no idea what he was talking about. "You want me to plan a ball," she repeated.

"Yes." Danny inched closer to her. "You've been to fancy balls before, right?"

"I have."

"So you know what they involve. You'll know how to impress the upper classes. And you'll know where I could host the right sort of event."

"I—" Phoebe continued to feel off-balance. The conversation wasn't at all what she thought it would be.

"We'll consider this your rental payment," Danny went on.

That surprised Phoebe even more. "*This* is what you want as rental payment?" she asked, baffled.

Danny's mouth pulled into a wicked grin. "What did you think I was going to ask you for?"

Heat flooded Phoebe's face and her eyes fluttered down. He knew exactly what she'd been thinking. Knowing that made her feel as exposed as if he'd torn her blouse wide open.

"Hey," he said softly, stepping close enough to rest a hand under her chin and tilt her head up to him. "Didn't I say you shouldn't do that anymore?"

"Do what?" Her voice shook.

"Get that sad, defeated look. It doesn't suit you." He moved closer still, so close she could feel the heat of his body.

"I'm sorry," she said, trying to look down again on

instinct. Her motion met the resistance of his hand, which kept her chin up.

"Don't be sorry," he said. "Ever."

He leaned into her, slanting his mouth over hers and stealing the breath from her lungs with a kiss. Phoebe couldn't believe she'd let herself be lured into a kiss yet again, but this one was as astounding as the last. She gave into it without a fight, letting him devour her mouth and tease her lips and tongue with his own. It felt so good that her eyes fluttered shut and she let out a sound of surrender before she could stop herself.

As soon as the sound was made, Danny pulled abruptly back, sucking in a breath. "If you start with that, I'm not going to be able to stop," he said in a rough voice. He took another step back and cleared his throat, then boomed. "No time for indulgence. We have a ball to plan."

CHAPTER 8

*T*here was nothing Danny loved more than a good challenge. Beating Cosgrove at his game was one of the most exciting challenges that had come his way in years. Partially because it involved more than just land deals, it involved Phoebe. Cosgrove wanted her, but Phoebe wanted nothing to do with him. That gave Danny the chance not only to step up and be her champion—a role that he rather liked the more he thought about it—it meant he could thwart Cosgrove on two fronts at the same time. And men like Cosgrove deserved to be taken down a peg or seven.

But there was an additional level of challenge to the Earl's Court deal that interested Danny—the one presented by Mr. John Dandie. Danny was sympathetic to the plight of any group of people that was ignored or denigrated by the ruling classes. While he didn't have a lick of interest in other men the way Dandie implied his friends did, Danny loved the idea of flying in the face of society's norms by giving those men a place to live. He didn't believe a word of the nastiness the papers printed about them or their depravity. Men like that weren't the cause of the moral degeneracy that the papers said threatened the city, men like Cosgrove were. So if he could help out one group and thumb his nose at another, he was all for it.

Which was how he found himself knocking on the open doorway of a discreet office tucked into a neglected corner of The City on Monday morning.

"Hello?" he bellowed, even though the front room of the office was only half as big as the common room of his pub. "Is this where Mr. John Dandie works?"

The two men at the desk on one side of the office glanced up from what they were doing. The man seated at the desk was young and slender, with blue eyes, a pale complexion, and a keen eye for fashion. The man standing over him, looking as though he were pointing out the way the open ledgers on the desk were organized, was tall with dark hair and eyes and a decidedly serious look. Based on what Dandie had said at the pub the other day, Danny assumed the seated man was the newly hired office manager and the standing one was the partner, David Wirth.

"Mr. Long." Dandie himself strode out of the back office, all smiles and welcoming. "What a pleasant surprise to see you here this morning."

Dandie crossed the room, offering Danny a hand. Danny shook it boisterously. "So this is your office, eh?"

"This is it," Dandie replied with a broad smile. "We're rather proud of what we've built. This is my partner, Mr. David Wirth."

"I've heard all about you," Danny said, crossing the room to shake Wirth's hand, pleasantly surprised by how firm the man's handshake was.

"And this is our new office manager, Mr. Lionel Mercer," Dandie went on, moving to the desk and gesturing to the fashionable young man.

Mercer stood and reached over the desk, surprising Danny with yet another strong handshake. "It's a pleasure," Mercer said, a flash of appreciation in his eyes.

Danny laughed in spite of himself. He'd never been so overtly sized up by a man before, especially not one who didn't seem at all fussed about letting on what his tastes were. "Looks like those interviews you had to rush off to the other day bore fruit, eh, Dandie?" He turned back to Dandie.

"They did." Dandie nodded. "Mr. Mercer had the finest credentials and the most glowing recommendations of any candidate we spoke to."

"And the most intriguing connections," Wirth added with a sideways look to the young man.

"You flatter me," Mercer said modestly, but in a way that conveyed absolute certainty in himself.

Danny could tell in an instant that the man was a

wealth of adventure just waiting to be tapped, but he turned to Dandie, intent on discussing business. "So, what can you tell me about this proposed property development you'd like me to undertake once I win the Earl's Court deal?" he asked as though the deal were a foregone conclusion.

Dandie shrugged. "Mostly what we discussed before. I envision a square—much like the ones that are already being planned and executed in that part of the city—which contains terraced apartments which will be rented to members of a certain organization we belong to." He nodded to the other two men.

Danny's mind tickled with curiosity to know what organization they were talking about, although he suspected it was one he wouldn't be allowed access to for a variety of reasons.

"Are you certain you'll be able to win the contract?" Wirth asked before Danny could pry for details.

Danny figured he was trying to protect his own by deflecting Danny's interest. He let the topic go, shrugged, and said, "I'm as certain as I am of anything. Though getting around Cosgrove's bid for the contract could prove more of a hurdle than I want it to be."

"Are you certain Cosgrove's bid for the contract is strong enough that Parliament would consider it?" Dandie asked.

Mercer stepped around the edge of the desk. "Is this Lord Richard Cosgrove?" he asked with keen interest that surprised Danny.

"It is." Danny faced him. "Do you know the man?"

"Not personally," Mercer said with a shrug. "I am particular friends with a few gentlemen who have spoken freely about him on occasion, though."

Danny's eyebrows inched up. "What have they said when they spoke freely? Is he a true threat for the Earl's Court contract?"

Wirth and Dandie seemed as interested in the question as Danny was. All three of them glanced to Mercer.

Mercer tilted his head to the side slightly, as though he enjoyed being the center of their attention and the one whom they all looked to for knowledge. "He has been putting a great deal of effort into land development," he said. "Or, at least, charging his solicitor, Mr. Grey, with putting effort into it. It seems his hereditary estates are in dire need of updating. The income they provide is more on paper than in reality. He needs the Earl's Court development and the income it would provide to shore up his home defenses, as it were."

Danny gaped at the man. "How do you know all that?" he asked, grinning at the man's cleverness.

Mercer answered the question with a coquettish smile. "As I said, I have quite a few friends who are mutual acquaintances of Lord Cosgrove."

"And half of the rest of England," Dandie added in a low voice. "Those are the credentials that earned him the job."

"Gossip," Danny laughed. "They gave you the job because you know all the gossip."

"I prefer to call it sensitive information of an important character," Mercer said with a coy grin.

Danny crossed his arms and stared at Mercer in challenge. "All right, then. If you've got all the dirt on all the nobs, tell me this. I'm planning a ball to sway those parliamentary toffs whose job it is to decide who gets the contract. Well, Lady Phoebe is planning it for me, really. How can we—"

"Lady Phoebe?" Mercer blinked as though the mention of Phoebe's name had sparked something in his mind. "That wouldn't be Lady Phoebe Darlington, would it?"

Danny's amusement at Mercer's seeming omniscience turned to a wary need to protect Phoebe from whatever threat strangers knowing her business might present. "That's her," he said carefully.

"And you say she is working with you to plan a ball with the intent of undercutting Lord Cosgrove's bid on the development contract?" Mercer asked on.

Danny writhed inwardly at the man's astuteness. "Yes. And she's under my protection." He probably didn't need to add the last bit, but he felt better staking his claim all the same.

"I'm glad to hear it," Mercer said, surprising Danny yet again.

"You are?" Wirth asked, as baffled by the whole exchange as Danny was. Dandie looked impressed with Mercer's knowledge as well.

Mercer paced around to the front of the desk, tapping

his lips with one finger as though lost in thought. He came to rest with his backside against the front of the desk. "Lord Cosgrove was friends with Lady Phoebe Darlington's father, if that sort of character can be said to have friends."

"I looked into him," Danny said. "The man was a waste of time and space, if you ask me."

"He most definitely was," Lionel said with a look of complete knowing. "I could tell you stories…." He shook his head. "Some other time. Lord Cosgrove, as I said, was Lord Darlington's friend. He knew far more about Lord Darlington's affairs than most people realize." He paused again, brow knitting in thought. "It is my understanding that Cosgrove has been pursuing Lady Phoebe. Do you know if this is true?"

Something visceral ignited inside of Danny. "He is, but he won't get anywhere with her," he growled. "She's mine."

Mercer's eyebrows flew up. "Interesting. I must say, I'm glad to hear she has a protector. She'll need it with what Cosgrove is planning."

"How in God's name do you have any idea what Cosgrove is planning?" Dandie asked, clearly baffled, and yet also amused by the oracle that was Lionel Mercer.

"The solicitor I mentioned," Mercer said. "Mr. Grey. He was also Lord Darlington's solicitor. He happens to be prone to extensive pillow talk and sharing more than he should."

Danny's brow shot up so fast he was surprised his

eyebrows didn't fly right off. So that was how Mercer got his information, was it?

Mercer went on, pushing away from the desk and pacing across the room, knowing he had the full attention of all three men. "There is a point of contention in Lord Darlington's will," he said.

"But Darlington died years ago," Wirth said with a confused shrug. "Hasn't the will been processed yet?"

"It hasn't," Mercer said. "For a particular reason. Cosgrove and Grey have deliberately sought to delay proceedings, though I'm certain they've come up with some sort of excuse to tell the dowager marchioness and her daughter about the delay." He paused, tilting his head to the side. "If they even know about it at all. Grey was the one they would have dealt with, and since he has a stake in keeping the whole thing secret...."

"What are you talking about, man?" Danny boomed when Mercer seemed to disappear into his own thoughts.

The outburst shook Mercer back to attention. "There is an issue of whether the estate of the late Lord Darlington is entailed away to a male relative or not. As I understand it, it may be inheritable by Lady Phoebe after all."

Danny's jaw dropped. "Are you saying that Lady Phoebe might not be as poor as a church mouse after all?"

Mercer winced and shrugged. "It's hard to say. She could inherit the property in question, but whether it is profitable or not remains to be seen."

"Can we see it?" Danny asked, not a clue how inheritance worked with the aristocracy.

A mysterious smile formed on Mercer's face. "We could pay a visit to Grey and ask."

"You're joking," Danny laughed. It was laughable. There was no possible way that the solution to Lady Phoebe's problems could be as simple as marching into a solicitor's office and asking if she was an heiress.

"I never joke in matters of business," Mercer said. An impish grin crossed his lips, and he added, "I can take you there right now, if you'd like." He glanced to Wirth and Dandie. "If my new employers wouldn't mind. Grey's office is only a block away."

"I wouldn't mind," Wirth said, eyes wide enough to indicate he was amazed by the turn of events.

"This is why we hired you, after all," Dandie added.

"Then we'll just be off," Mercer said. He crossed to the stand by the door to fetch his overcoat and hat.

Danny followed him. He hadn't removed his hat or coat in the first place, so he simply followed Mercer out the door.

As they reached the street, Danny leaned closer to Mercer and asked, "So were you a rent boy, then?"

Mercer sent him a look that was equal parts offense and confirmation. "I prefer the term 'particular friend'."

Danny laughed. "I'm surprised working in an office pays more than working in a bedroom."

"It doesn't," Mercer said with sudden seriousness. "But I have other reasons for changing professions."

Danny shrugged. "I don't suppose your former one is the sort anyone would want to stay in, if they could avoid it." Mercer didn't answer. "Still," Danny went on. "It sounds like it's set you up right nice to work with Dandie and Wirth."

"I believe it has," Mercer said, his smile returning. "We've arrived."

"What, already?"

They'd only walked the length of the block and crossed a side street to reach the front of a building that looked the same as any other on the dull street. Mercer marched through the front door and along the foyer to a door marked with a small plaque that read "Grey and Young, Solicitors". He entered without knocking.

"Good morning, Healey," he said to the clerk at the front desk in the small, cramped reception room, treating the man to a wider than usual smile. "What a delight to see you again."

"Lionel." The man behind the desk lit up like the new, electric streetlights popping up all over the city. He stood and skirted the desk to greet Lionel with a handshake that looked as though it wanted to be something more.

"Listen, Healey," Mercer said, tugging the man so close Danny wondered if he should be there to witness the exchange. "We're in a bit of a hurry. We need to take a look at Lord Richard Darlington's will. Can you help us?"

"After the way you helped me," Healey said with a flicker of one eyebrow, "I'd do anything for you."

"You're such a precious doll," Mercer cooed, stroking a hand along Healey's smooth cheek. "Could we view it somewhere private? I'm not sure Percival would be happy to know you let me have a look." He glanced down at the man's trousers as though asking to look at something else entirely.

"Certainly," Healey said in a rough voice, gesturing for Mercer and Danny to follow him to a room off to one side. He had to unlock the door with a key kept in his pocket, but once they were inside of what looked to be a dusty, old records room, he left the door open. "It's this one right here," the man went on, scrambling to fetch a flat box from one of the alphabetized shelves.

He placed the box on the table and gazed at Mercer as though seeing Apollo himself. It was all Danny could do not to burst into snorting laughter at the young man's eagerness, or at Mercer's cunning.

"You're a tricky little cunt, you are," Danny said, nudging Mercer with his elbow after Healey left the room to see to some other business.

"I have been called that before," Mercer said with a teasing, sideways look.

He removed the cover from the box and rifled through the pages. There wasn't much to rifle through. Lord Darlington's will was one of the few documents the box contained, though it was as long as a novel, as far as Danny was concerned.

"I'll never be able to read through this fast enough to find mention of Lady Phoebe's claims," Danny lamented, starting in on the first paragraph.

"It's all a matter of knowing how to read a will," Mercer said, taking the pages and thumbing through them. "Wills follow a prescribed pattern. Much of the language is the same in any one you look at. The specifics of inheritance, particularly when it comes to property claims, are generally located in the same—ah! Here you go."

He handed the will back to Danny, pointing at a certain spot farther down the page. Danny read it with a frown. He knew his way around legal language, considering how many real estate contracts he'd dealt with, but it never failed to frustrate him. Worse still, the particular terms of the will were as convoluted as he'd ever seen.

"The estate in Herefordshire goes to Lady Phoebe, provided she's past her twenty-fifth birthday. If not, it should be administered by her mother?" Danny glanced at Mercer in horror. "God save us all from that. If Phoebe isn't yet twenty-five, Grey and Cosgrove might be doing us all a favor."

"Read on." Mercer nudged him.

Danny did as he asked, fairly certain Mercer had managed to read the entire page in full already. Once he saw what must have put the sly grin on Mercer's face, he glanced at the man again.

"If Phoebe marries, the whole kit and caboodle goes to her husband?" Danny slammed the will pages together. "Women really do get the thin end of the wedge, don't they."

"They most certainly do," Mercer agreed. "But think about it. Why else would Cosgrove be so adamant about courting Lady Phoebe? If he marries her, he gets the estate."

"And if there's any chance of Darlington's estate making so much as a cent, he stands to profit handsomely, the nasty bugger."

"Careful who you assume is nasty, sir," Mercer said with pretend offense. It was clear to Danny that Mercer was enjoying the investigation and the subterfuge of it all as much as he was.

Their fun was interrupted by voices from the main part of the office, though. Particularly Mr. Healey's overly loud greeting of, "Lord Cosgrove. How unexpected to see you today."

Danny leapt into giddy motion, rushing to the door and shutting it as far as he could while still leaving enough of a crack for them to hear whatever conversation might take place with Cosgrove. Mercer joined him at the door. The two of them turned their ears to the inch-wide crack like daft schoolboys about to pull a prank.

"I'm here to see Mr. Grey," Cosgrove said.

"Lord Cosgrove," a new voice—Danny was certain it was Mr. Grey—greeted Cosgrove. "What brings you to my office today?"

"I need your help, Grey." Cosgrove crossed so close to the cracked door to the records room that Danny and

Mercer both held their breaths. "I need you to free up a bit of funding for an important project I must undertake."

"You don't sound too happy about it, whatever it is," Grey said.

"I'm not," Cosgrove grumbled. "It's this damnable Earl's Court land deal."

"Oh? I thought you were enthusiastic about that," Grey said.

"I was," Cosgrove said. "Until I discovered I have competition. I cannot lose that deal, Grey. I need to convince the members of Parliament who are on the committee to award the contract that I am the one they should award it to."

"What did you have in mind?" Grey asked. Their voices moved farther from the door, and Danny feared the two would step into another office and seal themselves away before he could hear what he needed to.

"Something," Cosgrove said. "Anything. Some sort of fete to show the gentlemen a good time and remind them whom they should be dealing with."

"A day at the races?" Grey suggested. "A musical evening? A ball?"

It was all Danny could do not to snort, even though Cosgrove and Grey disappeared into another room and their conversation became too muffled to hear.

"I told her he would bloody well try the same thing I'm trying," he said to himself.

"Her being Lady Phoebe?" Mercer asked.

"Exactly." Danny stood straighter, stepping out of the

room. There was no need to hide, now that Cosgrove and Grey were safely tucked away in a back office, but he didn't want to overstay his welcome, now that he knew what he needed to know. "She's in more danger than I thought." The thought brought a scowl to his face.

"Thank you, Healey," Mercer whispered as he and Danny hurried out of the office.

"Wait. When can I see you again?" Healey chased after them.

"I'm afraid I'm out of the game now, love," Mercer called back to him. "But we'll be in touch."

They rushed out of the office, leaving a disappointed Healey behind.

"Heartbreaker," Danny teased Mercer once they were on the street, elbowing his arm again.

"I'm surprised you view me so cavalierly, Mr. Long," Mercer said with genuine surprise.

Danny shrugged. "When you've come from where I come from and seen all that I've seen, you take humanity as it comes, not as society says you should take it." He picked up his pace as they strode back toward the offices of Dandie & Wirth.

"How very progressive of you," Mercer said with a smile. "Lady Phoebe is a lucky woman."

Danny laughed, though his laughter had an edge to it. "She hasn't been lucky so far. After reading that will, it seems to me that the very people who should have helped her all this time have, in fact, dealt incredibly poorly with her."

He had never meant his words more in his life. Phoebe was entitled to so much more than anyone was giving her. She shouldn't have had to struggle and work in a shop to put a roof over her head. She had money coming to her, or an estate at the very least. Even if the estate wasn't profitable, he could think of a thousand different ways to develop it for her and make a pretty penny.

But if Phoebe did inherit and became an independent woman of means, she wouldn't need to rely on him anymore. And he could already feel that pull of reliance on him, though their acquaintance was short. He might not have been a rogue, like Cosgrove, but he'd be lying if he didn't admit to himself that he liked being able to be Phoebe's champion. If she inherited the way she was supposed to, there was a fair chance she would leave him behind, and he wasn't sure he was ready for that.

CHAPTER 9

*P*hoebe was a bundle of nerves as she approached the door of Campbell House after her early shift at Harrods on Monday afternoon. She stepped back as soon as she'd rung the bell and adjusted her new gloves nervously. The gloves Danny had gifted her were the only nice thing she owned anymore, and considering the importance—and the audacity—of her mission, she needed every little hint of refinement she could get.

She was surprised when the door was opened not by Lady Cecelia Marlowe's butler, but by Natalia.

"Good. You're here," Natalia said, reaching through the doorway, grabbing Phoebe's hand, and pulling her into the grand, Mayfair house. "And not a moment too soon."

"Have you taken to answering doors now?" Phoebe

asked, her nerves bursting into a full-blown butterfly riot in her gut.

Natalia laughed aloud. "I knew you were coming," she said.

"It was your idea," Phoebe whispered as Natalia dragged her farther down the hall.

And it certainly was Natalia's idea for Phoebe to seek the help of the May Flowers with Danny's ball. Phoebe never would have dreamed of approaching her old acquaintances for anything, let alone help with an event of this magnitude. She had met Natalia at church on Sunday and spilled out the problem of hosting a ball for members of Parliament without any resources or even a location, and Natalia had come up with the May Flowers as a solution.

"They're meeting in Cece's conservatory," Natalia whispered, lowering her voice as she tugged Phoebe to the end of the hall. "They've been arguing since they arrived about whether to support the new, more radical movement for women's suffrage that is beginning or whether to take a quieter, more domestic approach.

"As I understand it, that's the same argument they've been having for years," Phoebe said.

Natalia giggled as she led Phoebe to the entrance of the conservatory. "Don't tell them that. The May Flowers certainly aren't what they used to be when Henrietta led us and we were deeply involved in The Irish Question."

"Are you still a member?" Phoebe blinked in surprise.

She'd thought that perhaps Natalia had been ousted for marrying beneath her.

"As long as Cece has any sway with the group, I am allowed to attend," Natalia said. She held a finger to her lips and pulled Phoebe into the conservatory.

"This new, radical approach is scandalous," Lady Maude was in the middle of saying. Phoebe's heart sank at once at the sight of the young woman. It hadn't even been a week since she and Lady Jane had come to Harrods to pester her. "How are we supposed to convince the men of Parliament to grant rights to women if we behave like hellions instead of the stable, domestic, moralizing force that we are?"

"How can we hope to gain a voice at all if we continue to relegate ourselves to mere household decorations?" Lady Diana Pickwick argued. Phoebe was shocked to see the usually soft and demure woman standing and gesturing as though she were about to go to war.

Lady Maude scoffed at her. "The only reason you despise being seen as a household ornament is because you are still a fixture in your father's house at, what age are you again, Lady Diana?"

Lady Diana's expression was downright thunderous. "I believe I am a month younger than you, Lady Maude. And where are you currently residing?"

Lady Maude snapped her mouth shut, her face turning puce with embarrassment. "I, at least, have a beau," she said in an undertone.

A strange feeling of otherness hit Phoebe square in the chest. The argument seemed somehow small and petty in her eyes. Two ladies of wealth and breeding, with every advantage the world could give to them, with upstanding and noble parents and fortunes that were secure, were arguing about being unmarried in their mid-twenties. She peeked down at her work skirt, noting the frayed edge of its hem, and became aware of the way her feet ached and pinched from standing behind a shop counter all morning. There was so much more for a woman to worry about than her marital state. Just as there were so many more ways for a woman to be proud of herself and her place in the world than having a husband.

Danny would approve of her assessment.

The thought struck her out of nowhere, causing her to draw in a quick breath. Or perhaps that intake of breath was due to the fact that Lady Maude spotted her standing by Natalia's side in the doorway.

"Well, well. What have we here?" she asked with a venomous smile.

"This meeting is for members only," Lady Jane said, rising to stand by Lady Maude's side. "And it is certainly not for common shop girls."

A flutter of shocked whispers spread through the room. Some of the ladies seemed horrified by Lady Jane's comment. Most merely widened their eyes and stared between Phoebe and Lady Jane, as if the curtain were rising on a stage drama.

Lady Cecelia rose from her seat and walked regally to

Natalia's side. "Lady Phoebe is here by my invitation," she said, taking Phoebe's arm with a kind smile and leading her deeper into the room.

Phoebe glanced warily at the serene woman, anxiety pooling in her stomach. She had no idea Lady Cecelia even knew she was coming, let alone that she had issued an invitation. It made her wonder how much of the whole thing Natalia had shared with her sister-in-law in advance.

"Is this the level to which we have sunk?" Lady Maude commented, taking her seat in the circle of chairs that filled the room and tilting her nose up. "Is anyone allowed to address our assembly now?"

"Lady Phoebe is the daughter of a marquess," Lady Cecelia reminded all of the women assembled, not just Lady Maude. "It is my understanding that she has come to us with a request for help."

The stiff reaction from most of the members of the May Flowers did nothing to ease Phoebe's worry.

"And why should we help her?" Lady Agnes Hamilton asked from farther back in the assembly.

Phoebe's heart sank. She'd always considered Lady Agnes an ally, if not a friend.

"It is our duty to help one another whenever possible," Lady Cecelia answered her gently.

Lady Agnes's expression hardened, as did the expression of several others around her. "Lord Darlington was responsible for the near ruination of my brother," Lady Agnes said, crossing her arms and glaring at Phoebe.

"Chauncey was just starting out in life, but that black-guard came close to bankrupting him and ruining his morals at the same time."

Heat infused Phoebe's face. She was under no illusion as to her father's character.

"Lord Darlington importuned my aunt," another of the assembly, Lady Heldon, spoke up from the back. "She was so distraught by the incident that she returned to the country and has not come back to London since."

"The bastard killed my cousin," yet another lady, Lady Dennison, said, staring daggers at Phoebe, as though she'd like to return the favor.

"Did he?" the woman sitting next to her gasped.

Lady Dennison squirmed in her chair. "Perhaps not directly, but poor Arthur was found murdered in an alley, and the last person to see him was Lord Darlington. At a gaming den. Where he'd just lost a fortune playing cards with Arthur."

"That isn't proof that the man was a murderer," the woman beside her said.

"It isn't proof that he was innocent either," Lady Dennison said.

Phoebe gulped and tried to still her racing heart as more of the women assembled grumbled and raised complaints about the sins of her father. She'd known her father was the worst sort of man possible, but being faced with it all at once, having all of the ire that he should have received for his sins directed at her, was almost more than she could bear. Natalia's idea of coming to the May

Flowers for help was a dismal one. If none of the ladies assembled had been willing to help her and her mother with something as simple as finding a place to live because of her father's wickedness, there was no chance they would help her host a ball.

Still, as more and more invectives were directed against her, she kept her chin up. In spite of every instinct within her that wanted to lower her head and her eyes, as she had a hundred times before whenever faced with the shame of her father or her life as it had become, she looked straight ahead. It was as if she felt Danny's hand under her chin telling her not to back down.

"I am truly, deeply sorry for the pain that my father caused," she managed to say, though her words were drowned out at first by the complaints of the women around her. They quieted when they realized she was speaking. It gave her just enough courage to go on. "I can assure you that whatever ill-fate and hardships have befallen you and your families, those hardships have rained down tenfold on me and my mother."

"As if we should care about you," Lady Jane sniffed.

Far too many people agreed with her.

Holding her head up became as difficult as climbing the Matterhorn with her bare hands. Phoebe swallowed and forced herself to take a breath. "I am truly sorry," she said, her voice shaking. "I can see now this was the wrong quarter in which to search for help. Good day to you all."

She curtsied politely, then turned to leave before she

could burst into tears. A buzz of indignant chatter rose up in her wake as she fled the room.

Once she reached the hall, she clapped a hand to her mouth to keep from sobbing and picked up her pace, racing toward the front door.

"Wait," Lady Cecelia called after her, dashing into the hall.

Phoebe paused long enough to see Natalia, Lady Henrietta O'Shea, and Miss Lenore Garrett follow Lady Cecelia into the hall. She wavered on her spot, desperate to leave, but knowing it would be terribly unmannerly of her to do so.

Lady Cecelia exchanged a glance with Lady Henrietta as they reached Phoebe. "Natalia has told us the sort of help you were going to request," she said.

"You are in need of help hosting a ball?" Lady Henrietta asked, nothing but kindness in her eyes.

Phoebe bit her lip, everything within her wound so tight that she thought she might shatter. "As a favor for a friend," she said, her voice tiny and rough with misery. "I am simply trying to repay his kindness by assisting with his business ventures."

Lady Cecelia and Lady Henrietta exchanged another look, drawing Miss Garett into the exchange as well.

"We're very familiar with Mr. Long," Lady Henrietta said. "He was instrumental in helping my husband bring the men who attacked and injured him to justice."

Phoebe blinked in surprise. She hadn't realized Danny had played a part in the tragic events of the attack on Lord O'Shea that had blinded him in one eye and left him in a wheelchair.

"He also helps my sister-in-law, Lady Clerkenwell, and her husband raise funds for their charitable endeavors," Lady Cecelia said.

Phoebe did remember that. One of those events was where she had first met Danny, even though she barely remembered it.

"Freddy and Reese think very highly of Mr. Long," Miss Garrett added. "I would say it's the least we could do to offer him help in return."

"You should have come directly to us instead of addressing the May Flowers," Lady Henrietta said.

"Believe me," Phoebe said with a sharp exhale, "I am beginning to think that as well."

They all glanced to Natalia, who flushed and stiffened. "I thought this could be a good way to reintroduce Phoebe to society," she said uncomfortably. "You know it is terribly wrong how badly she has been snubbed. Phoebe is the kindest, gentlest soul on the earth, and she certainly doesn't deserve the treatment she's been given. Those ladies should be glad to have a friend like Phoebe." Natalia's voice and energy rose as her speech progressed until she was pointing angrily at the room behind them. "It simply isn't fair," she finished, crossing her arms.

As grateful as she was to Natalia for her friendship at a time when few others were willing to walk on the same side of the street as her, Phoebe had to admit that the young woman still had a lot of learning and maturing to do.

"Thank you for your considerations and for your efforts," she said with a sigh, glancing to the front door, ready to leave. She looked back to Lady Cecelia. "I am sorry to have bothered you with my problems. I suppose I will have to look into halls Mr. Long could rent for his ball."

"Nonsense," Lady Henrietta said, stepping forward and taking Phoebe's arm. She walked with her toward the door. "We'll have the ball at Hopewell House."

"Yes, that's a brilliant idea," Natalia said, hopping into step with Phoebe and Lady Henrietta.

"It's the perfect venue for a party," Miss Garrett said. "I would love a chance to actually plan a grand, London ball instead of just attending one."

"You...you would?" Waves of gratitude washed over Phoebe as she glanced around at her unlikely saviors.

"Certainly," Miss Garrett said with a wide smile. "I love a good party."

"We'll all help you," Lady Cecelia said. "Whether the May Flowers want to be involved or not. We'll consider this our own, private endeavor."

"And perhaps, if the ball is the success that I know we can make it, those bitter old tarts will welcome you back into their society with open arms," Natalia said.

Phoebe glanced askance at her over the comment. It sounded a great deal like her mother's arguments for why she should accept Lord Cosgrove's suit. Even though

Natalia meant well, something felt wrong about the nudge toward the life Phoebe once led. It was as if they were pushing her back toward the cliff she had only barely managed to climb over.

"I cannot thank you enough," she said graciously all the same. "I'll go and tell Mr. Long at once that the ball can move forward."

"Send me a letter letting me know when you would like me to hold it and I'll put things in motion," Lady Henrietta said.

Phoebe left Marlowe House with her spirits renewed, but with a lingering feeling of anxiety all the same. She'd gotten what Natalia had invited her to the meeting to get, but she couldn't shake the feeling that she'd lost something in the process. Now she knew beyond a shadow of a doubt just what the ladies of her former acquaintance thought of her. Even ones who hadn't purchased gloves from her at Harrods. The chasm between her old life and her new one seemed larger than ever.

Those thoughts remained on her mind as she walked across the breadth of Mayfair and up to Oxford Street, then on to Fitzrovia and her new home. The light was already waning and The Watchman was filling up, but she made the decision to enter the pub in order to tell Danny the good news instead of going straight home, like any proper young lady would do.

The contrast in the world of the pub and that of Lady Cecelia's conservatory was like night to day. It was still early, but the crowd that was gathering at the pub seemed more boisterous than usual that evening. Someone had brought a concertina with them and several slightly inebriated customers had broken into song in one corner of the common room. It was a bawdy, cheery tune that Phoebe was embarrassed to admit she knew the words to. Several patrons at other tables were laughing loudly and flirting with the barmaids as they delivered food and pints.

"Lady Darlington, there you are!" Danny's voice was louder than anyone else's as he called to her from where he was addressing a table filled with surprisingly well-dressed men. "The evening is complete!"

He cut his way through the tables to reach her, greeting her with a wide smile and heat in his eyes.

"It's Lady Phoebe, not Lady Darlington," she reminded him with a smile that she couldn't stifle.

"Can it be just Phoebe?" he asked with a sudden air of innocent hope.

Phoebe grinned in spite of herself, charmed by the way he was a man of command and action one moment and a playful boy the next. She rolled her eyes, sighed, and said, "I suppose."

"Lovely."

His single word carried so much heat that she glanced around, acutely aware of the crowd around him. As aware as she was of the memory of his lips against hers and the need that had pulsed through her at his touch twice now.

"I came to tell you that Lady Henrietta O'Shea has

agreed to host your ball at her London home," she said, switching to her mission so that she could flee to the safety of her flat and her feelings without Danny's devilish gaze on her.

"Oh?" He seemed to become even happier and livelier than he already was. "That's brilliant. I knew you could do it."

"It wasn't me, really," she protested. "In fact, I was certain that the May Flowers would chase me out of Lady Cecelia Marlowe's house with torches and pitchforks."

"Is that so?" A sharp edge filled Danny's words, and he crossed his arm.

"I think I'm better off without them," Phoebe said, surprised that she actually meant it. The afternoon had certainly given her rich food for thought. She blinked and glanced up at Danny once more. "Lady Henrietta asked me to send her word of when you'd like to have the ball."

"As soon as possible," Danny said with the businesslike gleam in his eyes that she found even more alluring than his impishness. "Could she do it on Friday?"

"I don't know, but I'll send word to her," Phoebe said.

"Good." Danny's expression lit with confidence all over again. "We'll beat Cosgrove at his game yet."

"I'm sure we will," Phoebe laughed, enjoying the sense of competition, mad though it was.

But even as she shifted into mischievousness, Danny's expression took on a thoughtful, clouded, almost anxious look.

"There's something I found out," he began, but snapped his mouth shut. He stared at her, brow knit.

When Phoebe's anticipation rose to towering levels, she blurted, "What did you find out?"

Danny's jaw clenched, as though he wanted to say something but couldn't. At last, he said, "I found out that Cosgrove is planning a similar event to our ball. That's why we need to get things done as fast as possible."

"Of course." Phoebe let out a breath, surprised that she was relieved by his statement. She'd worried it could have been much worse. "I'll express as much to Lady Henrietta when I write to her. Which I plan to do immediately."

She turned to go, but Danny caught her arm. When she whirled back to him, he grinned and asked, "Would you accompany me to the ball?"

Bursts of heat and giddiness filled Phoebe's chest. "Are you asking me especially?" she asked, her voice almost too low and shy to be heard.

"Of course," he said, his smile growing. "I wouldn't want to go with anyone else."

Again, the comparison between Danny and Lord Cosgrove—or any other man of her acquaintance—was all Phoebe could think about. Danny's invitation was almost bashful. He didn't assume she would give a favorable answer. It was the most endearing thing she'd ever known.

"I would love to attend the ball with you," she said, lowering her eyes, but for an entirely different reason than shame. She felt so much like a fairy princess accepting the invitation of a prince that the noise and vulgarity of the pub seemed to vanish around her, leaving nothing but the soaring hope in her heart.

"Excellent," Danny said with a strong nod and a bright smile. "I'll purchase a new suit tomorrow. And I want you to buy yourself a new gown as well," he went on.

"Oh, I don't have the money to spare for that. I'll remake something I already own," she said.

"You will not," Danny insisted. "I'll pay for it. It's the least I can do, seeing as you've helped me so much."

"That's...that's so generous of you." Phoebe's heart fluttered, though she wondered how much money Danny had to spare.

He leaned in closer, winking at her as though they were alone. "Love, you haven't even begun to know how generous I can be."

He spoke the words as though they were an embrace. It left Phoebe certain beyond a doubt that the sort of generosity he was speaking of had nothing to do with money or gowns or balls. And mad as it was, she found herself longing to experience what he was claiming and wishing her original assumptions about how she would pay her rent were true after all.

ithin ten minutes of the beginning of the ball at Hopewell House, Danny was convinced that the entire form of entertainment was mostly pointless. At least as a means of having fun. As he stood near the entrance to Lady Henrietta O'Shea's ballroom, greeting guests the way Phoebe had instructed him to, the collar of his new and ridiculously expensive suit choking him and the starch in his shirt itching, all he saw were a bunch of self-congratulatory nobs posing and preening as a means to impress each other.

"Shouldn't there be music and dancing?" he murmured to Phoebe out of the side of his mouth, leaning closer to her than was probably appropriate, given the setting.

"The dancing will start within the half-hour," Phoebe whispered back. "It is necessary to give the guests time to arrive and be seen first."

"The ball began at eight o'clock," Danny argued. He slipped his gold pocket watch out of his tight, brocade waistcoat—something he'd been told was too colorful and arresting for the current fashion, not that he cared—and checked the time. "It's nearly nine already. Where is everyone?"

"Have you never heard the term 'fashionably late', Mr. Long?" Lady O'Shea herself said, slipping up to Danny's side with a mischievous grin. She pushed her husband, the inimitable Lord Fergus O'Shea, with her.

"Have they never heard the phrase 'the early bird catches the worm'?" Danny replied, knowing his voice was already growing too loud. He added in a quieter tone, "You're looking well, Fergus. Is that a new eye-patch?" And flashed him a teasing grin.

"It's only a shame I can't make the reply I'd like to make to that comment with ladies present," Fergus replied, grinning himself. "And you'll get used to this lot and their fickle ways soon enough." He paused to grunt out a laugh, then added, "The way things are going with your property empire, you'll displace us all in no time, regardless."

Danny laughed, but his chest went tight. He peeked sideways at Phoebe to see what she made of the comment. As far as he could discern, she still hadn't figured out that he was more than just a pub owner and a landlord. And after what he'd learned about her chances of inheriting an entire country estate, he wasn't sure he wanted to spill his whole story to her.

The wariness caused by Fergus's comment doubled to bloody annoying anxiety at the memory of how he'd lost his nerve to tell Phoebe about her possible inheritance the other day. He still couldn't put his finger on why he hadn't solved all of her problems and brought joy back to her life by telling her all was not lost and she could go on being the grand, aristocratic lady after all. Except that he did know. If Phoebe took up possession of her inheritance and returned to her old life, she'd be done with him. And damn him, he wasn't ready to let her walk out of his life. Not by a long shot.

"Guests," Phoebe whispered, startling Danny into realizing that he'd been staring at her like a lovesick fool. "You have guests to greet."

Danny sucked in a breath and stood straighter, extending a hand to the stodgy old fellow who stepped up to greet him.

"This is Mr. Esslemont." Lady O'Shea made the introduction. "He is the Member of Parliament for Aberdeenshire East." Excitement sparkled in her eyes.

Danny took his cue without hesitation. "Mr. Esslemont," he said in as refined an accent as he could muster. "What a pleasure to meet you. I'm Daniel Long of Long Property Ventures." He hated using his full name, hated speaking like a toff, and generally felt like the worst sort of impostor.

But Mr. Esslemont's expression brightened as they shook hands. "Mr. Long. The pleasure is all mine. I've read your proposal to the parliamentary committee on land development, and I must say, I was quite impressed."

"Perhaps we'll have a chance to discuss it more this evening," Danny played along with the whole charade. He couldn't keep it up, though. "Though if you ask me," he went on, falling into a lower-class accent, "we're here to have fun, eh?" He slapped Esslemont on the arm.

Esslemont laughed—clearly shocked by the gesture— but unoffended, before moving on.

Danny glanced to Phoebe. She stared back at him with an uncertain look.

"I know, I know," he said, his shoulders dropping. "That's not how nobs behave with MPs. But you can't expect a leopard to change his spots that readily."

He expected censure, but found curiosity in Phoebe's eyes instead. "No, indeed," she said, though there wasn't as much judgement in her voice as he expected.

Lady O'Shea cleared her throat, then introduced the next guest. "This is Mr. Phineas Mercer," she said, nodding to the tall, sandy-haired man with spectacles that had just taken his place in front of Danny.

Danny shook the man's hand, narrowing his eyes. There was something familiar about the man. "Mercer," he said. "You wouldn't know a Lionel Mercer, would you?"

Mr. Mercer's eyes widened and took on a slightly squirrely look behind his spectacles. "He is my brother," he said, then asked with hesitation, "Are you a friend of his?"

Danny laughed too loudly. "Not in that way, mate." He thumped Mr. Mercer on the shoulder. "I have some business dealings with the solicitors he recently began working for."

Mr. Mercer's expression filled with understanding. "It is a pleasure to meet you," he said, finishing with the standard greeting, then moving on into the room.

Danny watched him blend into the growing crowd in the ballroom. There was something different about Phineas Mercer. Something he couldn't put his finger on. No one seemed to notice him as he made his way to the far end of the room, and yet Danny could see in an instant that he noticed everything.

"What's he all about?" he asked no one in particular.

"Mr. Mercer?" Lady O'Shea shrugged. "He's a country gentleman. Word is that he's been searching for a wife, which is why he's in London. He always seems to be invited to even the most exclusive parties, and yet as far as I've seen, no ladies have set their cap for him yet."

"Does he even like the ladies?" Danny asked, realizing too late he'd spoken the daring thought a little too loud.

"Yes," Fergus said. "And that's all I am at liberty to say about that."

Danny chuckled and turned his attention to the next guest arriving. "And you are?" he asked without any grace at all.

The man balked and blinked rapidly. "Charles

Schwann, sir. Member of Parliament for Manchester North."

Danny winced internally and offered his hand, adjusting his whole demeanor to the mission in front of him. "Daniel Long. I am honored that you would accept my invitation to this little event," he said with what he hoped was a gracious smile. He peeked at Phoebe to see if she approved.

Phoebe's cheeks were an alluring shade of pink that matched her lips. Lips she'd obviously been chewing with nerves over his performance.

"Ah, Mr. Long," Mr. Schwann said. "So pleased to meet you. I was just speaking with one of my colleagues on the land development committee about your ingenious proposal."

Danny let out an inward sigh of relief and exchanged a few more words with the man before he moved on.

"Does this greeting business ever end?" he muttered to Phoebe after a few more guests arrived.

"Soon," Phoebe whispered back.

Danny made an impatient sound. "Why doesn't everyone just come in and get a drink?"

"Because this isn't your blasted pub, man," Fergus answered from Danny's other side.

Danny grumbled, but continued with greetings. His back was stiff and he was restless from standing in one place for so long. He wanted to move about the guests, ensuring that everyone had a drink and was enjoying themselves. So far, the entire ball seemed more like the crowd standing around in a theater lobby during inter-mission of a particularly dull show than a party.

He was ready to give up and go home when Cosgrove stepped into the ballroom, forgoing the line of greeting entirely, but sending Danny a vicious glance as he did.

"Who invited him?" he boomed, stepping out of his place in the greeting line.

"I did," Phoebe whispered, grabbing his arm and pulling him back, stopping him from marching after Cosgrove. "He needs to see that you are viable competition."

Danny stepped back to her, his brow raising in surprise. "Well, aren't you a clever little minx?" he said with a broad smile.

Phoebe flushed a darker shade of red and tilted her head down in that coy way she had. It was a different sort of lowering her head from when she felt ashamed, one he actually liked.

"Why don't the two of you take a turn about the room, conversing with the guests," Lady O'Shea said with a knowing look.

"I think that's a brilliant idea," Danny said.

He offered his arm to Phoebe, who took it and started into the heart of the ballroom with him. The orchestra members were in the process of taking their seats and tuning their instruments as they skirted the chattering, preening guests.

"Good," Danny told Phoebe in a low tone. "It's about

time the dancing started. This party is as dull as dust so far."

Phoebe laughed quietly. "There is an order to these things. It is necessary to give everyone a chance to show up and position themselves, and to share the latest gossip."

"I'll bet I'm the center of the gossip now for throwing this blasted ball in the first place," Danny grumbled.

"Undoubtedly," Phoebe said.

They passed by Mr. Mercer, who seemed to be studying the two of them with intense curiosity. Phineas Mercer wasn't the only one who saw the two of them as something to look at. A dozen other toffs at least watched them as they skirted the room. Danny sought out the Members of Parliament he'd already been introduced to and attempted to wedge his way into their hoity toity conversations. But everything everyone was talking about was either boring or a topic he didn't have the least bit of understanding about. It put him on edge.

It didn't take long for his ignorance of society matters to come back on him.

"I simply do not understand why Parliament is even considering the proposal of a miscreant from God only knows where," Cosgrove was in the middle of telling a group of MPs as Danny and Phoebe approached. He sent Danny a look that made it clear he knew he was standing right there. "I say that matters of such importance should be left to the noble class."

To Danny's frustration, the men with Cosgrove—

men whose support he needed—hummed and nodded in agreement. He couldn't let Cosgrove undermine him.

"Gentlemen," he greeted them as Phoebe tensed on his arm. "I would think that Parliament would want to grant the land development rights to men who know how to develop land."

Cosgrove sent him a pitying smirk. "And you think that gentlemen who have managed vast estates for generations do not know about developing land, sir?"

Danny shifted his weight to a challenging stance. "And how much money did your estate make last year, my lord?"

He knew before he'd finished the question that he'd committed a cardinal sin. The gentlemen with Cosgrove balked and looked as though he'd brought up a question of knickers for prostitutes.

"The profitability of my estate is not a subject that should be discussed in front of delicate ears," Cosgrove said in a condescending voice, sending Phoebe what he must have thought was a charming smile. In fact, he looked more like a badger with gas.

"Profitability is precisely what the men considering which company to grant a development deal to should be considering," Danny said, falling back on his strengths. God only knew that class and initiation into the secret club of nobs was not one of them. "The housing shortage in London has reached dangerous proportions," he addressed the other men. "With the increase in industry in and near the city, families are pouring in from the country and living a dozen to a room. Conditions of sanitation in these tenements are appalling and have led to the spread of disease. Any developer worth their salt would understand the necessity of providing safe and sanitary conditions for the burgeoning middle class in a manner that allows them to maintain the solid, respectable values that all Englishmen aspire to."

It was all tripe as far as Danny was concerned, but his speech hit its mark. The MPs looked impressed with his savvy, appearing to reassess him.

Cosgrove's face twisted into a bitter pout. "This from a pub owner." He sniffed.

"Mr. Long is much more than that," Phoebe defended him.

Danny grinned at her fondly, in spite of knowing how inappropriate it would look to the MPs. She was as sweet as honey, and she was right, even if she didn't know the full extent of what she was talking about. "Thank you for the endorsement, my lady," he said, then winked at her. Let the MPs make of that what they would.

The orchestra finished tuning, paused, then burst into a waltz. Danny sent a short, gloating look to Cosgrove, then turned to Phoebe to ask, "Would you care to dance, my lady?"

Phoebe's smile was the most gorgeous thing in London. "I would love to, Mr. Long."

Danny sent a victorious grin Cosgrove's way before leading Phoebe out onto the dance floor. Cosgrove looked ready to snatch up the nearest candlestick and throw it at him. Several other sets of eyes—including Mr. Mercer's—followed them onto the dance floor as well. Danny couldn't blame them. It must have been a sight to see a noblewoman who had fallen on hard times dancing with what they probably considered to be a dressed-up monkey.

"Do you know how to waltz?" Phoebe asked in a whisper as he took her into his arms and waited for the dance to start.

"Do I know how to waltz," he said with a snort and a shake of his head.

The prelude ended and the song began in earnest. Danny moved fluidly into the steps of the waltz, sweeping Phoebe around the center of the dance floor as though they were skating on a pond.

"You do know how to dance," she said, glancing up at him with a delighted smile.

"More than just toffs dance the waltz, you know," he told her. "Though it's far from being my favorite dance."

"What is your favorite, then?" Phoebe asked, her face aglow.

Danny made a show of thinking, contemplating all of the ribald, nameless dances he'd engaged in during long nights at noisy music halls. He didn't think those dances were the sort Phoebe expected him to answer with, so he shrugged and said, "The galop."

Phoebe's smile widened. "We should ask the orchestra to play a galop, then."

Danny stopped where he was and turned to the

orchestra. "Oy!" he shouted at the top of his voice, bringing every conversation in the room to a stop. The orchestra's playing degenerated instrument by instrument into silence as well. "Play a galop," he demanded.

The members of the orchestra exchanged surprised looks, turning to their conductor—a chap playing the violin who sat near the front. The ball guests all gaped at Danny, some of them whispering behind their hands. At last, the conductor shrugged and said something to his players, they all shuffled through the music on their stands, and within seconds, they burst into a lively galop.

"That's more like it," Danny said, loud enough for half the room to hear, though his words were directed to Phoebe. He adjusted the way he held Phoebe, then launched into the bouncing, exuberant steps of the dance.

Phoebe laughed, though her face was bright red and she glanced around, knowing full well everyone was watching them. Danny was impressed with how easily she was able to keep up with him as they bounded around the dance floor. The galop was a respectable enough dance that after a few bars, several other couples joined in with them.

Within a minute, what had begun as a dangerous gamble on Danny's part completely changed the mood in the ballroom. The stiff, stodgy conversations around the room gave way to laughing of a sort that was more in line with his pub or a dance hall. The posing and pretention of the aristocratic guests gave way to smiles and couples rushing onto the dance floor to join the mad crush.

"Does no one with a title or fancy estate ever let themselves have fun?" Danny asked as he whirled Phoebe through a series of steps that would position them to travel across the center of the dance floor.

"No, I don't believe they do," Phoebe laughed, then added, "They wouldn't dare."

"Well, I dare," he said, setting off through a series of traveling steps that spun them right through the center of the dancing crowd.

Suddenly, he understood. He understood why nobles would go through all the trouble of dressing up in ridiculous finery, spending shocking amounts of cash on orchestras and decorations and food. He understood why women would make themselves up like peacocks and stand like works of art to be admired so that a gent would come along and whisk them out to the dance floor. Because it was all damn good fun. There was nothing like spinning and laughing in time to well-played music, working up a sweat by moving in unison with another person. It was rather like his other favorite activity with a woman. And as repressed as most of the people around him seemed to be, it was no wonder they craved the relative excitement of the dance floor to let their hair down.

"I've got an idea," he panted as the vigorous galop stopped and the orchestra returned to a more sedate waltz.

"What is it?" Phoebe's eyes glowed with marvel as

Danny drew her off the dance floor and toward the orchestra.

"These nobs are desperate for a good time," he said as they ducked around a few clusters of guests—all of whom watched them with startled curiosity. "I can't beat Cosgrove when it comes to having a stiff upper lip, but I can run circles around him as far as making friends and having fun."

"And you think that will win you a land development contract?" Phoebe seemed entirely unconvinced.

Danny wiggled an eyebrow at her as they neared the orchestra. "You'd be surprised how far a good time can go to make friends. And how quick friends are to help each other out."

He turned to the conductor—who was in the middle of playing but eyed Danny sideways as he did. "Mate, could you be sure to play as many polkas and galops and whatever other dances you'd play in Chelsea."

Still playing his waltz, the conductor grinned and said, "Right you are, mate."

It was an immeasurable boost of confidence to find that the conductor was closer to his end of the social spectrum than to the nobs he was playing for.

"Right," Danny said, leading Phoebe away from the orchestra. "That's a start."

"What's next?" Phoebe asked breathlessly, following him around the side of the room.

"Which of the ladies here are game?" he asked her.

Phoebe blinked as they paused to survey the guests.

147

"Do you mean—" she lowered her voice, inching closer to him, "—which of them have questionable morals?"

"Of course, love," Danny said with a wry grin and a wink. "We've got to convince them to dance with the MPs."

Phoebe's answering laugh was all the gratification Danny needed for his plan. Phoebe came through as well. She discreetly pointed out all of the ladies with a less than shining reputation as they moved about the room. As he'd requested, once the orchestra finished their waltz, they burst into a polka.

Danny broke every rule of high society and propriety there was, and probably a few more that were invented on the spot just for him, as he moved around the ball-room, plucking the ladies Phoebe had pointed out to him away from their conversations and whisking them along to the nearest MP he needed to impress. Shocked looks and expressions of indignation followed his actions, but within ten minutes, the entire mood of the ball had changed from just another stodgy way for nobs to show off their nobbishness to a genuine good time. Danny used his years of practice as a pub owner and host to chat up the guests as he threw them together in different combinations. He measured the success of his efforts by how broadly the MPs he needed to impress smiled and how long they danced.

At last, he swept Phoebe back into his arms and led her out to the dance floor as the orchestra settled into another waltz as a way to give people a chance to calm down and catch their breath.

"You are absolutely mad," she laughed as he swung her through a series of close steps. "This is pandemonium."

"But it's working," he said, glancing around.

Sure enough, everyone seemed to be having a good time. More than one of the MPs nodded to him or smiled to express their appreciation. He was far from saying he'd made friends of the men, but he'd made an impression.

"You'll never be invited back into society again after this," Phoebe went on as he was forced to pull her close against his chest to avoid colliding with another couple. "The upper class might enjoy a novelty like this once, but you'll be made notorious through gossip by morning."

"Excellent," he said. "Notoriety is a good thing."

"I'm not so sure about that," she said, starting to lower her head the way he hated. The fact that she stopped herself and looked up at him instead of sinking into her misery was the grandest victory of the evening, as far as Danny was concerned. Everything else paled in comparison.

"Why don't you let me worry about my reputation, love," he said, smiling and willing her to smile as well.

"All right." She relaxed into his arms, letting him whirl her around the dance floor.

He was ready to leave. The ball had accomplished what he needed it to accomplish, and more than anything, he wanted to take Phoebe home. Not to her flat either. He wanted to take her *home*. With him. Forever.

But duty and business needed his attention for another hour, and then another one after that. He chatted up as many nobles as he could get to speak with him. He laughed over the progress of their plan with Fergus, Rupert, and his other friends. He noted the way Phineas Mercer continued to watch him and Phoebe, and he wondered whether he would need to drag the man out into the garden to have a serious talk about his intentions.

All of that faded into unimportance when the clock struck midnight and Phoebe sighed, "I don't think I've ever been so exhausted in my life."

Danny jumped on the cue. "Then let me take you home," he said, sliding his hand into hers and escorting her immediately from the ballroom.

Phoebe went with him willingly, but she glanced repeatedly over her shoulder at the still-active ballroom as they went. "Don't you want to stay until it's over? You could speak to more men and win more people over to your cause."

"I think I've caused enough scandal for one night," he said, though if he were honest with himself, everything he planned to do next had the potential to cause more scandal by far.

"Shouldn't we say goodbye to Lord and Lady O'Shea and thank them for hosting the ball?" Phoebe asked as they neared the door to the hall.

It was a stroke of luck that Fergus and his lovely wife were still at their posts by the door.

"Oy, Fergus," Danny boomed without slowing his steps as he made his exit. "Thank you for the lovely time, but I need to escort Lady Phoebe home so that she's not accosted by some ill-intentioned miscreant."

Fergus sent him a look that said he knew full well Danny was the ill-intentioned miscreant.

Lines of carriages were waiting in front of Hopewell House to take guests home. Danny helped Phoebe into one, giving the driver directions home. He and Phoebe spent the short ride poring over the events of the evening and assessing Danny's chances of winning the development contract away from Cosgrove as a result. Danny could hardly focus on business, though. Now that they were alone in a quiet carriage, he drank in all the details of Phoebe that he hadn't had the time to appreciate earlier—the way the pink of her new gown accentuated the honey-blond of her hair, the softness of her skin where its neckline swooped low, the way she smelled of flowers and spice. Everything he hadn't had time to notice before flooded in on him at once.

When the cab stopped between The Watchman and the flats, he all but leapt out and helped Phoebe down. He paid the driver far more than the trip cost, took Phoebe's hand, and sped her into the building.

"I think I'll be able to sleep for a decade after a night light like that," Phoebe laughed lightly as they started up the stairs. "It's a blessing I don't have to work tomorrow."

"You don't?" Danny's heart sped up as they climbed higher, toward his flat.

"No, I asked permission to switch my shift to another —wait." She attempted to tug him to a stop as they passed the second-floor hall. "My flat is down this way."

"But mine is up another flight," he said, glancing to her with heated mischief in his eyes.

"Oh." Deep color flushed Phoebe's face. Knowing filled her eyes. But instead of demanding he stop and return her safely to her mother and their flat, she continued on with him.

CHAPTER 11

*E*very last ounce of Phoebe's exhaustion vanished in an instant as she let Danny lead her up the stairs to the third-floor, then down the hall to his flat. She went from aching for sleep to aching for an entirely different reason so quickly that her head spun and her heart seemed ready to beat out of her throat.

"You're about to see something that few others have seen before," Danny told her with a mischievous flicker of one eyebrow, fishing a key out of his pocket and unlocking the door.

"Oh," Phoebe said. The single syllable was filled with a wealth of emotions she couldn't begin to describe. Had few people truly seen his flat? If so, did that mean women too.

He pushed open the door and drew her inside.

"Oh," she breathed, brimming with an entirely

different set of emotions as she glanced around the spacious main room of the flat.

His flat was twice the size of the one where she and her mother lived, and possibly more. The front room was decorated with an understated elegance that Phoebe would have expected to find in the townhouse of a titled lord. The furnishings were sumptuous, but simple, displaying excellent craftsmanship more than ostentatious cost. They were costly, though. The windows, which looked out to the street, were hung with rich, blue drapes tied back with gold cords. A bookshelf stood against the wall facing them, and unlike the shelves of so many of the noblemen she'd known, it was actually filled with books. Though Danny had a curio displaying interesting, foreign-looking objects and several pieces of art as well.

"What do you think?" he asked, his accent particularly low and his grin teasing. "Will it do?"

Phoebe spun in a circle. Her thoughts twirled with her. She'd underestimated Danny in ways she was only beginning to understand. She finished her turn by facing him, wonder in her eyes as she reassessed everything she thought she knew about him.

"You *are* more than just a pub owner and property developer, aren't you?" she asked, a little too breathless for her liking.

"No," he said with an honest shrug. "That is what I am. I own a pub. I develop properties. I own land and buildings." He inched closer to her, the heat of admiration for her in his eyes.

"But, surely—" She couldn't think of anything to follow those words. Shame for not knowing more about the world of property development wriggled in her gut. She suddenly felt like the worst sort of fool for assuming that wealth came only with title or industry. And clearly, Danny had wealth.

"Do I meet with your approval?" he asked, stepping closer to her still. "Or am I just a silly fool who caused a scene at a ball and who enjoys thumbing his nose at the nobs."

A tremor started deep within Phoebe's gut that spread quickly through her, like warm honey. "Can it be both?" she asked, surprised by her daring. Something about Danny urged her to be bold, though, as if he demanded she meet his level of temptation. She'd never met anyone as magnificent or alluring as Daniel Long in her entire life.

He closed the last of the distance between them, slipping his hand around to the small of her back and tugging her tight against him in a possessive gesture that came close to making Phoebe forget her name. "Love, it can be anything you want," he said in a deep, rich voice.

He leaned into her, tilting her chin up with his free hand and slanting his mouth over hers. His lips felt so good against hers that she knew in an instant she wouldn't resist anything he wanted from her. Indeed, she would embrace it, just as she raised her arms to embrace him. His tongue brushed along the seam of her mouth, teasing her into opening for him. As his tongue invaded her, claiming her as his own, she made a sound of surrender.

"God," he breathed heavily. "You make the most amazing sounds. They make me want to do wicked things to you."

As far as Phoebe was concerned, the wickedness wasn't in her sounds, it was in his voice. He was a rogue and a devil, and she was about to give him everything.

She lifted to her toes and pressed her mouth inexpertly against his. He made a sound of approval and held her tighter, taking command of their kiss and molding his lips against hers. He knew what they were doing so much better than she did, but all she wanted to do was learn from him.

He pulled back suddenly, sucking in an unsteady breath. "Are you certain," he whispered. "Are you absolutely certain?"

"Of?" she asked, drinking in the sight of his kiss-reddened lips, unsure if she would ever be able to form a coherent thought again.

"That you want this," he said. "That you want me."

The implied question was so much more serious than anything anyone had ever asked her. It wasn't just a flippant inquiry into whether she wanted to go to bed with him. He was giving her a choice in her own life, in her own fate. If she gave in to him, there would be no going back. He was leaving the decision of whether she wanted to change her life irreversibly to her.

"God, yes," she said with passion, throwing herself into another kiss.

Whether he knew how important the moment between them was or not, he responded enthusiastically, kissing her again with abandon. He moved with her toward an open doorway to one side of the room, maneuvering them both expertly through and into a finely-appointed bedroom. Phoebe didn't have the wherewithal to take in all of the details, but she noted that the predominant color of the room was blue, and that the enormous bed in the center of the room looked like something Henry VIII would have had in his bedchamber.

Even those thoughts fled her mind as Danny grabbed the shoulder of her gown and tugged it down so that he could kiss her neck and shoulder. Phoebe had never had a man's mouth anywhere close to that part of her before, and even though it was just her shoulder, the way he kissed and nibbled her sent electric jolts of excitement through her.

"You are the most beautiful woman I've ever seen," Danny murmured as he continued to kiss her, his hands reaching behind her back in search of the fastenings of her ball gown. "I have wanted to ravish you from the moment I first met you."

Phoebe was touched that he had wanted her so much

and for so long, but she was completely incapable of speech. Particularly when he inched her bodice down far enough to slide a hand between the fabric and her skin to cradle her breast. She gasped and shivered at the sensation, suddenly wishing her lovely new gown, which she had adored when she put it on for the first time earlier that day, didn't exist.

As fast as that thought came to her, Danny withdrew his hand and turned her so that he could speed through undoing the fastenings at the back of her gown in earnest.

"If I rip it, I'm sorry," he said, desire and mischief mingling in his deep voice.

"I don't care," she panted. "Just get it off."

Danny laughed at that and pulled at the two sides of her bodice, sending pearl buttons flying. He worked fast to loosen the entire thing enough to push it down past Phoebe's hips. The whole thing pooled on the floor around her feet, several seams probably ripped in the process.

Danny didn't stop there. He lifted her right out of the pile of her gown and set her down on the edge of his bed. He took a moment to remove his jacket and waistcoat and to toe off his shoes, but that seemed to be the extent of his patience. He surged over her, causing her to spill back onto his bed, and kissed her passionately. His mouth magical, as far as Phoebe was concerned. He showed her what mouths were for and why God had invented lips and tongues. She could have lay there letting him kiss her for hours and been perfectly content.

But there was more to learn, more that she could feel Danny wanted from her. He moved his hands to the hooks of her corset, working it open and spreading it to the side so that he could stroke his hands across her belly and breasts—over the thin fabric of her chemise at first, and then under it, his hands against her bare skin. Phoebe sighed at the pleasure his touch gave her, wriggling inside and out with an urgency she didn't entirely understand.

"I am going to ravish you like no woman ever has been before," he rumbled, kissing the heated flesh of her belly as he drew her chemise up. "You won't know what to do with yourself when I'm done."

"I don't know what to do with myself now," she panted, rubbing her legs together restlessly.

"Then let me show you, love," he said, taking hold of her thighs to stop her impatient movements.

He nudged her thighs apart, slipping a hand between the split in her drawers. She gasped hard as his fingers brushed the most intimate part of her. A light of victory came to his eyes as he explored her, tracing circles around that wet part of her and opening her in the most intimate way. It was shockingly intimate, but at the same time, nothing had ever felt more perfect. She let out a plaintive sigh as he slipped a finger inside of her, and then another, but it was when he danced his thumb across her clitoris that she let out a cry of pure, carnal shock and excitement.

"Dear God," he murmured, shaken himself. "You want it."

It was almost as though he were speaking in a sort of code that was only just being revealed to her, but she understood everything he meant. The sensations he drew out in her were so potent and overwhelming that she felt as though she were about to lose herself. But at the same time, she wanted to lose herself. Instinct told her that losing herself to him would be the greatest gift she could possibly give him.

He continued to tease and stroke her intimately. The flash in his eyes was almost as if he were daring her to become herself and testing himself to see how far he would take things. And mad though it felt, all Phoebe wanted to do was please him, which proved easy to do as the sensations he pulled from her had her completely in his thrall.

She felt as though she were about to drown for a moment as her whole body wound tight with tension, then burst into pleasure so new and intense that she cried out with it. Danny cursed passionately as she did, his touch intensifying, as if he could draw the sensations on and on for both of their benefit. Even after the initial burst subsided, leaving her feeling as though she were floating on a cloud of pleasure, she was happy.

"I knew you would be an angel," he said in a rough voice, pulling back enough to finish undressing himself.

Phoebe caught her breath as she watched him pull his shirt over his head, then unfasten his trousers. The tension and tremors that whatever he had done to her had satisfied swirled back through her as he shed the rest of his clothes, then stood naked before her. He was the picture of masculinity, all hard lines and strong planes, with a tantalizing spread of dark hair over his chest and belly. But it was the firm spear of his penis, standing at attention in a way none of the statues she'd seen at London's museums ever had, that caught her attention.

"I'll be as gentle as I can be," he said with sudden tenderness, leaning in to remove the last of her clothes. "And if it hurts, it'll only be for a moment."

A rush of trepidation shook Phoebe. As beautiful as he was, she would be lying to herself if she said she wasn't intimidated. He seemed far too large for her body, no matter how glorious he'd just made her feel.

But she'd told him she wanted him, and she refused to let herself back away now. She still wanted him. Intimidation hadn't changed that.

He seemed to sense her thoughts.

"Frightened?" he asked with a teasing grin as he joined her on the bed, throwing back the bedcovers and repositioning both of them so that her head rested on his pillows.

"A little," she admitted, lowering her eyes.

"Well, you should be," he said in a mock villainous voice. "Because I'm about to do very, very bad things to you."

Phoebe laughed. She couldn't have stopped herself if she'd tried. He was teasing her to put her at ease, which was the dearest thing imaginable, as far as she was concerned.

"You've already done very, very bad things to me," she told him with a grin of her own.

"Not like I'm about to, love," he said. He nudged her legs apart, reaching down to hook his hand under one of her knees and to bring her thigh up to his hip. "You have no idea what naughtiness I have in mind for the two of us," he growled, stealing a kiss as he adjusted himself to fit tighter against her. "By the time I'm done with you, you'll have been converted into such a wanton that the newspapers will print scandalous stories about you." He stole another kiss.

Phoebe giggled, her already satisfied body warming and loosening even more for him. She circled her arms around his back, pressing her fingertips into his muscles.

He kissed her lips, her neck, her shoulder, then her lips again. "I'm going to use you in such wicked ways that you won't be able to—"

He pushed into her with a firm and decisive stroke, taking her completely by surprise. Phoebe gasped at the quick shock of pain, as if something inside of her had torn free, but it happened so fast and she'd been so distracted by his teasing that she hadn't had time to panic. The sensation of him filling her, almost past a point she thought she could tolerate, was erotic and amazing. And Lord help her, but she liked it.

Danny's silliness became smoldering purpose in an instant. He moved gently inside of her at first, giving her body a chance to adjust to his. "You all right, love?" he murmured against her ear as he moved.

Phoebe had the distinct impression he was holding back. She nodded, making a high, squeaking sound and digging her fingers harder into his back.

"It'll feel much better in a moment," he promised her, then increased the intensity of his movements.

He was absolutely right. The more she adjusted to him, the better it felt. Her tension drained away, and as it did, he moved faster and more intently. Which made it even better for her. Within seconds, the cycle of passion came around to the point where she was sighing and mewling in time to each of his thrusts as they gained in intensity, and before long, she was teetering on the brink of another, miraculous orgasm.

She came apart with a cry, clenching around him. He matched her cry, and all sense that he was holding back vanished. With a few more thrusts, his whole body went tense, and he let out a cry that was as beautiful as it was raw. Phoebe knew enough to know he'd spilled his very soul inside of her, and as dangerous as that was, she loved it. She would remember the moment for the rest of her life.

The raw intensity of making love quickly gave way to an entirely unexpected feeling of relief and contentment. If the throes of passion made her feel as though she and Danny were in the storm together, the aftermath was as gentle as a summer breeze, but twice as intimate. Danny collapsed to his back, gathering her into his arms, even though they were both too hot and sweaty for such an intimate embrace.

"That was lovely," he panted, stroking her hair and her arm as she snuggled into an embrace at his side.

"It was," she agreed drowsily.

That was all the thought she was capable of. The toll of the ball and making love was too much, and she drifted into sleep before she could stop herself. A tickle of a thought in the back of her mind whispered that she must love Danny to be able to fall asleep in his arms after doing something so scandalous. She couldn't bring herself to feel a lick of guilt, though. She couldn't recall a moment in her life when she'd ever been happier.

Her happiness followed her into sleep, but it was disturbed some time later—she had no idea how long—by a furious knocking at the door to Danny's flat. They'd neglected to shut his bedroom door, so the sound was as loud as if someone were mere yards away.

"Danny! Danny! Wake up!" someone shouted from the hall.

Danny stirred by Phoebe's side, grumbling and stretching. "Go away," he said, though not loud enough for whoever it was in the hall to hear.

"Danny!" Whoever it was continued banging. "Get up!"

"Go away," Danny called louder.

Phoebe grinned at his surly shouting in spite of herself, charmed by his rough ways, even though she shouldn't have been. She giggled, hiding her face against his shoulder.

Her good humor vanished in a flash a moment later as the banging continued and the voice in the hall shouted, "Danny! The pub is on fire!"

CHAPTER 12

*I*f Danny hadn't fallen asleep so quickly and thoroughly after what was absolutely the best experience of love-making he'd ever had in his life, he would have seen the ominous orange glow through the uncurtained windows of his bedroom.

"Fire?" He dragged himself into full wakefulness, in spite of his body urging him to stay nestled under his covers with Phoebe, and leapt out of bed. Instead of rushing to answer Umbridge's banging on his door, he flew to the window and peered out, craning his neck toward the front of the building and his beloved pub across the street. "Dear God."

Not much was visible from his bedroom window, which looked out on a side street, but even without a clear view, he could see the flickering orange and red, and when he threw open the window, he could smell the acrid stench of smoke.

"I'm coming!" he shouted to Umbridge. "Stay here," he ordered Phoebe, whirling back into his room and lunging for his wardrobe. The fancy ball things that were scattered across the floor of his room would never do for the mission he was about to embark on, so he wrenched open his wardrobe and put on whatever clothes came to hand, regardless of whether they went together or not. He cursed every long second it took to put his shoes and socks on, but as soon as the laces were tied, he leapt away from his bed and Phoebe—who had a look of determination in her eyes that he wasn't sure he liked as she got up and gathered her ball things—and dashed into the main room.

Umbridge was pacing the hallway anxiously when Danny threw open the door. "It happened suddenly," the man said as Danny charged down the stairs with him. "Bob had closed up less than an hour before. The place was empty, thank God, but the way it all went up so swiftly."

"The flats above the pub," Danny said, voicing his deepest concern. "Did the people get out in time."

"As far as we know, they did," Umbridge said. "Which is all on Bob. He hadn't gone to bed yet and smelled the first of the smoke. Says he saw four men running away from the place too."

Dread clenched Danny's gut as he and Umbridge shot out of the building of flats and into the street. Men running away from the scene of a fire meant arson. There wasn't a doubt in his mind.

His stomach lurched at the sight that met him. The street was bright as day as flames engulfed the entire building housing The Watchman. More than one fire brigade had already arrived—although it looked as though they had only just arrived and were still in the process of unfurling their equipment to pump water from the tanks on their carts—and lines of people with buckets had already formed in an attempt to douse the conflagration and protect the buildings to either side. Already, the fire looked as though it would catch on those buildings, potentially destroying the entire side of the street.

"More water!" Danny bellowed, making a quick survey of the situation and taking charge. "Anything to stop those flames."

He was fighting a losing battle from the beginning and he knew it. The fire had already advanced far beyond what even the combined efforts of the entire street and several of the surrounding neighborhoods could manage. The fire brigades exhausted their supply of water in what felt like the blink of an eye and left to get more. Those wielding buckets kept up the fight valiantly, and before long, Danny had a glimmer of hope that they might be able to save some of the rest of the buildings on the street.

"Tell me what I can do to help." Phoebe's voice startled him out of his single-minded focus as he dashed between the men with buckets, a few stalwart women helping the occupants of the adjacent houses to safety,

168

lest their homes catch fire as well, and the general mayhem of onlookers who were too startled to help.

Danny turned to her, eyes wide with energy. Phoebe was dressed in simple clothes, far different from how she'd looked at the ball mere hours before. Every instinct within him wanted to wrap her up and move her to complete safety, but the determination in her eyes wouldn't stand for it.

"There are women and children fleeing the flats all around the pub. Make sure they get to safety," he said, then turned back to the fire, trusting Phoebe to know how to carry out his order.

The work was exhausting. In no time at all, Danny was covered with soot and sweat, singed in places where he had run too close to the fire in an attempt to beat back the flames. With impossibly hard work and the efforts of nearly a hundred people from the neighborhood, they were able to extinguish the main fire in the pub and stop it from spreading beyond the two buildings abutting The Watchman.

By the time dawn began to break over the blackened, weary street, the fires were out, but The Watchman and two other buildings were a complete loss. Danny's body ached from exertion and his heart was shattered by the loss. After Tuttle—who had come halfway across London to help when someone made the journey to fetch him— ordered Danny to rest, Danny sat heavily on the steps of the building with his and Phoebe's flats and stared at the blackened hull of his pub. His soul felt hollow and splintered. The pub had been in the family for three generations. While it wasn't the original property his great-great grandfather had won in his fateful poker game, it was one of the first his grandfather had purchased with the profits of that transaction. The Watchman wasn't just a place of meeting and drinking to him, it was his family, his legacy. And now it was gone.

He buried his head in his hands, elbows resting on his knees, consumed by grief. He would have stayed that way for who knew how long, if Phoebe hadn't quietly slipped onto the steps with him and sat beside him. She silently rested her hand on his shoulder. The simple gesture was as sweet and intimate as anything they'd done during the night. Driven by instinct and affection, he turned into her, resting his sooty forehead against her shoulder and letting out a shaky breath that he didn't want to admit was a sob. And bless her, Phoebe wrapped her arms around his shoulders and held him close.

He wasn't sure how long they sat there like that before Tuttle approached and cleared his throat. Danny glanced up, then straightened at the serious look in Tuttle's eyes.

"One of the men say this note was left for you by the men who did this," Tuttle said, presenting Danny with a slip of paper.

Without a word, but with anger flaring in his gut, Danny took the note, opened it, and read it.

"For every thing you take from me, I will take something precious from you."

The note was unsigned, but there wasn't a doubt in Danny's mind who had sent it, or who had burned his pub to the ground.

"Cosgrove," he growled, shooting to his feet.

Phoebe had taken the note from him and read it herself before rising and standing next to him. "I agree," she said in a quiet voice. "This is very fine stationary, not something available to many but the upper class."

Her confirmation energized him. He glanced around, looking for any of the numerous police officers who had arrived on the scene to assess the situation. Several of them had joined the bucket brigades or offered help in other ways, but a few had done nothing but stand back and observe. They had to be supervisors of one sort or another.

"You!" he bellowed as he spotted the stodgiest of them all. He started toward the man, Phoebe trailing him.

The officer blanched when he saw Danny striding toward him, but that wasn't enough to convince Danny to soften his demeanor.

"I want you to go after the man who did this and bring him to justice," Danny continued to shout all the same as he reached the officer.

"I—I...th-the man who did this?" The officer stammered and backed away from Danny.

"Yes," Danny said. "Lord Cosgrove."

In an instant, the officer's whole countenance changed. He stood straighter, lowering the arms he'd put up to defend himself, and made a scoffing noise. "And what makes you think a gentleman like Lord Cosgrove would have anything to do with a pub burning down?"

Dread gripped Danny at the man's suddenly dismissive tone. "Because we're rivals in business," he said, adjusting his accent to the loftiest tone he could manage, knowing he would need it. "Because I bested him yesterday evening in a personal matter as well."

He glanced to Phoebe. She stood confidently by his side, looking as outraged by the officer's sudden switch in manner as he felt. There was so much she still didn't know—about him and about her own situation and why Cosgrove would see the way he had won her over as a mortal blow.

The officer scoffed at Danny's statement, drawing his attention back to the matter at hand. "Look, you. I know you're upset about your pub burning down, but you can't just go and accuse a lord of that sort of criminal act."

"Even though I know he did it?" Danny demanded, his temper rising as fast and hard as the flames that had engulfed his pub.

The officer's look turned condescending. "What would a nobleman possibly want to do with a chappie like you?"

"Mr. Long is a businessman," Phoebe jumped to his defense. "He is in competition with Lord Cosgrove for a land development deal before a parliamentary committee."

The officer glanced to Phoebe with as dismissive a

sneer as he was now using with Danny. "And what would you know about parliamentary committees, little missy."

Danny bristled. "This is Lady Phoebe Darlington, daughter of a marquess. You will treat her with the respect she is due."

"And I'm the bloody Duke of Clarence," the officer laughed.

Danny clenched his fists at his sides to keep from pounding the man across the face. "I tell you, this fire was arson, and Lord Cosgrove is responsible."

The officer rolled his eyes. "Pubs burn down all the time, what with all the alcohol lying around."

"We have proof," Phoebe said, holding up the note.

The officer took it and looked at it. "This is nothing." He shrugged and tore the note into pieces.

Phoebe yelped in indignation. Danny teetered on the brink of violence.

"I demand to speak to your supervisor," he said in a deadly voice. "No, I demand to speak to Lord Clerkenwell."

The officer snorted. "And who do you think you are that a man like Lord Clerkenwell would speak to the likes of you?"

"He is a personal friend," Danny seethed.

"Oh, yeah?" The officer clearly didn't believe him or believe that a man of his social status had any right to help from the law at all. "I think we're done here," he said, stepping away from Danny as though he were nothing at all and gesturing toward his men. "That's it, lads. We're leaving."

"Without performing an investigation?" Phoebe demanded, as gobsmacked as Danny was.

"No investigation needed, miss," the officer said with a sniff. "A pub caught fire, probably do to sloppy handling of alcohol and lack of cleanliness."

"Danny's pub was meticulously cared for," Phoebe argued.

The officer ignored her. "Tragedies happen. There's nothing that can be done about it. Brush off your losses and go find another hole to hock your wares out of."

"Now, you see here," Phoebe started to rail against the man as he walked away without giving her or Danny a second look.

Danny caught her shoulder and held her back as she tried to follow him. "Don't," he growled. "He's not going to help us."

"But why not?" Phoebe whirled toward him. "Your pub was burned down in an act of arson. Homes were lost, and lives could have been lost with them."

"He doesn't care," Danny said, eyes boring holes in the back of the officer's back as he walked away. "We're nothing to him."

"But we're people," Phoebe insisted.

"Not to him." Danny shook himself and glanced away from the retreating officer, whose men had stepped away from their efforts to help in order to follow him, and looked at Phoebe's distressed but still beautiful face instead. He rested a dirty hand on her soot and sweat-streaked cheek, affection and fury warring within him. "Men like him don't care about the working-classes. We're no better than animals to decent, middle-class people," he infused his words with sarcasm, "or to stuck up nobs either."

"But you're not working-class," Phoebe said. "You're something else. And so am I." Her expression turned confused, as though she didn't know what she was.

"It doesn't matter, love," he said. "This is England. It's about nothing if not class and rules and lines that cannot be crossed. A place for everyone and everyone in their place. And the likes of him, and of Cosgrove, have decided where our places are. God help anyone who dares to rise above their birth, or sink below it." He leaned in and kissed her lips lightly.

"I won't accept it," Phoebe said, glowering. "I won't accept anything this unfair. Lord Cosgrove is responsible for burning your pub as surely as my father was for burning down any hope that I might be a part of high society, and he won't stand for it." She turned to march toward the building with their flats.

"Phoebe, where are you going?" he called after her, then followed when she didn't stop.

"I'm going to wash up and change my clothes," she said over her shoulder as she entered the building. "And then I'm going to demand justice from Lord Cosgrove myself."

. . .

In the very back of her mind, Phoebe wondered if her mission to demand justice from Lord Cosgrove at his club—where she was certain he would be on the morning after a ball that had seen him defeated in more ways than one—was a wise one. She didn't think any sort of show of determination on her part would actually bear fruit or make Lord Cosgrove confess to his crimes. But after witnessing the way Danny was dismissed so summarily by a police officer who wasn't worthy of shining his boots, and all because of some perceived sense of class, she was too livid not to proceed.

"Wait up, love," Danny called after her before she could reach the end of the street. He'd bathed and changed into clean clothes as well, but the distress of everything that had happened in the night and the losses he had incurred were visible in the dullness of his expression. "I'm not letting you go alone."

"Good," she said, taking his arm as though he were a gentleman escorting her on a promenade through Hyde Park. "Because I'm going to need you to rail at Lord Cosgrove right along with me."

His only answer was an exhausted, lop-sided grin. And though that was only a tiny expression, it meant the world to Phoebe. He wasn't going to stop her. He would march right by her side up to the gates of Hell, if she's asked him to, to demand justice. Even though their chances of getting that justice were virtually non-existent. She could feel his need to stand up and be heard as surely as she could feel her own.

He was perfect in so many ways. If the last dozen or so hours had shown her nothing, it had shown her that. Danny made her heart sing in ways she didn't fully comprehend. He'd been magnificent at the ball, cutting a dashing figure and looking far more handsome than any of the rigid gentleman of her former acquaintance, even though his hair was unfashionably curly and unkempt and his suit had been better suited to the theater than Hopewell House. He's been lively and endearing as they danced far more than a respectable couple should have, and to dances that most of the nobles of her acquaintance would never admit to knowing, let alone dancing in public.

And when he'd taken her home and made love to her, he had shown her a whole new world that she never would have known existed without him. He was brilliant in every way. Her body longed for him, even now, and her heart was his as surely as if he had coaxed it from her body and attached it to his own in the middle of their passion. She didn't think it would ever be fully hers again, but she also felt as though part of his heart was hers now.

The tenderness of those thoughts was clipped short as they finished their journey through busy, London streets to arrive at the front door of Lord Cosgrove's club.

"Do you intend to storm the place like the revolution-aries stormed the Bastille?" Danny asked as Phoebe let go of his arm and marched up the steps to try the front door.

"If I have to," Phoebe said, glaring at the door. The

handle wouldn't turn. The door was locked. She banged on it with her fist. "I demand to be let in," she called out.

"Phoebe, darling," Danny said, the barest hint of humor in his voice as he stepped up behind her and rested a hand on her shoulder.

He didn't have a chance to go on. The door swung open, and a stiff man with grey hair and impeccably tailored livery stood in the doorway, both as greeting and clearly blocking her way. "Can I help you?" he asked.

"I'm here to see Lord Cosgrove," Phoebe told the man, squaring her shoulders and drawing on wells of courage she didn't know she had. "We both are." She glanced to Danny behind her.

The doorman sniffed, barely showing any sort of emotion as he stared down his nose at both of them. "Women are not permitted here," he said. His lip curled as he glanced to Danny and added, "Nor are street toughs."

He attempted to shut the door without another word or glance, but Phoebe slammed her hand against the wood to prevent him.

"We *will* see Lord Cosgrove," she demanded. "He has horrible crimes to answer for."

"You will not," the doorman said, pushing on the door.

Phoebe didn't have the strength to stop him from slamming it, shutting her and Danny out without a further word. Fury more potent than any of the frustration she'd felt in the years since her father's death boiled through her. She'd been made fun of, insulted, and tossed aside; she'd been dismissed by former acquaintances and shouted at by members of the May Flowers, but she'd never had a door literally slammed on her by a man who saw her as little better than a stray dog in the street.

"I have never been so insulted in my life," she seethed.

"I have," Danny said, reaching for her hand and leading her away from the door. "So much for the genteel manners and graciousness of the titled class, eh?"

It was a bitter pill to swallow. Her whole life, she'd believed she'd been born into privilege, but now she could see that that privilege was nothing more than bullying when put to bad use. It took far more than someone's status in life and the family they'd come from to make them a good person.

"Come away, love," Danny urged her, slipping a hand to her waist and escorting her back to the street. "We don't need them anyhow."

They started back the way they'd come, but before they got more than a few paces, one of the windows on the ground floor of the club flew open.

"Good gracious, Lady Phoebe. What are you doing with an oaf like that on a morning as lovely as this?" Lord Cosgrove said, sticking his head and shoulders out the window.

Phoebe nearly saw red. She marched to stand directly under the window, facing Lord Cosgrove, "You, sir, are a villain of the worst sort," she shot up at him.

Lord Cosgrove had the audacity to look affronted by her comment. "Me, my lady? Why, what have I done but shown you utmost kindness and consideration?"

"You have shown me nothing of the sort. You have egregiously wounded my dear friend, Mr. Long, by burning down his pub," Phoebe shouted back at him, not caring how many people on the street around her were staring at her in alarm.

Lord Cosgrove looked just as alarmed. "I am wounded by your unfounded accusation, Lady Phoebe," he said, pressing a hand to his chest. "As you well know, I was in attendance at Lady O'Shea's ball last evening."

"It was Danny's ball," Phoebe seethed.

"And I have several sources that can confirm I went straight home at midnight, slept like an angel, and came here first thing this morning," Lord Cosgrove ignored her. Several grey-haired old men just behind him in the room hummed and guffawed in agreement. "So you see," Lord Cosgrove continued, "there is no way I could have set fire to anything. And why would I concern myself with a *pub*." He sniffed.

"You know damn well why," Danny growled, standing protectively behind Phoebe. "And you didn't have to light the fire yourself to be responsible. Your men were seen. You left a note."

"Did I?" Lord Cosgrove blinked innocently. "That doesn't sound like me at all. I haven't written a note or a letter since my dear mama died these twenty years ago."

The men in the club behind him laughed at the joke.

Phoebe was ready to scream in frustration. "You will not get away with this," she said, as furious as she was helpless.

"Lady Phoebe," Lord Cosgrove said in a condescending tone, utterly ignoring her threat. "It would seem that you are in dire need of being rescued. That blackguard clearly has you in his clutches and has poisoned your mind. Please, consider my suit. My offer of marriage still stands. I would gladly swoop in, like your knight in shining armor, and rescue you from the clutches of a devil like him." He wrinkled his nose as though Danny stank and nodded at him.

Danny might still have smelled of smoke, but it was the scent of a man who had been wronged and who had worked until his hands bled to save something that was really and truly his. Men like Lord Cosgrove inherited their land and lived like leeches off of it. Danny had inherited his pub and poured his blood, sweat, and tears into it to make it and his other properties better.

"I know who the beast is in this scenario," she said, tilting her chin up and standing with pride and, she hoped, grace. "It is not Mr. Long."

"If ever you need—"

"I would no more marry you than I would marry a sea serpent," she cut Lord Cosgrove off before he could spout anymore nonsense. "You can offer me nothing, whereas Danny can offer me everything."

Her deliberate use of Danny's given name caused Lord Cosgrove to blanche. A moment later, his expression took on a bitterness that twisted his features into ugliness. "Suit yourself," he sniffed, leaning back into the room. "I shall not be responsible for the consequences."

Without another word, he slammed the window shut and disappeared deeper into the room.

"That went well," Danny said with deadly humor.

Phoebe didn't even crack a smile. She turned away from the club, taking Danny's hand and marching along the street. "If he wants a fight," she said, "then we will give him one."

CHAPTER 13

"It's tragic, simply tragic," Phoebe's mother said several days later as she glanced out one of the large windows of their flat at the charred remains of The Watchman pub. "It's absolutely pitiable."

Phoebe was in more of a hurry than usual, buttoning her high collar and searching the main room of the flat for her purse as she rushed to get ready for work. "Yes, Mama. It is a terrible tragedy that Mr. Long's pub was destroyed."

Her mother turned away from the window, the frills of her morning robe flapping as she did. "No, not that. Although that is terribly sad in its own right."

Phoebe eyed her mother askance. "Then what?" she asked, dreading the answer.

"It's a tragedy that the smell of smoke now pervades everything I own," her mother said.

Phoebe sighed and rolled her eyes. She had neither

183

the time nor the patience to deal with her mother's arrogance. She found her purse and started toward the coat rack beside the door. The only thing that prevented her from chastising her mother outright was the fact that Mr. Waters had expressed his concern to Phoebe just the day before that she had the faint whiff of a fireplace about her.

All the same, her mother huffed and went on with, "You've no idea how embarrassing it is to take a pleasant stroll in Hyde Park with one's friends while smelling of smoke."

Phoebe reached for the door handle, but paused and turned back to her mother. "Is Lady Denbigh speaking to you again?"

"What?" Her mother looked both offended and intrigued by the idea. "Heavens, no," she said with a dismissive wave of her hand. "I was referring to Lord Cosgrove."

Phoebe's heart dropped to her stomach. She stepped away from the door, storming across the flat to glower at her mother. "Mama, how could you, in good conscience, spend a single moment of time with that despicable arsonist after what he did to Mr. Long?"

Her mother reeled back, nearly toppling into her chair at the table by the window. "Good heavens, Phoebe. How could you stoop to make such an accusation of such a fine man as Lord Cosgrove? And when he has so generously offered for your hand when no other man will."

Phoebe's mouth dropped open, but her indignation

was so fiery that it took a moment for her to sort through the wealth of offensive things her mother spewed to find an answer. "Lord Cosgrove all but left his calling card at the scene of the fire, Mama. He is guilty. And for the last time, I have no intention of marrying him. Ever."

"But he's a viscount," her mother argued.

"I don't care if he's the bloody King of Siam." Phoebe jerked away from her mother, marching to the door.

"Mind your tongue, girl," her mother called after her. "You've been spending too much time in company with that Mr. Long. He's corrupted you thoroughly. And no well-born man will want to marry a woman who has been corrupted."

Phoebe's face flared hot at her mother's words. On the one hand, she was absolutely correct. Danny had corrupted her thoroughly. More thoroughly than her mother could ever know. One night of passion and bliss was bad enough, but she'd utterly thrown caution to the wind and crept up to Danny's flat just the night before for a repeat performance. She'd told herself that Danny was heartbroken over the loss of his pub and that he needed comfort, but if she were honest with herself, that was merely an excuse for what she wanted. And what she'd wanted was to be naked and free, wrapped around Danny's powerful body, with him hard and thick inside of her. He'd given her exactly what she wanted and more.

But the deeper reason that she blushed and sped from the apartment without addressing her mother's accusations was because she knew deep down in her soul that if Danny would ask her to marry him, she would say yes without hesitation. Nothing would have made her heart happier than to be Mrs. Danny Long. Her. The daughter of a marquess, who had been presented to Queen Victoria at her coming out and who had been offered up as a potential bride for men of title and standing. She thrilled at the idea of marrying a low-born pub owner who spoke too loud, laughed too heartily, and who had made a spectacle of himself in front of high society.

She loved him. That thought put a smile on her face as she marched across Oxford Street, skirting the grand houses of Mayfair, on her way to Harrods. She loved Danny Long to a degree that was almost ridiculous. She'd given her body to him joyfully, in spite of having the wickedness of such a thing drummed into her from earliest youth. He made her smile when she was at her lowest. He made her feel as though it didn't matter who her father was or what he had done, she was worthy of love and acceptance. She was loved.

"You're late, Miss Darlington," Mr. Waters said as Phoebe finally took up her position at the glove counter after speeding through preparations in the ladies' dressing room once she arrived at work. He took a small pocket watch from the pocket of his waistcoat and checked just to be certain. "Ten minutes late."

Phoebe breathed a sigh of relief. She'd been afraid she would be twice as late after her mother's shocking revelations. She'd made up part of that time on the walk to work.

"I'm terribly sorry, Mr. Waters," she said, eyes downcast in spite of knowing how much Danny detested when she looked that way. Where Mr. Waters was concerned, an act of contrition went a long way, so she used that fact to save her skin. "My mother was poorly this morning, but I raced here as quickly as I could." She also knew that Mr. Waters had a weak spot for mothers, seeing as he'd adored his own, who had passed away shortly after Phoebe had been hired.

Sure enough, sympathy, and a certain amount of grief, softened Mr. Waters's features. "Understood, Miss Darlington. Just see that it doesn't happen again."

"No, sir." Phoebe added a curtsy that would have made the Prince of Wales proud.

As soon as Mr. Waters left, Phoebe blew out a breath and set to work, readying her station for the moment when the shop's doors opened. A strange sense of pride came over her as she straightened up rows of gloves in their trays, added the newly-arrived stock from the boxes that had been stored under her counter to the display, and dusted the shelves behind her. She wondered if the maids who had worked in her father's country estate in Herefordshire had taken as much pride in her work.

That thought led her into wondering how those maids were fairing, how the entire staff of Credenhill Grange was faring, as the first customers began to drift down the aisle, perusing everything the shop had to offer. She'd loved Credenhill Grange, had grown up there. The estate was beautiful and filled with the only happy memories of her childhood. Her father's transgressions had mostly involved London, so the country estate had always felt like a refuge. She had no idea what had become of it now. It had likely been entailed away to some distant, male relative, or sold to pay off the last of her father's debts. Her mother had been too distressed and distracted to make inquiries of her father's solicitor— not to mention blanching at the idea that she, a woman, should have anything to do with something as masculine as business—and Phoebe hadn't dreamed she could make those inquiries herself. Not as an unwed daughter with no friends and no help from any quarter.

She wasn't that same, lost, weak woman she'd once been now, though. And she had friends. Perhaps Danny could help her search out her father's solicitor to determine what had happened to the estate. Though it would break her heart if it had fallen into the hands of someone who didn't care and hadn't maintained it. Perhaps if she—

"There she is, Maude," Lady Jane's voice shook Phoebe out of her conflicted thoughts. "The starlet of the hour."

Phoebe clenched her jaw and took a deep breath, steeling herself to face Lady Jane and Lady Maude yet again. The gorgons seemed to have nothing better to do anymore than to pester Phoebe at work.

"Good morning, Lady Jane, Lady Maude," she greeted them with a smile that was little more than her gritting her teeth. "How may I help you today?"

The two ladies exchanged wicked looks, sending dread straight to the pit of Phoebe's stomach. Lady Jane held a journal of some sort that was printed on pink-tinged paper. The snakes in Phoebe's stomach writhed harder. She had a sinking feeling she knew exactly which periodical Lady Jane had.

Lady Maude, tilted her nose up and surveyed Phoebe as though picking out a race-horse to bet on. "Yes, the resemblance is unmistakable. It's her, all right."

Phoebe shrugged as casually as she could. "I've never pretended to be anything other than who I am."

Lady Jane ignored her, unfolding the journal and clearing her throat before reading a passage. "*Lady X was a vision of false innocence. The angelic gleam of her blond hair stood in direct contrast to her sensual mouth and tempting figure. The way she swept through the ballroom, all purpose and energy, would have been irresistible to even the most staid of men. But the impostor was not bound by rules of society or propriety. He followed her with a wolfish gleam in his eyes, knowing that he would have her by the end of the evening.*"

Lady Jane lowered the periodical and smirked at Phoebe. "I wonder if the other descriptions given in the story are as accurate."

Phoebe swallowed, a tremor forming inside of her. "May I see?" she asked, cursing the crack in her voice, as she held out her hand for the journal.

Lady Jane looked reluctant to hand the paper over until Lady Maude said, "Oh, give it to her. I want to see her face when she finds out she's been *exposed*." She added extra emphasis to the final word, along with a gloating grin.

Lady Jane sniffed and handed the journal to Phoebe. "I want that back."

Phoebe ignored her, poring over the page Lady Jane had been reading from. It was near the beginning of what appeared to be a serialized story. Along with a description of a ball and of a leading lady that seemed very much like her, the page described a man that was undoubtedly Danny. Phoebe scanned further along the story to find exactly what she expected to find—a shockingly erotic account of passion...that wasn't entirely unlike what had actually occurred between her and Danny after the ball.

She flipped back to the first page of the journal, unsurprised to find herself holding the latest edition of *Nocturne*. Her curiosity about the sensational journal flared into a sense of anxiety. So she and Danny were the latest victims of the unknown author's fantasies, were they?

She feigned indifference as she handed the paper back to Lady Jane. "I'm surprised that you've corrupted your morals to the point of reading erotica and flashing it about in public as though it were a moralizing pamphlet."

Lady Jane's smirk vanished and Lady Maude's smugness turned to disappointment.

"You know that's you and that horrid beast from Lady O'Shea's ball the other night," Lady Maude said.

Phoebe shrugged. "It could be anyone. The details

are vague at best." They weren't, but Phoebe wasn't about to let on that she and Danny had, in a way, been discovered. "I don't concern myself with wickedness like this."

As soon as Lady Jane took her paper back, Phoebe busied herself tidying trays of already neat gloves. Both Lady Jane and Lady Maude looked painfully disappointed in her reaction.

"You realize your reputation will be destroyed because of this," Lady Jane said.

Phoebe glanced back to her with a sharp laugh. She held her hands to her sides, glancing around her area of the shop. "What reputation? Any standing I had with your lot evaporated years ago. Don't you agree?"

Lady Jane looked downright bitter at that thought. "Well," she sniffed, tucking the salacious journal under her arm. "I simply thought you would like to know what is being said about you and that man after your performance at Lady O'Shea's ball."

"Everyone who the mysterious author of *Nocturne* has written about has seen their social standing tumble," Lady Maude added.

"How fortunate for me, then," Phoebe said with a smile. "I cannot tumble any farther than I already have. Good day, ladies."

Lady Jane and Lady Maude weren't used to being dismissed. They stood where they were for a moment, fiddling with their purses, biting their lips, and looking generally disappointed. At last, they gave up and walked away.

As soon as they were gone, Phoebe blew out a breath, shoulders sagging. She wished she'd thought to keep the copy of *Nocturne* so that she could read through the entire story to find out just how bad it was.

"Psst!"

Phoebe jerked out of her thoughts as Hilda whispered to her from across the aisle. When she glanced up questioningly, Hilda said, "I know where to buy copies of that *Nocturne* thing," with a mischievous glint in her eyes.

"Do you?" Hope—and trepidation—filled Phoebe's heart.

"Oh, it's all the rage at my boarding house," Hilda said. "You wouldn't believe the things written in there. Every time I read it, I think my eyes are going to fall right out of my head. That author leaves nothing at all to the imagination."

"Oh, dear," Phoebe sighed. She'd heard as much about the publication, but now, knowing that she and Danny had somehow been made the subjects of the author's fantasy, she wasn't sure if she approved. Even if she did burn to read the story now.

She had to wait until her entire, long shift was over to do anything about it, though. It made the day creep by. She was bristling with impatience by the time she left work and made her way to the newspaper stand Hilda had told her about to purchase a copy—a ridiculous process that involved speaking to a particular man selling the thing and using a code to ask to buy it. Once the paper was in her hands, she took herself to Hyde Park and found a bench in the shade where she could read it.

"Oh, Lord," she sighed as she skimmed through the dazzlingly explicit details of the erotic story. Though truth be told, it was fascinating and filled her with a naughty urge to act out the things the mysterious author had imagined about her and Danny.

A thought struck her that wiped the coy grin from her face halfway through a description of Danny doing shocking things between her legs with his tongue. Whoever the author was, they had to have been present at Lady O'Shea's ball. There were too many distinct descriptions for them to simply have made everything up. She leafed through the rest of the issue in her hands. Everything it contained had its origin at the ball. The details of decoration and food, even what the orchestra had played, were explicit in more ways than one. Phoebe felt as though she were on the verge of discovering the identity of the author, and the one thing she knew about *Nocturne* was that London had been anxious for months to discover who that author was.

A second thought struck her as she stood, tucked the journal under her arm, and made her way out of Hyde Park, heading toward Mayfair. Journals such as the one she'd just read genuinely could make or break reputations. She'd heard rumors that the authors of scandalous rags like that made small fortunes blackmailing their subjects. Whether blackmail was involved or not, appearing in print could damage someone's reputation. Her reputation was already long gone, but Lord Cosgrove's wasn't. Yet. And a man without a reputation was the sort of man Parliament would never grant a contract for land development to.

She reached the door to Hopewell House within fifteen minutes and knocked eagerly. Lady O'Shea's butler smiled as he opened the door to greet her, which filled Phoebe with confidence.

"Is Lady O'Shea at home?" she asked, stepping into the house as the butler gestured for her to come in.

"For you, my lady, I'm certain she is," the butler said, gesturing for her to follow him down the hall. "We were all so delighted with the ball the other night," he went on. In spite of his august years and stiff posture, he leaned closer to her and said, "We servants don't ordinarily get the chance to enjoy ourselves as much as our betters while serving during a ball. You and your friend, Mr. Long, provided as much joy for us as you did for the esteemed guests."

"Why, thank you, sir," Phoebe beamed in response.

She didn't have a chance to say more, as the man led her to an afternoon parlor where Lady O'Shea was taking tea. She wasn't alone, though. Miss Garrett sat with her, as did Natalia, who Phoebe had come to see.

"Phoebe!" Natalia yelped leaping out of her chair and rushing across the room to hug Phoebe. "We were just talking about you. Come and have some tea."

"I don't want to disturb you, Lady O'Shea," Phoebe said, following Natalia into the room. "I came to have a word with Natalia."

"Have a word with all of us," Lady O'Shea said, gesturing to the sofa where she sat. "Miss Garrett and Natalia and I were just discussing your grand entry into the realm of fiction, something I see you have discovered as well." Her eyes practically glittered with mischief as she nodded to the pink-tinged paper under Phoebe's arm.

Phoebe blushed furiously as she had a seat. "I'm a bit alarmed by the whole thing, to tell you the truth," she admitted.

"Nonsense." Natalia fluttered about, fixing Phoebe a cup of tea. "How exciting to be made the subject of such a popular and scandalous journal."

Phoebe sent her a wary look. "If my reputation wasn't already nonexistent, I would be devastated."

"But you aren't devastated?" Miss Garrett asked.

Phoebe considered the question seriously. "I'm not sure I have farther to fall," she admitted. "But reading this story has given me a wicked idea."

"I should say so," Miss Garrett said, her eyes sparkling with wickedness of her own. "Particularly if there is any truth to the association it implies between you and Mr. Long."

Phoebe blushed harder. "Well, as to that, it's not something I feel as though I should discuss."

Her answer was a dead giveaway, which all three of the others knew in an instant.

tes
tes
"Well," Lady O'Shea said with an excited smile, sipping her tea.

"That's not what I came to discuss, though," Phoebe said, taking a sip of her own tea before changing the topic. "I trust you've all heard about the fire that destroyed The Watchman pub and surrounding buildings."

All three of the others instantly lost their cheer, their grins replaced by grimaces and frowns.

"Yes," Natalia said. "And I think Lord Cosgrove is horrible to do such a thing."

Phoebe's brow shot to her hairline. "So you've heard the speculation that Lord Cosgrove was responsible?"

"Of course," Lady O'Shea said. "Remember that your friend, Mr. Long, is friends with my husband and Natalia's brother."

"And Freddy and Reese," Miss Garrett added. Phoebe found it particularly interesting that she didn't refer to Lord Harrington as her fiancé, even though he was.

"The man should be drawn and quartered," Natalia said with particular vengeance.

"I will admit that I agree," Phoebe said. "He was positively dreadful to me and Danny when we went to confront him at his club the morning after the fire."

The other three ladies exchanged looks as though highly impressed by Phoebe's initiative.

Phoebe went on before they could steer the conversation away from the idea that had formed in her mind in

196

Hyde Park. "After reading this delicious story, presumably of me and Danny, I had an idea."

"What sort of an idea?" Lady O'Shea leaned closer to her.

"An idea to strike back at Lord Cosgrove the same way he sought to strike at Danny," Phoebe said. "Surely, a parliamentary committee would not award a development contract to a man whose reputation has been brutalized in the press."

"If that were true, then the story in *Nocturne* would discredit Mr. Long and take him out of the running for the deal," Lady O'Shea said circumspectly.

Phoebe had thought of that, but she shook her head all the same. "This bit of frippery is the sort of thing men pat themselves on the back over," she reasoned. "If you ask me, it might actually improve Danny's standing in the eyes of the men on the parliamentary committee."

"That's certainly true," Miss Garrett agreed.

"But if the information printed were of a more damaging sort, if it were an account of the misdeeds and crimes a man was guilty of by association to a man who is already well-known to have ruined a great many members of the aristocracy—"

"Your father," Lady O'Shea said, leaning back with a smile, as though Phoebe had announced "checkmate".

Phoebe nodded. "All I need a journal willing to print a story implicating Lord Cosgrove in the crimes my father committed. His reputation would be ruined in a substantial way, Danny would win the development contract, and perhaps my mother would finally stop trying to convince me to marry the bastard, Cosgrove."

The other three looked as though Phoebe had just presented them with a marvel.

"Why, Phoebe," Natalia said, giggling. "I had no idea how ruthless you were."

Phoebe sat straighter. "I've had to become ruthless to survive. And no, I have no qualms about bringing down a man associated with my father who has caused me so much personal distress." Her shoulders drooped slightly as another thought came to her. "I have no idea how to start the thing, though. I don't know a single newspaper editor, or anyone of any importance, really."

"Oh, but I do," Miss Garrett said, her grin growing in size and cheekiness. "I've spent enough time in London now to make a few friends who might be of use. One more recent friend in particular." She reached across and patted Phoebe's hand. "You leave this to me. I know exactly how to proceed."

CHAPTER 14

"The good news is that the pub, the entire building, actually, was insured," Tuttle said from across the table and a pile of paperwork in Danny's dining room. "Not many property owners are taking advantage of the new insurance schemes, but I've always tried to steer you in the right direction."

"I know," Danny said, wanting to sound thankful, but too frustrated to so much as smile. He'd been in a terrible mood for days, since the fire itself and his and Phoebe's confrontation with Cosgrove at the man's club. More than just the stink of smoke lingered in the air. As he stared out the window at a cloudy, London sky and the dull building across the mews from his flat, he writhed with the need to do something, to wring someone's neck. The only time he hadn't felt like marching back to that club, dragging Cosgrove out of the place by his ear, and pounding his fist repeatedly across the man's face was when Phoebe had snuck up to visit him in the middle of the night the previous evening.

It had been a glorious visit at that. Just when he'd begun to wonder if he'd taken things too far between the two of them and shocked her sensibilities by behaving like such a lion after the fire, she'd reassured him of her affection by coming willingly to his bed. And she'd been a dream, sighing with pleasure and meeting his passion with her own, in spite of her inexperience. Her eagerness to make love with him was the only thing that had kept him from sinking into anger and despair to the point of doing something rash.

"Demolition crews should begin work taking down the destroyed buildings before the end of the week," Tuttle went on, shuffling through the papers on the table, "which means—"

"By the end of the week?" Danny sat up straighter, pulling his full focus back to the conversation at hand. "What about the arson investigation?"

Tuttle pressed his lips together, looking as sheepish as he did irritated. "The police refuse to look into the matter further," he said.

"Refuse?" Danny boomed, gaping at the man.

"The officer who filed the initial report, Officer Mull, says it's a clear case of accidental fire," Tuttle said with a wince. "He dismissed your claim that Lord Cosgrove was responsible."

"How dare he?" Danny pounded on the table, standing. "Everyone knows Cosgrove was behind it. Cosgrove himself didn't deny it, not really."

"Whether Cosgrove was behind the arson or not, Scotland Yard isn't willing to investigate," Tuttle said.

"Have you appealed to Jack Craig yet?" Danny asked, beginning to pace his flat. "Jack would do something about it."

"Lord Clerkenwell was very responsive to my appeal," Tuttle told him. "But when he attempted to press the matter internally, he was refused in no uncertain terms."

"And why was that, I wonder?" Danny fumed, shoving a hand through his hair.

He didn't need Tuttle to answer, but the man did anyhow. "As far as Scotland Yard sees it, you're a middle-class pub owner at best, and you're accusing a member of the aristocracy. Not a soul is going to touch that claim."

"Bloody English values," Danny growled, tempted to snatch up a vase on his mantelpiece and dash it to bits in the grate just to smash something. "I'm sick and bloody tired of the upper classes being so untouchable. As if their shit doesn't stink."

Tuttle spread his hands in a hopeless gesture. "'Twas always thus and always thus will be'," he quoted.

"Well, it shouldn't be," Danny grumbled.

He continued to pace for a moment, unable to shake the irritation that bunched the muscles of his back and made him grit his teeth. Tuttle sat silently at the table, alternately glancing between the papers containing all of the business dealings involved with the demolishing and rebuilding of the fire-damaged buildings. Because Danny sure as hell was going to rebuild. He wouldn't let Cosgrove cow him in the least. His new construction would be bigger, better, and more modern than anything that part of the city had seen.

At length, Tuttle cleared his throat. "Am I correct in understanding that your chief frustration is the lack of respect you receive from authorities and those in positions of power?" he asked.

"Yes!" Danny shouted, spinning to pace toward the man. "I'm richer than all of them, so why shouldn't they treat me as their equal?"

"Birth," Tuttle answered with a shrug, but rushed on before Danny could do more than laugh bitterly. "You could, of course, do what industrialists and entrepreneurs have been doing for a hundred years and more."

Danny crossed his arms and frown. "And what is that?"

Tuttle chewed his lip nervously before saying, "You could marry into the aristocracy."

Danny knew in an instant what Tuttle had in mind. He'd be lying if he said he hadn't thought of marrying Phoebe in every single waking moment that wasn't already consumed by the business of his pub and the land deal. He wanted her more than he'd ever wanted a woman before. She was goodness and light. She was stronger than she thought she was, and at the same time, she needed him to protect her. In short, she was everything he'd ever looked for in a woman and the only woman he could see himself living out the rest of his life with.

"There is the matter of her inheritance," Tuttle went on, hitting exactly the nerve that had stopped Danny from proposing to Phoebe and pledging his life to her when he was between her legs the night before. "According to what you told me about her father's will, she is set to inherit a country estate and everything that goes along with it. And that estate would pass to her husband once she marries."

"I know, I know," Danny grumbled, the twist of guilt that usually came with thoughts of the whole thing gnawing at his gut.

"You cannot change your birth," Tuttle continued, "but you're extraordinarily wealthy. I've made a few initial inquiries, and your investments are more than enough to cover the debt that Credenhill Grange has accumulated. I might have a few suggestions for men who could be hired as land stewards as well. A country estate is the ultimate accessory of high society. The daughter of a marquess would be another trapping of importance and respectability that money cannot buy."

Danny huffed a frustrated breath and rubbed his hands over his face as he returned to pacing. It was all so easy, so simple. He loved Phoebe. He wasn't too proud to admit it. He was reasonably certain she loved him. For now. But how would she react if he married her, or even proposed marriage, only to find out later that he was well aware of her true value and the social advancement marriage to her would provide him with? She was too intelligent not to believe he was using her for his own gains.

Or worse still, if he told her about her inheritance before proposing, there was a chance she would drop him and everything her life had become to return to society. He'd seen the way she smiled at everyone in that ballroom at Hopewell House. It was the happiest Danny had ever seen her. Well, the happiest he'd seen her with clothes on. There was no denying she loved that life, loved the clothes and the music and the company. He had much to offer her, but he wasn't sure he could compete with the entire, bloody English aristocracy.

"I'm not some brute, like Cosgrove, who wants to collect a woman of substance for all the things she can do for me," he said aloud, voicing his prickliest concern. "I'm not going to use Phoebe as a pawn for my own advancement." If he proposed now, he would be every bit the mercenary that Cosgrove was.

"I don't think you'd be using her," Tuttle said, rising and gathering his papers. "You are a man of honor and integrity, Danny. You always have been. I can see clearly that you're worried any matrimonial offers you might make to Lady Phoebe would be seen as self-serving, but I know you as a person as well as a business associate. You love her. I believe she loves you. And love trumps business."

Tuttle's words were a bit of a comfort. They were

certainly something Danny would have to consider. The other aspect of the whole, mad muddle was that he hated making decisions quickly. He hadn't taken the business built by three generations of his family and grown it into an empire by making rash decisions.

A knock sounded at the door as Tuttle stuffed his paperwork into his satchel. Danny crossed to answer it. His heart leapt and his mood improved vastly at the sight of Phoebe standing in the hall.

"I have the perfect plan to ruin Lord Cosgrove," she announced, her eyes bright with mischief.

"God, I love you," he burst out, her declaration pushing him over the edge. He leaned into the hall, scooped his arm around her waist, and tugged her both into the apartment and up against him. Before she could say another word, he slanted his mouth over hers, kissing her with all the passion he could muster and then some.

She sighed deep in her throat, looping her arms over his shoulders, and making the most delicious noise of surrender as he danced his tongue along hers in imitation of something else he wanted to do to her as soon as possible. That adorable sound turned into an alarmed squeak, and she leapt back as she noticed Tuttle grinning at them from the table.

"Oh! I didn't know you had company," Phoebe stammered, pink-faced and lovely in so many ways.

She tried to pull away, but Danny held her firmly around the waist. "What, Tuttle? He was just leaving," he said, grinning like an imp. The contrast in his mood before she arrived and now that she was in his arms was so sharp that it made him dizzy.

"I was just leaving," Tuttle repeated, crossing the room to fetch his hat from the rack by the door. "You think about what I said," Tuttle charged Danny. "It could solve everything. Good day, Lady Phoebe." He nodded to Phoebe.

As soon as Tuttle was gone, Danny swept Phoebe fully into his arms again and kissed her, raising his hands to undo the buttons of her blouse. He had every intention of getting her flat on her back in his bed as quickly as possible, and he wasn't afraid to show it.

"What could solve everything?" she asked with a plaintive sigh that sounded more like she was begging him to love her than asking about his business.

"Do you know," he said between kisses to her mouth, cheek, and neck as he pushed the front of her blouse open, "I have no idea."

He finished with her buttons and pushed her blouse off her shoulders, sweeping his hands up her corseted sides to cradle her breasts. From there, he bent low enough to rain kisses across the swell of her breasts while raking her nipples through the fabric of her corset and chemise with his thumbs. They responded pertly as she made beautiful sounds of enjoyment.

"I hope you don't mind being thoroughly loved in the middle of the afternoon," he said, backing her toward his bedroom. "Because more than anything in the world right now, I need to be buried deep inside of you."

"Oh," she sighed shakily. "And I haven't even shown you the scandalous story written about us yet."

Danny stopped, standing straight and grinning down at her. "What story?" Anxiety that someone had printed something horrible about him in some newspaper threatened to destroy his amorous mood.

But Phoebe merely grinned and handed him a slightly pink newspaper. Danny let her go long enough to take it from her. He recognized it as a journal that published erotic stories and that had been circulating among the upper classes for the last few months as though it were made of gold and reading it would make your cock grow three inches.

"The Fallen Angel and the Beast?" he laughed at the title of one story that began on the front page. "Is that us?"

"Apparently, it is," Phoebe said, a naughty glint in her eyes.

That glint was enough to move mountains. He tossed the newspaper over his shoulder and swept her into his arms again. "I'll read it later," he said. "I'm a bit busy at the moment."

He lifted her into his arms, and she wrapped her legs around his waist as best she could in her dowdy skirt as he carried her to his bedroom and laid her across his bed.

"Don't you want to know my plan to ruin Cosgrove?" she asked breathlessly as he unfastened her skirt and tugged it off her legs, along with her petticoat and stockings.

"Does it involve beating him over the head with an iron bar, stuffing him into a burlap sack, and throwing him in the Thames?" Danny asked, towing off his shoes and fumbling his way through removing his own clothes. Clothes were such a nuisance.

"No," Phoebe giggled, unfastening her corset and wriggling out of the rest of her clothes. "But it does involve exposing Cosgrove's connection to my father and all the wickedness he was involved in, thus ruining his standing in the eyes of society and the parliamentary committee."

Danny had his shirt off and his hands working through the fastenings of his trousers as she finished her speech. He paused, then said, "Love, the only thing I care about being exposed right now is your gorgeous pussy."

Phoebe's eyes went wide for a moment. Then she squirmed out of her drawers, tossed them aside, and opened her legs for him.

His cock jumped at the sight of her, already glistening and wet. His hands shook with such eagerness that he had a hard time undoing the fastenings and shucking them. His grateful prick sprang to full attention as he straightened. She'd thrown off the rest of her clothes by then and lay naked on her back, legs still spread, breasts pink and full, nipples hard, with an expression of invitation that stopped his lungs from working.

"You're the most beautiful thing I've ever seen," he growled, grabbing his cock and working it for a few, blissful strokes, just to see the hunger in her eyes.

"And you're magnificent," she panted.

It would be torture to pace himself, but he did his best as he climbed onto the bed over top of her. He leaned down to kiss her, teasing her with only the barest of contact between their overheated bodies. His cock ached to be inside of her, but he wanted to make her come first. Blessedly, since sex was so new to her and her desire was monumental, that hadn't proved hard to do in their times together.

He broke away from her mouth, shifting to suckle one of her breasts while balancing himself above her as best he could. "I know that journal, by the way," he said between kisses and raking her nipple with his tongue. "I know the sort of things that author writes."

"I found the bit that I read exceptionally intriguing," she said, breathless and high-pitched. "Particularly the bit about what the hero got up to with his mouth between the heroine's legs."

A shiver of excitement shot down Danny's spine tightening his balls and pushing him alarmingly toward the edge. He balanced himself above her. "Love, did you just give me an order about what you want me to do to you?"

She bit her lip, cheeks pink, body flushed, mischief in her eyes. "Is it an order you'd obey?" she asked.

He laughed, then lifted her around the waist, twisting so that they lay the right way around on the bed, Phoebe with her head resting on the pillows. Once that was taken care of, he scooped his hands under her knees, prying her legs wide apart and bending her knees to give him full access. She gasped and cooed deliciously at everything he did, resting her arms on the pillows with her hands over her head in a position of blissful surrender.

"You're going to be the death of me," he growled before bending down to rake his tongue along the wet slit of her pussy.

She gasped and bucked, but he'd only just begun giving her what she wanted. He wasn't sure she actually knew what she was in for, which was the most arousing thing he'd ever experienced. He threw his heart and soul into pleasuring her, using his tongue and fingers, licking and stroking and plunging inside of her. She rewarded him with a maddening series of mewling cries, vocal gasps, and impulsive movements against him. Her pleasure was raw and entirely artless. Just feeling the way she abandoned herself to pleasure made Danny want to forget everything else in his frustrating life.

When she came, she came hard, her breath turning to a series of anticipatory pants as the pleasure built within her, then bursting with a sensual cry as her cunny throbbed with pleasure. It was so powerful that Danny moaned along with her. He couldn't resist partaking fully in her release and quickly adjusted his stance so that he could plunge deep into her before she finished squeezing. He held himself there for a moment, reveling in her body's response before seeking his own release.

She was hot and tight, and every inch of her drove him wild. It was more than being inside of her, the friction glorious and sensual. It was the way she wrapped her arms and legs around him, the sound of her full-throated sighs as she welcomed him within her, and the way she reached down to grasp his arse, urging him on. He lost his head, thrusting powerfully into her over and over, losing his mind a little more with each movement and with the way she moaned in ecstasy in time to his thrusts.

He wanted it to last forever, but with a burst of lightning and adoration, the tension within him became unbearably huge, and he exploded, his soul unraveling within her even as his seed rushed into her. It was brilliant on every level, light and pleasure and everything pure and good in the world surging through him with sensations that were almost unbearably hot.

As fast as those sensations overtook him, they tumbled into the peaceful glory of completion and the disjointed feeling of becoming one with her that came with it. He moved inside of her until he couldn't anymore, then collapsed to her side, careful not to crush her as he did.

"Marry me, Phoebe."

The words floated out of him, with spent passion that came straight from his heart, before he could stop himself.

Her panting stopped abruptly as she held her breath. He settled on his side, pulling her overheated body against his, searching her eyes for an answer. Those eyes were wide and stunned, but also hazed with passion.

"Marry you?" She breathed again, her chest rising and falling, stars in her eyes.

The cat was out of the bag, so he might as well let it run free. "I'm serious," he said, stroking her hair away from her damp face. "I love you. I love you like I've never loved anyone before. You're beautiful and intelligent, and you're the only woman I could ever see myself spending the rest of my life with. And after these last few days, who knows? You might already be carrying my child." He stroked a hand down to her belly, feeling her shiver as he did. "Marry me," he repeated.

She sucked in a breath of wonder, then sighed, "Yes! Yes, of course, I'll marry you."

She threw herself against him, knocking him to his back in her enthusiasm to kiss him. He laughed, letting her ravish him as thoroughly as she wanted to. What she lacked in experience, she made up for in energy.

"Give me a moment, love," he continued to laugh as she kissed his neck and chest. "Give me a few minutes to rest and we can go again."

"Well, hurry up," she panted, returning to his mouth, which she kissed mercilessly.

It was the most beautiful, wonderful thing he'd ever experienced. And yet, part of him knew he was committing a cardinal sin that would come back to bite him.

CHAPTER 15

She was engaged. Phoebe breathed a happy sigh at the thought as the first rays of sun peeked through the curtains, bathing Danny's room in hazy light. Against all odds, she had met the most wonderful, original man in the world, fallen deeply in love with him, and he had asked her to be his wife. She snuggled against him, throwing her bare leg over his equally bare thigh and nuzzling his shoulder. She wouldn't have to work at Harrods anymore, although she would miss Hilda and Imogen. She doubted that Danny had the means to keep her in luxury, but she would be the very best middle-class wife to him that she possibly could, even if her mother—

Phoebe snapped to full wakefulness with a gasp, sitting bolt-upright. Her mother.

"Oh, dear," she whispered into the scant light.

"What?" Danny's drowsy voice said next to her. He

reached a hand to rub her back. "Come back to bed, love, it's only—shit."

Danny sat abruptly beside her as he glanced to the carriage clock sitting on the mantel of the fireplace across from his bed. It was nearly nine o'clock.

"Oh, no," Phoebe gulped, throwing her legs over the side of Danny's bed and nearly tumbling to the floor. "Mama will be wondering where I am. She'll want to know why I didn't come home yesterday."

Danny climbed out of the other side of the bed and lunged toward his wardrobe as Phoebe picked up the bits and pieces of her clothes from the floor. "Maybe she won't have noticed," he said without any confidence.

"I wasn't home for supper last night," Phoebe said warily, sending Danny a foreboding look as she dressed as quickly as she could. "We always eat supper together. Mostly because she cannot cook for herself."

"You've been doing all the cooking?" Danny asked, a small, impressed smile interrupting the anxiety of his features.

"Who else is there to do it?" Phoebe said. In all honesty, she was proud of her newfound ability to cook, although the meals she was able to manage weren't anything like the sumptuous feasts she'd enjoyed growing up.

There wasn't time to think about the past, though. Only the miserable present and the dressing down she was certain to get when she stumbled back into her flat and faced her mother, looking as debauched as her night with Danny had made her. She caught sight of herself in a small mirror in the corner of Danny's room and groaned. She looked worse than she thought.

But she felt magnificent. There was that, at least. And Danny had asked her to marry him. She hadn't done anything that thousands of other women before her hadn't done.

"We need to move fast today if we're to find further proof Cosgrove was responsible for burning down the pub," Danny said once he was dressed. "I have a few ideas, and I wouldn't mind your company as I explore them."

"I'll need to freshen up first," Phoebe said with a sheepish, sideways look.

Danny grinned. "I suppose we did get a bit mussed up last night."

Phoebe giggled. "With any luck, Mama will still be in bed," she said, finishing dressing and starting for the main room of Danny's flat. "She has taken to lying in since we moved here."

"I'll come downstairs with you to make sure she doesn't tear your head off or run you through if she thinks the worst," Danny said, following her out of the bedroom, shirt and waistcoat unbuttoned, carrying his shoes instead of wearing them.

Phoebe turned at the flat door to look at him and ended up laughing. "In your present state, I'm afraid you'll cause more trouble for me instead of alleviating what is sure to come."

Danny bent to stomp into his shoes as Phoebe waited for him by the door. As he straightened and glanced down at his appearance, he laughed. "I'll just tell your dear mum that I can look however I want or do whatever I want with my bride."

A girlish giggle escaped Phoebe before she could do anything to make herself look like less of a lovesick ninny. She pulled open the door and stepped out into the hall, happier than she'd been in ages.

But as they headed to the stairs, she noticed Danny's smile fade.

"Love, there's something I need to tell you," he said as they descended one floor and set out into the second-floor corridor.

"Oh?" Phoebe glanced over her shoulder at him as she reached for the door of her and her mother's flat. "Something good, I hope."

His face pinched and he rolled his shoulders. "It is good, if you ask me. In a way. At least, I hope you'll find it good. You see, I was at John Dandie's office the other day, and I ran into a bloke named Lionel Mercer, who is on familiar terms with quite a few people, including solicitors."

Phoebe listened to his story without understanding what he was talking about as she opened her flat door and stepped inside.

Danny continued with, "Anyhow, Mercer and I—"

"Oh. There you are."

Phoebe froze two steps into the flat, her heart

squeezing its way up to her throat as her mother greeted her from the table by the window. She was dressed in her morning robe and old fashioned mob-cap, sipping tea and frowning. Danny stepped into the flat behind her, nearly bumping into Phoebe's back as she stopped so suddenly.

"And you, Mr. Long." Her mother's frown turned into a downright scowl. "I trust you enjoyed your little excursion?"

Phoebe's mouth flapped as she scrambled desperately for something to say that would make her look like less of a strumpet in her mother's eyes. "Um...er...."

Her mother sniffed and took a sip of her tea. "I am firmly against this practice of young ladies strolling about the city in the early morning hours, even if this new fad for athletic activity for women has become popular. Women should spend their mornings in the home. It would stop them from encountering unworthy company while wandering the streets."

Instead of putting Phoebe at ease, her mother's words made her gape harder. "I...was...out for a morning stroll?" she said, pressing a hand to her stomach.

"As I was telling my dear friend last night over supper at...at whatever the name of that fashionable place is in Leicester Square, young women these days have been given entirely too much license and should be treated with stricter discipline."

Phoebe swayed on her spot, hardly believing her luck. At least, she thought it was luck. "And how was your supper?" she asked in a weak voice, praying that her mother had been so distracted by her friend that she'd neither realized Phoebe hadn't come home for supper nor figured out where she might have been.

"It was divine," her mother smiled and sighed, sinking into her chair. Her face took on a far-away look. "We had roast beef and Yorkshire pudding. I haven't had beef in nearly a year. I could have eaten the entire cow, it was so delicious. And you should have seen what the chef did with the potatoes. They were—"

"Excuse me, Mama." Phoebe bolted past her mother, no interest whatsoever in hearing the contents of her supper inventoried, and headed for her room. "I have to... I have to prepare for work."

She didn't have to work until much later in the afternoon, but any excuse she could come up with to get away from her mother before she realized the truth was a good one. She glanced over her shoulder to Danny—who looked uncharacteristically rattled by the whole thing—before disappearing into her room.

She didn't hear a peep from the flat's main room as she threw off her soiled clothes, bathed with her wash-basin and sponge, and dressed as swiftly as she could in clean clothes. That meant that either Danny had left or her mother was refusing to speak to him.

The latter proved to be true, as she discovered when she flew back into the main room to find Danny standing in the exact same spot with his arms crossed and her mother nibbling on toast and perusing one of her ladies' journals—thankfully not *Nocturne*.

Phoebe wanted to make it out of the flat before her mother started up another conversation, but she didn't quite make it.

"I have a few things I want to discuss with you when you return," she said, dragging her eyes away from her journal to stare at Phoebe. "Important things."

Phoebe hesitated with her hand on the door handle. "I have things I need to discuss with you as well, Mama," she said, sending a quick look Danny's way. "But we're needed elsewhere."

"Very well, then," her mother sighed.

Phoebe wrenched open the door and flew into the hall, Danny following her. As soon as the door was shut behind her, she breathed a sigh of relief. At the same time, she felt like an utter coward.

"I should face her rather than avoiding the issue," she said as they headed down the hall. "She's going to find out eventually."

"I'll be there when you tell her about us," Danny said with a nod. He broke into a grin. "If only to see the explosion when she learns who her son-in-law will be."

Phoebe giggled as they started down the stairs. "Oh." She glanced over her shoulder at Danny as they crossed the downstairs hallway and stepped outside. "What was it that you wanted to tell me about Mr. Dandic and Mr. Mercer?"

Danny's expression took on a sudden, vaguely anxious look. "I wanted to tell you that—"

"Lady Darlington. What a pleasant coincidence." As

they stepped out into the street, they nearly ran headlong into Miss Lenore Garrett. "I was told this was where you lived."

Phoebe flinched at the sudden appearance of her new American friend but managed a smile for her all the same. Danny's face pinched, and he rolled his eyes slightly, likely over being interrupted.

"Miss Garrett," Phoebe said, reminding herself to try again at some point to ask Danny about Dandie and Mercer. "How lovely and surprising to see you this morning." She stopped herself from explaining that she should be addressed as Lady Phoebe, not Lady Darlington. Miss Garrett was American and couldn't be expected to keep track of titles, and soon it wouldn't matter anyhow. Soon she would just be Mrs. Long.

"I came because I was struck by the most brilliant way to wheedle a confession about the fire out of Lord Cosgrove overnight," Miss Garrett said, a devilish light in her eyes. She lost her impishness for a moment as she glanced across the street at the frightening hulk of the burned-out pub. "I'm so very sorry for your loss, Mr. Long," she went on. "Hearing about it is one thing, but I've been standing here with a broken heart, surveying the damage, for a good five minutes now." She sighed. "It's made me more determined than ever to bring Lord Cosgrove to justice."

"Thank you, Miss Garrett," Danny said, seeming not to have a clue what else he could say.

"We were just on our way to the offices of Dandie &

Wirth in The City, seeing as Danny has an idea about how we could enlist their help to accomplish the same end," Phoebe said.

"What a lovely coincidence," Miss Garrett beamed broadly, hooking her arm through Phoebe's and starting down the street with her. "I can accompany you and tell you all about this plan I've conceived as we walk."

Phoebe felt as though Miss Garrett were sweeping her away into a whirlwind of mischief as she escorted her down the street. Danny followed behind, watching the two of them with a look of pure amusement. If it weren't for the fact that she felt completely swept up and carried away by Miss Garrett, she would have marveled at how many outspoken people she suddenly had in her life.

"This is the plan," Miss Garrett said as they headed south along the major thoroughfares. "We invite Lord Cosgrove to tea. Just when he's feeling content and comfortable, we lead him on, asking leading questions, pretending as though we already have proof of his guilt, and implying that his reputation is already damaged and coming clean with the full details of what happened is the only way to redeem himself."

Behind them, Danny barked a laugh as though the idea were the most ridiculous thing he'd ever heard.

Phoebe didn't disagree with him. "Are you certain that would work?" she asked, not wanting to insult her new friend.

Miss Garrett only seemed to brighten. "It worked for my father," she said as they turned a corner onto a less crowded street and marched on. "Daddy was a poker player in his younger days, you see. Before heading west and setting up his ranch in Wyoming. He always said that the best way to win a high-stakes game was to bluff better than your opponents and to learn their tells. He used that many a time when solving disputes on his ranch. There are a pair of sisters in Haskell who are just dreadful—Vivian and Melinda Bonneville. Vivian is an absolute pill, but she's as ruthless as they come. She had some of her ranch hands swipe my father's prize bull in the middle of the night so that he could get amorous with some of her cows and save her the cost of buying a bull of her own. She thought she could call the whole thing an accident and say that the bull got out on its own."

"Oh." Phoebe blinked rapidly, feeling as though she were getting a glimpse into some sort of fantastical, fairy tale world that was far from real.

"It backfired on her, of course," Miss Garrett went on. "But the way Daddy proved to everyone that Vivian stole that bull on purpose was by hosting a party and acting like everyone already knew. By the end of the evening, Vivian had confessed her plot to anyone who would listen. She tried to make it sound like she was the victim, but Vivian isn't particularly bright."

"And you think that Cosgrove and your Miss Vivian are cut from the same cloth, do you?" Danny asked behind them, barely able to keep the amusement out of his voice.

"I do," Miss Garrett said. "There's no one as stupid as

someone who thinks too highly of themselves but who has done something underhanded."

Phoebe didn't know what to say to that line of logic. There might have been some truth to it, particularly in the details Miss Garrett laid out as they wound their way through London to Dandie & Wirth's offices. Danny managed to steer them in the right direction, even though Phoebe and Miss Garret walked ahead of him. Miss Garrett was just finishing the last details of the story of her father's plan as they stepped into a nondescript office building and on to a modest-sized office that looked as though it was in the process of being redecorated.

"Mr. Long. How lovely to see you again." They were greeted by an elegant young man in a fashionable grey suit with the most arresting blue eyes and perfect, pale complexion that Phoebe had ever seen.

He wasn't the man who truly caught her attention, though. Standing beside him with what looked like a book of swatches was a slightly taller man who bore a striking resemblance to him, only he wore a pair of neat spectacles. Phoebe knew him all too well.

"Mr. Mercer," she said dropping into a curtsy on instinct. She'd had no idea that the Mr. Mercer Danny had mentioned—and that could only be who the well-dressed man in front of her was—was in any way connected to Mr. Phineas Mercer, one of many gentlemen her mother had attempted to throw her at over the years. Though as far as she knew, Phineas Mercer was little more than the son of a baronet whose family money had run out.

"Lady Phoebe." Mr. Phineas Mercer set aside the swatch book he was holding to greet her. "What a pleasure to see you again." He took her hand and greeted her with perfect elegance.

"You two know each other?" the other Mr. Mercer asked, a spark of delight and calculation in his eyes.

"Lady Phoebe and I are both on the fringes of the same circles," Mr. Phineas Mercer said, shifting his attention to Miss Garrett. "And Miss Garrett and I met at Lady O'Shea's ball last week."

"I remember," Miss Garrett said, taking Mr. Mercer's hand and inching closer to him as he bent over it. "I seem to recall you asking me quite a few impertinent questions as we danced."

"Impertinent questions are the very best sort," Mr. Mercer replied, smiling at her.

Phoebe's eyes went wide, and she stole a quick look at Danny. In all the time she'd known him, Mr. Phineas Mercer had only ever been a dull, reclusive man that stood at the edges of social gatherings, watching without participating. Not once had she seen him look as warmly at anyone as he did at Miss Garrett. If he'd looked half as fetching at any of the events where Phoebe had encountered him, she might have considered her mother's insistence that she make herself biddable to him. Though the thought seemed ridiculous to her now, newly engaged to Danny as she was.

The entire, intriguing situation was interrupted as two men, one of them Mr. John Dandie, entered the office in the middle of a conversation. That conversation stopped abruptly once they saw how full the office was.

"It appears we have guests," the man with Mr. Dandie said, stepping forward to greet Danny with a smile. He had dark hair and eyes and had a businesslike air of competence about him.

"Danny. Good to see you again," Mr. Dandie said, moving to shake Danny's hand when the other man stepped back. "And Lady Phoebe." He moved to greet Phoebe. "This is my partner, Mr. David Wirth," he introduced the dark-haired man.

Phoebe noted the slight flinch and what she could have sworn was a hint of jealousy from the other Mr. Mercer.

"And our newly-hired office manager, Mr. Lionel Mercer," Mr. Dandie said, formally introducing the man.

"It's a pleasure." Phoebe smiled at him. "And this is my friend, Miss Lenore Garrett."

Short though they were, the necessary round of introductions felt like an interminable delay to Phoebe. She was grateful when Danny burst out with, "These two lovely ladies think they have a plan to corner Cosgrove into admitting he's behind the fire that destroyed The Watchman. I remain unconvinced that Cosgrove would fall for anything so quaint and simple, though," he finished, sending Phoebe a guilty look.

She was stung that he would more or less call Miss Garrett's plan silly, even if she half agreed.

"What is the plan, then?" Mr. Wirth said, crossing his arms and tapping his lips with one finger as he prepared to listen.

"The plan is a brilliant one," Miss Garrett said with absolute confidence. "In a nutshell, we invite Lord Cosgrove to tea, converse as though we already know he was responsible, convince him everyone knows he was responsible and that the only way for him to redeem his reputation is to come clean about the whole thing."

Danny failed to hide his snort as Miss Garrett finished her explanation. Phoebe glanced warily at him. Charmingly, he looked duly chastised under her scolding look.

"It's a sweet plan," he said with a wince. "I'm just not convinced a man like Cosgrove would fall for schoolroom tactics."

Mr. Dandie and Mr. Wirth looked as though they were inclined to agree.

"It's a brilliant plan," Miss Garrett defended herself. "Don't you think so, Mr. Mercer?"

Mr. Phineas Mercer looked as though he were suddenly on the spot. But it was Mr. Lionel Mercer who answered, "That is a brilliant plan."

Everyone glanced to him with varying degrees of incredulity and doubt, but Lionel's gaze remained unfocused, as though he were thinking through the plan.

"It is simplistic and juvenile," he went on, tapping his lips in what was perhaps an unconscious imitation of Mr. Wirth. "But so is Lord Cosgrove. Any man of his age who adds color to his hair to appear younger and wears those ridiculous clothes he puts on is vain to the point of idiocy. Men like that will scramble to protect their reputations before they stop to think about what they say. And Cosgrove has more than the average man to defend himself against."

"So you actually think the plan would work?" Mr. Wirth asked, seeming both impressed and reticent as he studied Lionel.

Lionel shrugged. "Yes, I think it might. The nobility can be painfully obtuse about matters of reputation sometimes."

Phoebe agreed with the comment and nearly laughed when Mr. Dandie and Mr. Phineas Mercer glanced anxiously in her direction, as though Lionel's words might offend her. "I happen to agree," she said with a shrug.

"It's settled, then," Miss Garrett said with a satisfied nod. "I'll make arrangements for Lord Cosgrove to be invited to tea, either at Hopewell House, where I'm staying with my fiancé's sister, or elsewhere."

"You're betrothed to Lord Frederick Harrington," Lionel said, not as a question, but sounding as though he were filing away a particularly odd piece of information for later use.

"I am," Miss Garrett answered, then sent a coy look

to Mr. Phineas Mercer. "We have a special arrangement, Freddy and I."

Phoebe couldn't begin to understand what the trio must have been thinking, only that all three of them suddenly looked as though they were speaking in a code that the rest of them didn't understand. Mr. Wirth appeared too lost in thought to care about the conversation, but Mr. Dandie grinned and rolled his eyes.

"I'm glad you stopped by the office this morning, Danny," he said, stepping into the middle of their group and gesturing for Danny to break off to the side with him. Phoebe went with them. "I've just heard word that the parliamentary committee charged with deciding on the Earl's Court development deal is close to making their decision."

"Are they?" Danny's expression lit with an entirely different light of hope. Phoebe marveled as his entire countenance shifted to that of the astute businessman taking care of his investments. "Have you heard anything about which proposal they're favoring?"

"From what I've been able to find out, it's down to you and Cosgrove," Mr. Dandie said with a slight shrug. "We'll know more in the coming days. I think you have a solid shot at it."

Danny smiled, though there was a hint of ruthlessness to his look. "Good," he said. "I would love nothing more than to beat Cosgrove at his game once and for all and show him and the rest of the aristocracy where the future of this country really lies."

CHAPTER 16

*I*n the past, Danny had taken a certain amount of enjoyment in dressing up in fancy clothes. Society was nothing if not laughably strict about how people from different classes dressed, and wearing clothes that were considered finer than a man of his status should have was one of his favorite ways to tweak the noses of those who still felt that he should know his place and stick to it.

The next afternoon, however, as he paced the main room of Phoebe's flat, waiting for her to finish last-minute preparations for the mad tea party they were about to embark on at Hopewell House, all he felt was that his collar was too tight and itchy, his new shoes pinched, and he looked like a trussed-up fool instead of the man he knew himself to be.

"Good heavens, Mr. Long," Phoebe's mother groaned, staring daggers at him from the small writing desk to one side of the room, where she was busy spewing out a wealth of what was likely gossip to who knew who in letter form. "You fidget like a child. If you're going to parade around pretending you are your betters, you mustn't squirm."

"I am very sorry, madam," Danny fired back, too loud and irritated to sound polite.

Phoebe's mother flinched at his harsh tone, her eyes going wide. Danny felt bad for offending her for all of two seconds before she sniffed and said, "If you were my son, I would turn you over my knee and smack you until you knew how to speak to your betters."

The vehemence of her reply, giving as good as she'd gotten, and the image her words raised in Danny's mind nearly had him sputtering with surprise laughter. Phoebe's mother was an absolute pill and a harpy, but deep in the back of Danny's mind, he began to wonder what kind of magnificent, sturdy woman she would have made if she'd been born low and had to fight her way up. He had a feeling she could have mastered that fight.

"I'm almost ready, I promise," Phoebe said breathlessly as she hurried out of her bedroom, fastening some sort of pretty bauble into her hair.

Danny's heart dropped to his gut and spread a decidedly carnal sort of warmth through him as he studied her. She was far and away the most beautiful woman he'd ever known. She wore her pink ball gown again, though she'd done something to it to make it more suitable for daytime hours. Her blond hair was caught up in an attractive style at the back of her head, and the hairpin she'd stuck in it was the perfect touch to make her look fresh and inviting. But it was the flash of excitement in her blue eyes, the determination that radiated from her, and, of course, her rosy lips—which he'd kissed into oblivion not more than a few hours before, in spite of Phoebe's insistence that they needed to be careful lest her mother discover their indiscretions at any moment—that captivated him most.

"You look lovely," he said, well aware that the way he spoke made him seem like a lovesick schoolboy.

Phoebe blushed under the compliment, smiling in that delicious, coy way of hers. "Thank you," she said as she headed to a small table by the window to fetch her purse. "You look quite handsome yourself."

Danny wanted to say more. Words didn't seem to be enough to describe how perfect Phoebe was to him. But before he could catch her in her flight around the room to gather her things and sweep her into his arms for a kiss that would likely make her mother pass out, there was a knock on the flat's open door.

"Message just arrived for you, Danny," Umbridge said, holding up a small, folded piece of paper.

"I don't know why you insisted on keeping that door open while you wait," Phoebe's mother said with a long-suffering sigh. "I detest being interrupted when I am in the middle of an exceedingly private correspondence."

"You were the one who insisted on keeping it open," Danny told her as he crossed to take the note from Umbridge. "You said it was improper for a man to be closeted alone with two helpless females, and that the door should remain open so the other residents could hear your screams when I murdered you." His mouth twitched into a teasing grin, especially when Phoebe's mother huffed and bristled and thrust her nose into the air.

"I can only imagine what sort of horrid thoughts go through the mind of a man like you," she said, pretending to go back to her correspondence.

"Mama," Phoebe said, stepping up to Danny's side as he read the note Umbridge had handed him. His mood improved even more at the short message's contents. "Mr. Long is a good and decent man, and you would do well to warm to him."

"Yes, you would," Danny agreed, smiling as he folded the note and thrust it into his jacket pocket. "Because I've just received inside word that the parliamentary committee on land development will be making their decision tomorrow afternoon, and that only me and Cosgrove are left in the running, with all signs pointing to me winning the contract. They want me there when the decision is made."

Phoebe made a delightful sound of happiness, but her mother snorted in disgust.

"Really, Mr. Long." She shook her head, turning away from her writing desk. "Your lack of regard and respect for men whom God has placed in a position above you is scandalous. And you must refer to him as *Lord* Cosgrove, as befits his station."

"Then *Lord* Cosgrove should refer to me as 'sir', because he is most surely not my better," Danny fired back, too pleased with the turn of events to do anything other than treat Phoebe's mother as though she were a particularly feisty barmaid. "And you should treat me with a little more respect too, ma'am, seeing as I am shortly to be your son-in-law."

It was as if lightning had struck the room and resounding thunder rippled throughout. Phoebe's mother's casual irritation flashed to dire shock, and all color drained from her face. Phoebe went pale as well, stiffening at his side, her eyes wide. It was as if a judge had handed down a death sentence when the accused expected to be set free.

"You will be my *what*?" Phoebe's mother hissed.

Danny frowned, turning to Phoebe. He already knew the answer, but he asked anyhow, "Didn't you tell her that we're engaged?"

Again, the reaction to his words wasn't at all what he expected it to be. Phoebe's shock switched to red-faced rage as she glared at him. "I was waiting to tell her in a gentler manner," she said. "But you had to go and blurt it out, like you always do."

Danny's mouth dropped open, but before he could speak, Phoebe's mother bleated, "You do not deny it, then? Are you engaged to this oaf of a man?"

Both Danny and Phoebe turned to her with scowls, though the scowls were likely for different reasons.

"Yes, Mama." Phoebe broke away from Danny and

approached her mother. "Danny proposed and I said yes."

"But...but Lord Cosgrove," her mother stammered.

"You know full well that I don't have the slightest interest in that old buffoon," Phoebe said, raising her voice in a way Danny was certain she wouldn't have done a fortnight ago. "I never have been interested. I love Danny." She whipped to face Danny. "Though at the moment I'm as like as not to box his ears for being an outspoken clod."

Danny's mouth still hung open. He wasn't sure if he wanted to laugh and capture her in his arms for a kiss or if he wanted to pick a fight so he could shout at her and vent his emotions in a different way.

"I might be an outspoken clod," he said, settling on speaking too loudly, but not quite shouting and not storming across the room to rail in her face, "but I am far more than either of you seem to think I am."

He regretted his outburst as soon as the words were out. There was so much he had yet to explain to Phoebe, beginning with his net worth and the extent of his land holdings. And he still hadn't worked out a way to break the news of her own inheritance to her. Considering how furious she was with him now—and all because he'd let slip to her mother that they were engaged at an inopportune time—he was more convinced than ever that learning of her inheritance would spell disaster for the two of them. That didn't ease the guilt of holding onto the secret for too long, though.

"I know you are," Phoebe huffed, stomping her foot. Her words, tone, and gestures were so at odds with each other that, again, Danny didn't know whether to laugh or to continue to be angry. Phoebe pressed a hand to her forehead. "I just want to get this afternoon's tea over with. I am not confident in the plan, and nervousness has made me irritable."

Danny blinked in surprise. It was a far more level-headed response than he'd been expecting. Then again, Phoebe always had been so much more than everyone gave her credit for.

"What tea are you going to?" her mother asked, eyes narrowed in suspicion as she glanced from her daughter to Danny.

"A tea in which your lovely daughter plans to catch *Lord* Cosgrove out and make him admit to causing the fire that destroyed my pub," Danny snapped.

Instantly, Phoebe was back to being furious at him. Danny had to admit that, once again, he'd spoken out of turn.

Phoebe's mother shot out of her chair, eyes wide with indignation. "How dare you confront a man who has offered so selflessly to help you for so long?" she asked Phoebe, practically quivering with indignation. "Why, Lord Cosgrove is the kindest, most considerate—" Words failed her for a moment before she tacked on, "He is a viscount!"

"I cannot continue with this," Phoebe said, marching

across the flat and shooting out into the hall. "I trust I will be back in time for supper, Mama."

Danny followed her into the hall, too many emotions assailing him at once to feel anything but woefully out of sorts. Part of him saw the ridiculous humor in the situation. People never did behave rationally when their hearts and futures were on the line. Another part of him was stung that Phoebe could be so bull-headed with him. She was the one who accepted his proposal, after all. Wasn't she proud to become his wife?

They barely spoke as Danny hailed a cab to take them across Mayfair to Hopewell House. Phoebe was clearly struggling with her feelings, and he needed all of his powers of concentration if he hoped to keep the frivolous plan to corner Cosgrove from spinning completely out of control. His mood was soured further when they reached Lady O'Shea's house only to discover that Cosgrove had arrived before them. To Danny, that felt too much as though the man had scored an early victory against him.

"What is *that man* doing here?" Lord Cosgrove asked, rising from the dainty chair where he'd been sitting in a parlor that was clearly designed for women to gossip and titter in.

"Mr. Long is a friend," Miss Garrett said, rising as well. She crossed to Lord Cosgrove's side and nudged him to have a seat as though he were an ornery cow on her father's ranch. "I invited both him and my other dear friend, Lady Darlington—"

Phoebe muttered something under her breath that sounded exasperated.

"—to join our lovely party this afternoon," Miss Garrett continued. "After all, we have so many things in common to discuss."

"Do we?" Frederick Harrington asked Phineas Mercer in a low mutter.

Danny was surprised to find both men there. He never would have dreamed either would be even slightly interested in Miss Garrett's mad scheme. Though Freddy was her fiancé—which was even madder than the tea party, considering what Danny knew of Freddy's devotion to Reese Howsden—and Mercer was.... Actually, Danny didn't know what Phineas Mercer was—to Miss Garrett or to anyone. That realization put him even more on edge.

"Please, have a seat," Miss Garrett went on, gesturing toward a fussy little loveseat as if she intended Danny and Phoebe to pile into it together.

"I think I'll stand, thank you," Danny said, marching around the back of the circle of furniture to the side of the loveseat.

Phoebe narrowed her eyes at him, shook her head, and crossed directly to the loveseat and sat.

"I was just telling Lord Cosgrove about Haskell, Wyoming," Miss Garrett said, pouring tea for both Danny and Phoebe from the service on the table between the various chairs and sofas. "Particularly about an incident my mother recently wrote to me about."

"It seems there was a fire on one of the ranches," Freddy explained, managing to keep a straight face, even though his eyes communicated to Danny that it was all part of the ruse. "A chicken coop that housed someone's prize roosters was destroyed days before a county fair where a prize for the finest rooster was about to be rewarded." The sheer volume of amusement in Freddy's eyes made it hard for Danny to maintain a straight face.

Fortunately, he was able to hide how utterly preposterous he found the whole situation to be as Miss Garrett handed him his tea. "Is that so?" he asked before taking a long drink. He had a feeling he'd need whatever fortification he could get to make it through the afternoon. Why he had let Phoebe and her friends go through with the insane plan was a mystery to him.

The only man in the room who seemed to be taking the topic of conversation seriously was Mercer. "And you said that your mother thinks the arson was committed by the owner of the prize rooster's rival in the county fair?"

"Yes," Miss Garrett replied, her eyes fairly glittering with excitement as she took a seat on the chair beside Mercer's.

The way she perched right on the edge of the cushion and leaned toward Mercer raised a dozen questions in Danny's mind, none of which had to do with the matter at hand. He peeked at Freddy to see what he thought, but Freddy seemed as amused by the pairing as he was by the story. Danny shook his head slightly and took another sip of tea. He would never understand the way the upper classes thought.

Hard on the heels of that notion, Mercer turned to Cosgrove and asked, "What do you think of the situation, my lord?"

Danny expected Cosgrove to laugh the whole thing off, but to his surprise, Cosgrove sputtered and choked on his tea. "I? Er…um…well, competition of course. And… er…no chickens were harmed, were they?" He shot a guilty glance Danny's way.

It was all Danny could do not to drop his tea and ask if Cosgrove were a raging idiot. He might not have heard the extent of the conversation before he and Phoebe arrived—anything could have been said to put the man on edge—but he couldn't possibly be so moronic that Miss Garrett's foolish plan would actually work.

"I'm afraid several chickens perished in the conflagration," Miss Garrett said solemnly. "But it was the property damage that caused the greatest amount of grief. Dozens of chickens were left homeless after the incident. Doesn't that make you feel pity, my lord?" she asked Cosgrove.

"Oh…I…pity, yes," Cosgrove stammered.

"And don't you think that the man who was responsible for so much destruction and displacement should behave as a true gentleman and own up to his mistakes?" Miss Garrett went on. "I, for one, would admire a man who was able to take responsibility for his actions and make amends."

"It...it does seem like the admirable thing to do," Cosgrove said, squirming in his seat. He went so far as to put his teacup down and to tuck a finger into his collar to adjust it.

Danny gaped at Cosgrove, hardly believing what he was witnessing. He simply couldn't help himself when he blurted, "Don't you see that the man they're talking about is you, you gigantic pillock?"

In an all-too familiar repeat of the way lightning had struck at Phoebe's flat earlier, the entire parlor went silent. All eyes snapped to Danny. Miss Garret and Mercer seemed annoyed, as though he'd interrupted their game. Phoebe looked downright livid, but her ire felt very much like the same sort she'd been harboring against him since the flat. Oddly enough, Cosgrove looked as though he'd been yanked out of the dark hole he was hiding in and thrust into the light. He looked like a man who had been caught red-handed.

"I...I don't know what you're talking about," he stammered, sinking back into his seat. "I don't know anything about the fire that destroyed your pub. I wasn't even there. I was...I was at the ball, here, at Hopewell House. You can't prove a thing. You've no way to connect me to the crime. Lady Phoebe, surely you believe I'm innocent, don't you?" The way the lout appealed to Phoebe made Danny see red.

His patience was at an end. Cosgrove's babbling was as good as a confession, as far as he was concerned. Somewhere in the back of his mind, a tiny voice acknowledged that Miss Garrett's plan had worked after all, but he ignored it as he marched around the loveseat, handing his half-drunk tea to Phoebe, to tower over Cosgrove in his seat.

"Admit it," he said in a menacing voice. "You masterminded the arson that destroyed my pub, and you did it to try to intimidate me into dropping my bid for the Earl's Court deal."

CHAPTER 17

*I*n the last three years, since her father died—
even longer than that, if she counted the long
descent her father's behavior caused—Phoebe had
watched her status and her pride be chipped away, piece
by piece. It had wounded her in ways she couldn't begin
to comprehend. But watching Danny charge through
what should have been a delicate situation—if it should
have been a situation at all, which she still wasn't certain
of—caused something inside of her to snap.

"Must you always be so bull-headed?" she asked,
setting both her and Danny's teacups down and standing.

Danny turned to her, the fury he'd directed at Lord
Cosgrove turning to surprise as she marched closer to
him. "I'm tired of being treated as though my property
and my ambitions don't matter, simply because I was
born to the wrong mother."

Phoebe laughed bitterly before she could stop herself, even though a thread of deep sympathy wound around her heart. "That is precisely how I feel," she said. "I am through with being a commodity in the eyes of men and of the helplessness thrust upon me by my father's actions. How do you think it feels to be left without a penny to my name?"

"But you have far more than pennies to your name," Danny fired back at her.

A tiny part of Phoebe thrummed with satisfaction that Danny would debate her with all the energy she threw at him, even though she was a woman.

"Now is not the time for this," Lord Cosgrove blurted, standing so suddenly he nearly tumbled back to his seat again.

Phoebe sent him a withering look. "Everyone in this room knows that you were responsible for destroying Danny's pub, my lord. There is no point in trying to deny it." Lord Cosgrove stammered, but before he could form words, Phoebe whipped back to Danny and went on with, "Just as there is no point in brow-beating the man into a confession with as much bombast as you use while entertaining a crowd in your pub."

Danny shifted his stance, crossing his arms. "Are you angry with me for being myself?" he asked. "Because I am what I am, love, and I have never pretended to be anyone else."

"Perhaps you would like to continue this discussion

in another room," Miss Garrett said judiciously, standing, but looking a little too wary to step into the fray.

Phoebe ignored her, even though the sting of knowing she was being rude to a woman who was just trying to help her was acute. "I'm angry because my life was taken from me without my consent," she said, feeling as though years' worth of bottled up emotions had come uncorked. "I'm angry because I lost my home, whatever sense of family I had, and my pride, just as you lost your pub."

"Then why turn harpy on me?" Danny demanded, though without the sharpness she would have expected from a man who was truly offended.

Phoebe felt as though she stood on the verge of releasing every frustration that had lashed at her for years. "Because you won't judge me for being furious," she said, coming close to shouting as the truth struck her.

"I won't," Danny bellowed, as though he were disagreeing with her instead of giving her exactly the answer that she needed.

"But, bloody hell, man. You're at a society tea party, not a boxing match. What good is it to browbeat a dolt like Lord Cosgrove when our friends are trying to get a confession out of him with finesse."

"Now, see here—" Lord Cosgrove started, raising a hand as though he would debate the matter.

He was thoroughly ignored by all.

"Finesse can only go so far in business," Danny fired back. "You've learned as well as I have that sometimes the direct approach, facing problems head-on, is the best way to go. You've learned it, and that's why I love you."

"Truly, the rest of us should leave the two of you to sort this out in peace," Miss Garrett whispered, gesturing to Mr. Mercer and Lord Harrington to stand and leave the room.

Looking duly embarrassed, the two men stood.

"You don't have to go anywhere," Danny told them. He turned back to Phoebe. "I'm sorry to have embarrassed you in front of our friends, love. I'm sorry that I behaved like I was at a music hall instead of a ball the other night, though you seemed to enjoy that well enough."

Phoebe glanced down in the manner of her old habit for a moment. She had enjoyed watching Danny flout the rules of society. She quickly tilted her head back up and met Danny's eyes.

"We'll just...." Miss Garrett whispered as she, Lord Harrington, and Mr. Mercer started toward the door.

Before Phoebe could say anything, Danny rushed on with, "If you are so ashamed of me and my brutish ways, why did you agree to marry me?"

Miss Garrett, Lord Harrington, and Mr. Mercer froze. Lord Cosgrove bristled. Phoebe came dangerously close to laughing at the way Danny had of bringing what felt like everything in London to a halt with a few words. Blast him, but she loved him for that mad trait.

"You *what*?" Lord Cosgrove barked before Phoebe could make any sort of reply.

Danny transformed from looking as though he had wasps in his drawers to gloating like a king as he turned to Lord Cosgrove. "That's right," he said in his broadest Cockney. "I asked Phoebe to marry me, and she said yes."

"Oh, how scrumptious," Miss Garrett said, clapping her hands together. Suddenly, it seemed as though she didn't want to leave them all alone after all.

"How dare you, sir?" Lord Cosgrove practically shook as he glared at Danny. "You are not worthy to pick up Lady Phoebe's handkerchief, let alone marry her."

"That's not what Phoebe thinks, do you, love." Danny winked at her.

Phoebe was reasonably certain she'd stepped through the looking glass into a mad, new world—a world where pub owners with low-born accents flirted with daughters of marquesses and winked at them in company. Worlds where ladies worked as shop girls and working class men were granted land development deals by parliament. Where American heiresses hosted tea parties and plotted with country gentlemen while their fiancés looked on without seeming to care. The world of order and propriety she'd known as a girl was completely gone, and she wasn't sure she knew what to do with the new world she found herself in.

"I will marry whomever I wish to marry," she said, squaring her shoulders and summoning as much of her pride as she had left. She glanced from Danny to Lord Cosgrove. "I will command my own destiny."

"That's right, love, you will." Danny nodded sharply.

"And who are you to speak thusly to a lady of Lady Phoebe's standing?" Lord Cosgrove demanded.

"We truly shouldn't be here," Miss Garrett whispered to Mr. Mercer over to the side.

"I'm not about to leave," Mr. Mercer muttered to her in return.

"I am the man who can make her happy," Danny said, turning to confront Lord Cosgrove. "And by the end of tomorrow afternoon, I am going to be Parliament's choice to develop the land in Earl's Court. Not you."

Lord Cosgrove bristled. "Can you be so sure?"

"On which account?" Danny asked. "Because I think we both know who Phoebe would choose between the two of us."

Lord Cosgrove flinched as though offended, but looked as though he, too, knew which way the wind was blowing on that score. "How can you be so sure you'll win the development deal?" he demanded instead.

A shrewd, almost frightening grin pulled at one side of Danny's mouth. "I want to make a deal with you, Cosgrove," he said in an ominous voice.

Phoebe's stomach flipped at the way he spoke, and she raised a hand to press against the butterflies that were beginning to rage.

"What sort of a deal?" Lord Cosgrove asked, eyes narrowed.

Danny glanced around at Phoebe, Miss Garrett, Mr. Mercer, and Lord Harrington, all of whom watched him as though witnessing a drama. "Everyone here knows you ordered the fire that destroyed my pub," he said.

Lord Cosgrove turned a disturbing shade of puce. "You can't prove it."

"Can't I?" Danny arched one eyebrow.

"I...I was so careful," Lord Cosgrove whimpered.

"I will make a deal with you," Danny went on, his smile growing. "I will drop any efforts to investigate the arson, and I will never tell another soul as long as I live that you were responsible."

Lord Cosgrove blinked. "Truly?"

"If you drop your bid for the land development contract in Earl's Court," Danny finished.

Phoebe's eyes went wide. She gaped at Danny, marveling at how easily, and apparently callously, he could drop his quest for justice.

"It's a deal," Lord Cosgrove answered immediately.

Phoebe turned her gape on him. "You would give up on your pursuit of the development deal so readily?" she asked Lord Cosgrove with as much incredulity as she wanted to ask Danny how he could give up on his pub.

"Shake on it," Danny demanded, thrusting out his hand.

Lord Cosgrove winced, then took Danny's hand. The two of them shook on the deal, looking as though they were each trying to crush the bones in the other's hand. "I will send word to the parliamentary committee immediately, telling them I wish to focus on my family's holdings instead of developing land in London."

"And I will pen a note to my friend, Lord Clerkenwell, at Scotland Yard to let him know the coppers won't need to bother with the investigation into the arson," Danny said.

Lord Cosgrove blanched the way a man might if the ship next to his had been exploded by cannon-fire while leaving his unscathed. Phoebe was more surprised by the fact that Danny had managed to get Lord Clerkenwell to open an investigation into the fire after all, in spite of it being deemed unimportant the last time she'd heard of the matter. Unless Danny were bluffing. She simply didn't know anymore. Men and their business dealings were enough to give her a raging headache.

"There," Danny said, his usual, cheeky grin returning. "I'm glad that's settled."

Rather than looking cowed and defeated, Lord Cosgrove grinned right along with him. "You truly are a mercenary bugger, aren't you?" he said slyly.

"In business, yes I am," Danny admitted.

"In your choice of a bride too," Cosgrove went on, glancing to Phoebe. "My solicitor, Mr. Grey, tells me that his assistant, a Mr. Healy, received a call from one Lionel Mercer and you, Mr. Long, just last week, and that you made inquiries about a certain will."

Phoebe's confusion doubled, particularly when Danny suddenly looked more anxious than she'd ever seen him. He stole a sideways glance at her.

"So you must, of course, have learned about the

conditions of Lord Darlington's will where it concerns his daughter's inheritance," Lord Cosgrove went on.

"I have no inheritance," Phoebe said. "Father left me and Mama nothing but debts." She was suddenly uncertain of the one thing that had guided her life for the past several years, as underscored by the smug look Lord Cosgrove wore and Danny's equally guilty look.

"Are you so very certain of that?" Lord Cosgrove said, his grin widening. He glanced to Danny as if he'd won the contest after all.

"I...." Phoebe couldn't say that she was. She'd been so busy trying to put a roof over her and her mother's heads and food on their plates for the last few years that she hadn't had time to question the way Mr. Grey had never fully answered her questions regarding the execution of her father's estate. She'd left the matter to her mother and trusted that her mother would handle things.

She'd been an utter fool.

"I have an inheritance after all?" she asked, blinking and feeling vaguely sick at the notion. At least, sick that she hadn't done more to find out about it earlier.

"Your father left you his estate in Herefordshire," Lord Cosgrove informed her.

"But the estate is entailed away," Phoebe said, feeling light-headed.

"No, it isn't," Danny told her, looking far guiltier than she was comfortable with.

"Not only is it not entailed away," Lord Cosgrove went on, "it belongs explicitly to you under the terms of your father's will. Unless you marry, of course. Then it goes to your husband."

Phoebe sucked in a breath, her heart pounding against her ribs. As much as she didn't want it to, everything suddenly made sense. Lord Cosgrove's interest in marrying her had nothing to do with his care of her in particular. As her father's friend, he must have known about the conditions of the will and the estate. Beyond that, he must have felt that he could use the profits from the estate to finance whatever developments he'd planned for Earl's Court, thus increasing his money. But if she married Danny, which Danny had announced she would, he wouldn't have the capital for any sort of land development. Backing out of the Earl's Court deal wasn't a concession to Danny's threat to bring him up on charges of arson, it would enable him to save face.

And as for Danny....

"You have always said that you dislike the way you're treated because of your birth," she said, barely above a whisper. "But marrying a titled heiress, inheriting an estate in the country, would change all that."

"No," Danny growled. "That's not—" He huffed out a breath through his nose, lowering his head and rubbing a hand over his face.

"Did you know before you proposed to me?" she asked, her voice shaking. She already knew the answer, as much as she wished she didn't, but she needed to hear him admit it.

"Not because of your inheritance," he insisted,

though his face had gone bright red. "Phoebe, I love you, and I would marry you if you were a match-girl without a single friend in the world. You are the sun and the moon to me." He reached for her hands.

Phoebe pulled her hands away the moment he brushed them, taking a large step back and nearly knocking into Miss Garrett—who continued to watch the scene unfold with wide eyes. "I don't know what to think," she whispered. Her heart told her one thing, but her pride insisted on another.

"You know that I will always stand by your side, Lady Phoebe," Lord Cosgrove said imperiously. "As a friend of your father's, and of your dear mother's, not to mention a fellow member of the aristocracy—" he shot a peevish look at Danny, "—I will always offer you help and solace wherever I can."

Phoebe glanced up at him, indignant that he would still press whatever excuse for a suit he had when she was in the middle of a crisis. She shook her head and took another step back. "I cannot face this mad situation right now," she said, frowning at Lord Cosgrove, then meeting Danny's eyes. "I need to think."

She turned and started out of the room.

"Phoebe," Danny called after her, jogging to catch up.

Phoebe stopped, turning to him and holding up her hands to ward him off. "Give me some space to think," she told him.

Danny's mouth hung open, but he didn't say

anything. Finally, he closed his mouth and let his shoulders drop. "All right," he said, taking a step back.

Phoebe stared at him for a long, lingering moment, then turned and fled the room, no idea what she would do with her life taking yet another strange twist.

CHAPTER 18

$\mathcal{H}$e'd gone and mucked up the best thing that had ever happened in his life. Danny was as certain of that as he was that Cosgrove would try another underhanded trick to yank the Earl's Court deal right out from under him. There was no point in loitering around Hopewell House once Phoebe was gone, so he made the politest goodbyes he could and stormed sullenly out into the streets of Mayfair. His mood was so rotten as he headed back to Fitzrovia that refined ladies and frightened children jumped out of his way, as if he were a bear that had been let loose in London.

He had to speak to Phoebe, to explain why he hadn't told her what he'd learned about her inheritance sooner. He needed to explain his own fortune and all the reasons why marrying her wouldn't be the mercenary act Cosgrove had painted it to be. It was long past time for him to stop teasing Phoebe by letting her persist in thinking he was nothing more than a pub owner and landlord. Except now that she believed he'd been devious about her inheritance, God only knew what she would think of him for conveniently hiding the full truth of who he really was.

"Phoebe?" He banged on the door to her flat once he made it back to Fitzrovia. "Phoebe, we need to talk," He banged again, then paused to consider that complaints about his brutish exuberance were what had sparked their earlier argument. He knocked more sedately and softened his voice to say, "Phoebe, please let me in."

The door across the hall opened and Mrs. Washburn, another of his tenants, popped her head out. "They're not at home," she said.

"They're not?" Danny's heart sank.

"The old one was all giddy about meeting up with a gent who wanted to discuss a proposal. And Miss Darlington had work, I believe."

Danny's heart twisted in alarm. "Thanks," he told Mrs. Washburn, then charged down the hall to the stairs. Leave it to Phoebe's mother to get wind of trouble between him and Phoebe right away. The proposal she had to discuss could only be the same, tired drivel of Phoebe and Cosgrove. Thank God Phoebe had made her feelings on that score abundantly clear to Cosgrove.

But as he strode down to Oxford Street, hailing a cab to take him to Harrods faster, doubts crept up on him. Phoebe had a mind of her own. She'd changed from a defeated dove to a woman of strength, even in the short time he'd known her. He could see her doing whatever it took to conquer the world that had once rejected her. Could that extend to marrying Cosgrove after all?

He couldn't entertain the thought, even though it continued to poke at the back of his mind. His cab reached Harrods, and he leapt out, overpaying the driver, and charged into the shop. He turned heads as he charged through the outer departments to the aisle of counters selling ladies' finery, where Phoebe worked. But the young woman behind the glove counter was not Phoebe.

"Where is she?" he asked, spinning in a circle and looking everywhere he could, as if she would pop out of the woodwork. Shoppers and staff alike flinched at his frantic energy and backed away from him. "Where is Phoebe?"

"She came in for a few minutes," the young woman behind a counter selling handkerchiefs said. "But she didn't stay."

"Dory had to rush in from hosiery to fill in for her," another young shop girl said.

The nest of anxiety in Danny's gut grew. It didn't help that Phoebe's pinched-faced manager, Mr. Waters, showed up on the scene.

"Can I help you?" he asked with a sniff, glancing down his nose at Danny, even though Danny was taller.

"I was looking for Phoebe," Danny said, annoyed, but without the patience to either play along with the man's assumptions about him or assume a superior air and put the man in his place.

"Miss Darlington is on probation," Mr. Waters said with a sneer.

The imperiousness of the way the man spoke shifted Danny from anxious to defensive on Phoebe's behalf. "What do you mean, probation?" he demanded.

"She failed to work her shift today," Mr. Waters said. "And she begged off on her shift tomorrow. She said she had a desperate family matter to attend to. That is the only reason I did not sack her on the spot. That, and the fact that she is one of my best girls."

Danny cringed at the way the man spoke, but he didn't have time to call him out for it. "Where is she now?" he asked, shoving a hand through his hair and already planning how he would fly to her.

"I don't know," Mr. Waters answered peevishly. "I do not track the personal lives of my staff like—"

Danny launched away from the man, no interest at all in anything he might say. He left Harrods and walked home, hoping to catch a glimpse of Phoebe somewhere in Mayfair or along Oxford Street as he went. He thought of searching through Hyde Park, pounding on the doors of every former friend she'd had, even going to Cosgrove's house and demanding to know whether the man had plans to marry Phoebe just to spite him.

In the end, all he could do was drag his exhausted body and troubled mind home. The sun was beginning to set by the time he made it to his flat. He'd tried knocking on Phoebe's door again, but still received no answer. All he could do was fix himself a pathetic supper from the bits and pieces he had lying around his flat, strip off his rumpled and soiled clothes, and flop into bed. Even then, he did nothing more than spend a restless night tossing and turning, worrying about what Phoebe must think of him, and plotting ways he could redeem himself in her eyes.

He was an utter mess the next morning. His head pounded, and dark circles made his eyes appear sunken. It was the morning of the hearing before the parliamentary committee for land development, though, and if he wanted to make a good impression on the men who would, he hoped, barring last minute hijinks by Cosgrove, award him a deal that would both enrich him and give Dandie's friends a safe place to live, he had to make a good impression. He forced himself to dress with care, shave, and groom himself to look like an enterprising businessman, even though his heart was no longer in it.

In a last-ditch attempt to make things right, he stopped by Phoebe's apartment on his way to the hearing.

"Phoebe?" he called through the door with what he considered amazing restraint, knocking instead of banging. "Are you there?"

To his surprise, the door flew open, and Phoebe stood there, eyes wide, as though she were surprised to see him. "Danny," she said in a flat tone.

He drank her in with a glance, his heart squeezing anxiously at what he saw. She would always be beautiful to him, but she looked a little worse for wear. Her face was wan and her eyes slightly red, as though she'd been crying, or as if she hadn't slept either. Her hair was arranged in a perfect, elaborate style, though, and she wore one of her finer gowns.

"Danny?" she asked when he'd done nothing but gaze at her for too long. "What do you want?"

Everything within him wanted to answer, "You," and to sweep her into his arms for a kiss that would change her mind about his boorishness and villainy—if, indeed, that was what she thought of him now—and make her want to spend the rest of her life with him.

"I...I'm on my way to the parliamentary hearing," he said instead, insides twisting awkwardly over how sheepish he felt.

"Good luck, then," Phoebe said.

She stepped back and attempted to shut the door on him.

Danny's heart nearly broke at the gesture. He wedged his foot into the doorway and slapped his hand against the door to keep it from shutting. "Please don't shut me out," he said.

She sighed heavily and stepped deeper into the room, allowing him to walk into the flat behind her. Phoebe's flat was always well-kept, but there seemed to be more dishes waiting to be washed on the counter that he could see through the kitchen door, and for some reason, her mother had what looked like every gown she owned strewn across the furnishings in the main room and was fussing over them.

Phoebe's mother glanced up from her fluttering and gasped, "He cannot be here," glaring at Danny. "Not now. Not when...when we have so much to do." She glanced covertly at Phoebe.

Suspicion pinched at Danny's insides, but he didn't have a chance to demand to know what was going on.

"He isn't staying," Phoebe said, drawing his full focus. She crossed her arms and glared at him.

"I'm sorry, Phoebe." Danny stepped closer to her, reaching for her. He considered it a small miracle that she let him rest his hands on her arms. "I'm so, so sorry that I didn't tell you about the inheritance. I only found out about it last week. And with so much else going on—the land deal, the fire, all of my other business—I never found the time to mention it."

"But you found the time to propose to me," she said, her eyes narrowing.

Danny pulled his hands back, squirming under her scrutiny, and running a hand through his hair. "Well, truth be told, that proposal came as a bit of a surprise to me too. The circumstances at the time were—" He glanced awkwardly to Phoebe's mother, who was doing a poor job of pretending she wasn't listening to the conversation.

Phoebe blushed a dark shade of red. She grabbed Danny's arm and dragged him out of the main room and into the kitchen. "Do you mean to tell me that you only asked me to marry you because you were caught up in the throes of passion?" she hissed, sending a wary look out through the kitchen door to make certain her mother wasn't listening.

"No!" Danny said, too loud as usual. "God, no. I had already made up my mind to marry you."

"After learning of my inheritance," Phoebe said in a flat voice.

"No, love, that's not it at all." He laughed in spite of himself, though the sound was bitter and tense. Everything he said was just digging his grave deeper. "Sweetheart, I have piles of money of my own," he told her. It was too late to worry about how she would react to the truth. The truth needed to be spoken. "I own property all over London, not just this building and my pub. My family has been investing in London real estate for four generations. Name the richest nob you know, and I can guarantee you that I'm worth twice as much."

Instead of lighting up at the idea, Phoebe crossed her arms and narrowed her eyes. "If you are so wealthy, why are you living in a three-room flat in Fitzrovia instead of a palatial townhouse in, I don't know, Kensington?"

"I don't want to live around a bunch of hoity-toity nobs who would be as like as not to turn up their noses at me and cross the street to walk on the other side when they see me coming," he said.

"Precisely," Phoebe said, letting out an exhausted breath and letting her arms and shoulders drop. "Danny, I've known you for long enough to know that money isn't as important to you as the way people see you. You want to be respected. You want to be treated as an equal by society. So, of course, marrying the daughter of a marquess would accomplish that for you."

Danny flinched, partially because she had sketched his character so well, and partly in aversion to the idea that she thought he saw her as a pawn in his game. "That's not true," he insisted. "You're so much more to me than that."

"Am I?" she asked, back to challenging him. "You knew who I was when I stumbled into your pub on that rainy day. You knew what I'd been reduced to. Are you certain you didn't see in me an opportunity to get everything you've wanted in life?"

He frowned. "And what about how you saw me? I offered you a place to live when you'd been turned out. Are you certain you didn't see me as a shot at a secure future?"

Her cheeks flared pink all over again, and she turned her face away.

Danny went on. "You needed something practical too, love. I gave it to you. Would you have loved me in your former life? Would you have gone to bed with me and made me the happiest man in the world if you really were just the daughter of a marquess and I was just a lower-class pub owner?"

She snapped her head back to him. "Do you realize that every time you have described yourself to me, you've said you are nothing but a lower-class pub owner?"

Danny blinked, uncertain what she meant.

She took a half step toward him. "Danny, you've just told me that you're amazingly wealthy and that you own real estate all over London. You're on your way to a parliamentary committee that is going to award you an extremely high-profile land development deal that will earn you even more money. A fact, by the way, that is not lost on me. Nor is the understanding that in order to carry out such a development, one must have capital first."

Danny shook his head. "Are you saying you knew about my money?"

"I guessed," she sighed, shrugging and glancing briefly out the window. "And also, Natalia is a terrible gossip who, I believed, greatly exaggerated your worth when I sought her solace and council about this whole matter yesterday evening."

A strange twist of relief filled Danny's chest. She'd gone to visit Natalia Townsend.

"So you knew," he repeated.

She stared square at him. "What I know, Danny Long, is that you may be worth a fortune, but you undervalue yourself. You long for the respect and appreciation of men who, frankly, will never fully give it to you— because of their own arrogance and not anything having to do with you. But the only person's respect you need is your own." She took another step closer to him and poked a finger into his chest. "You need to respect yourself. You need to embrace your own worth instead of forever seeking validation from the outside world. You need to decide if you are simply a pub owner or whether you are an entrepreneur and an economic emperor. Marrying the daughter of a marquess and inheriting her country estate isn't going to change how you feel about yourself."

Danny was so stunned by her words that when he opened his mouth to reply, nothing came out. He could only stand there, gaping at her, his heart swelling so tenderly that it came near to bursting.

"Phoebe!" Her mother stepped into the doorway, jolting Danny out of the astounded thoughts that had him frozen. "Hurry up," her mother hissed. "We cannot keep him waiting."

Phoebe huffed out a breath and marched past Danny into the main room. "I'm coming, Mama."

Danny turned to watch her gather her purse and hat. His attention was snagged as Phoebe's mother sniffed at him.

"You should have behaved with more decorum," she scolded him. "She has always been too good for you, and now everything will be as it should always have been." She punctuated her words with a nod before marching out of the kitchen.

Danny followed in a daze. Phoebe's mother flounced her way out to the hall through the open door that Phoebe held. Phoebe manned her post by the door until Danny stepped out of the flat. Then she shut and locked the door behind her with all the finality of someone snapping a book closed after finishing with it. Danny followed the two women to the stairs and descended with them, but his head was too full of the things Phoebe had said to rush after them to demand to know where they were going or what they were doing.

"Oh, good. You're downstairs. I won't have to climb all the way up there to discuss business with you before the hearing," Tuttle said, entering the building as Phoebe and her mother left.

"I'm not sure I have enough of a brain left to handle business at all, after everything I've just been through," Danny said, still watching the empty doorway where Phoebe had been moments before.

"Well, you'd better locate your brain forthwith," Tuttle said, slapping Danny's back. "I'd look in your trousers, if I were you."

On any other day, Danny would have laughed at the ribald joke. He was still too stunned to do anything but crack a smile, though.

Tuttle nudged him toward the door. "Good thing I'll be by your side at this hearing."

Danny hummed as they made their way to the street and hailed a cab. Phoebe and her mother were just visible at the far end of the street, walking toward what looked to be Mayfair.

"If you are, in fact, planning to take the plunge, we need to discuss your plans for marriage soon," Tuttle said as a carriage veered toward them. "And for securing Lady Phoebe's inheritance. If everything you told me was true, it might be a bit of a struggle to—"

"I'm not sure the marriage is going to happen,"

Danny said, giving voice to the deep-seated fear he hadn't been able to shake since the tea party.

"What?" Tuttle laughed as though Danny were joking. "I thought the two of you were madly in love."

Danny was still madly in love, but he couldn't tell about Phoebe anymore. She'd grown into a woman of her own mind, a woman who would run circles around him in every way. "We've had a bit of a tiff," he admitted, glancing off to the corner she'd disappeared around. "I honestly don't know what her thoughts on the subject of marriage are at the moment."

The cab had stopped at the curb, and Tuttle had opened the door. He gestured for Danny to get in. "Every loving couple fights now and then," he said. "It's a good way to clear the air. The two of you will be right as rain in no time, you'll see."

Danny hummed and hopped into the carriage, but he wasn't so sure. Not every deal came off without a hitch. Sometimes the things he wanted the most slipped through his fingers.

CHAPTER 19

*B*oth Phoebe's head and heart ached as she escorted her mother through the bustling, commercial streets around Oxford Street and deeper into the heart of Mayfair. She was still racked with confusion about everything that had transpired during and since the tea party Miss Garrett hosted. Her emotions were in an even bigger tumult after the conversation she'd just had with Danny.

Had he really not seen the depth of his own need to be accepted? The expression that had come over his face when she spelled things out for him was so profoundly startled that, for the first time, she began to see that he wasn't the ever-confident lion that she'd always assumed he was. In fact, she was beginning to wonder if all of his noise and bluster, all of his teasing and playing around with accents, dress, and the sensibilities of the gentlemen

267

he came into contact with was little more than a way for him to pretend he believed he was worthy.

It was ridiculous for Danny to think he wasn't equal with or superior to every other titled man Phoebe had ever known. She should have guessed he was wealthier and more powerful than he'd let on. Natalia hadn't truly told her anything new when Phoebe had gone to her for a shoulder to cry on the evening before. And if truth be told, Phoebe still loved Danny beyond reason, in spite of everything that had happened and everything that would likely happen next.

"You are too quiet, my dear," her mother said with too much cheer as they entered Mayfair. "This is a day for you to rejoice. It is a happy day indeed." Her mother chuckled and clapped her hands to emphasize her point.

"If you say so," Phoebe sighed.

She rubbed her pounding head. After her visit with Natalia, she'd come home only to fall straight into the middle of her mother's most outlandish scheme yet. She still couldn't believe that her mother had continued her plotting where Lord Cosgrove was concerned. And she never would have guessed things would turn out the way they were about to after all the water that had flowed under that bridge. She'd lain awake most of the night, racked with guilt about what her mother had planned without Phoebe even being aware of it. The irony of the whole thing was astounding.

"Smile," her mother ordered her as they turned onto Mount Street, where Lord Cosgrove's townhouse was located. "We're about to get everything we've wanted since your father died."

"Are we?" Phoebe sent her a sideways look.

"Yes. So stop your grousing," her mother snapped.

Phoebe clenched her jaw as they walked on, feeling lower than she had in weeks.

"It's that lout, Mr. Long, isn't it," her mother said when they reached a small cross street. "He upset you this morning."

"Anything between me and Mr. Long is none of your business, Mama," Phoebe sighed.

"You are my daughter. Your business will always be my business." When Phoebe didn't say anything, her mother went on with, "It's for the best that the two of you had a row. It will make everything else that much easier."

"Danny will be furious about this," Phoebe said, feeling how true it was down to the marrow of her bones. He would see the whole thing as a massive betrayal.

Her mother surprised her by stopping abruptly and spinning to face her. "Stop your pouting this instant, young lady."

"I have reason to pout, Mama," Phoebe snapped back.

Her mother looked equal parts exasperated and determined. "I have done what is best to secure our futures," she said.

"Have you?" Phoebe arched one eyebrow.

"You don't know what it was like," her mother said with sudden passion, her face pinching with misery. "You

269

don't know what it was like being married to your father. I never wanted the marriage to begin with. My father arranged it with his friend. Your father was an odious pig from the very start."

"Mama!" Phoebe's heart sped up, and she glanced around to see if anyone were listening in.

"He squandered my dowry within a year," her mother went on. "He got me with child, then ignored me, claiming that I was the defective one when you were born and proved to be a girl. He flouted his mistresses in my face, not to mention his illegitimate sons."

Phoebe gasped. "I didn't know he had other children."

"He had far more than that," her mother growled. "He had bastards and he had debts. He had wasted investments and he had loans with frightening terms. I know you felt the impact of his sin as the two of us watched everything we had—materially and socially—vanish without either of us being able to do a thing about it. But imagine how that made me feel. I was thrown into a situation not of my choosing, it destroyed me, and there wasn't a damn thing I could do about it."

Phoebe's eyes went wide at her mother's coarse language, and she pressed a hand to her stomach.

"I know you don't understand why I have championed Lord Cosgrove so heartily for so long," her mother went on. "I know you despise him. But believe me, my dear. I know from bitter experience what it is like to be cast out on your own. I know the pain and suffering that can cause. No, Lord Cosgrove is not the best of men, but neither is he entirely like your father. He is greedy and he is vain, but he is not profligate, and he is not a criminal. We might not like it, but we will be secure with him."

Phoebe was speechless in the wake of her mother's words. Her mother's line of reasoning was not new to her, but the passion with which she spoke, the strength of her convictions, was a side to her mother that she'd never seen before. Sudden guilt over the way Phoebe had discounted and diminished her mother for so many years —like too many others had washed their hands of her as a silly woman with silly ideas—gripped her. She'd never truly stopped to see their situation through her mother's eyes. She'd been too busy fighting and scraping to keep the two of them safe. Fighting her own way. She still wasn't convinced that her mother's way was any better than hers, but for the first time, she thought that perhaps she understood it.

"All right, Mama," she said, reaching for her mother's hand and squeezing it. "I understand. I'm sorry you had to endure all that."

"It was beyond endurance," her mother said, bursting into a sob.

Phoebe's heart went out to the woman. She surprised both of them by throwing her arms around her mother and hugging her. "I'm sorry," she repeated, squeezing her mother tight. "You know I'm not happy about it, but I'll go through with this whole thing. I won't fight it or protest anymore. I understand."

"Thank you, my darling girl." Her mother sniffed and snorted, stepping back and fishing in her sleeve for a handkerchief. "You have no idea how much this means to me.

Phoebe smiled at her and walked on toward Lord Cosgrove's house, feeling as though she were going to the gallows. It would make her mother happy, but all she could think was that Danny was going to be furious.

THE HEARING TO DECIDE WHICH PROPOSAL FOR THE development of the land in Earl's Court was not held in any of the grand chambers of The Palace of Westminster, nor on the floor of the House of Commons. A matter of everyday business, like land deals, was decided in a small office off of Whitehall, which was where Danny found himself, pacing the halls and wishing the whole thing would just be over.

"Steady as she goes, man," Tuttle said from his seat on a bench beside the door behind which the committee was meeting. "There's no chance of you losing the deal at this point."

Danny grunted, but that was all the response he was capable of. Cosgrove hadn't shown up for the meeting, which was a startlingly good sign that the man intended to make good on his promise to back out of the running for the deal.

He paced to the end of the hall, pushing a hand through his hair—which was standing out wildly, considering how often he'd repeated the gesture in the past half hour—to check around the corner that led to the staircase and the building's lobby. If Danny knew Cosgrove like he thought he did, the bastard would still try something. He might march up the stairs and down the hall to the committee meeting at any moment. He might demand his proposal be accepted over Danny's because he was a bloody viscount and Danny was nothing.

His heart caught in his chest at the track his thoughts had taken. Phoebe's speech that morning rushed back in on him. He wasn't nothing, but he'd been telling himself that he was for far too long. He'd been doing it without even realizing it.

He turned and marched back to Tuttle, who was watching him with a vaguely amused look.

"Tuttle, what would you say I am?" he demanded, stopping to stand in front of the man.

Tuttle's brow shot up at the question. "What are you?"

"Yes." Danny nodded. "If you had to describe me, what would you say I am?"

The corner of Tuttle's mouth twitched. "I'd say you were a male of the human species."

Danny appreciated the quip, but he shook his head and pinched his face. "No, no, I'm not playing around. What would you say I am?"

Tuttle took on a more thoughtful look. "You're a businessman. A shrewd one at that. You're one of the new

273

model of magnate, like Rothschild or Rhodes, or even some of those Americans, like Rockefeller or Morgan."

Danny took a step back, shocked at how flattered he felt at the comparison. "I am rather like those men, aren't I," he said with a smile.

"Was there ever any doubt?" Tuttle laughed.

"You would be surprised," Danny said, shaking his head. "I was surprised myself."

Tuttle's grin turned knowing. "Does this have anything to do with your lovely fiancée?"

Danny let out a sigh, his momentary good mood dropping. "I honestly don't know if she still wants to marry me, after the squabble we got into."

Tuttle looked surprised. "Why would any woman not want to marry you?"

"Because I'm a loud, crass fool who couldn't keep his mouth shut when he should have and who failed to say the things I actually should have said sooner?"

Tuttle shook his head. "You've far more endearing qualities than you think you do. I would be gobsmacked if Lady Phoebe came anything close to turning her back on you now."

"I wish I could be so sure," Danny grumbled, rubbing his face and falling back into pacing. "Something wasn't right about our conversation this morning. Her mother was acting oddly too."

Tuttle laughed outright. "I would bet that her mother acts oddly the majority of the time."

Danny shared Tuttle's wry humor for a moment, but

it didn't put him at ease. "No, I feel like she was even stranger than usual this morning. Like she knew something I didn't."

His thoughts had to rest there. The door to the committee room opened, and a clerk gestured for him and Tuttle to come inside. Danny leapt into action, practically bursting through the door. The dozen or so grey-haired, stuffed shirt gentlemen who sat around a long table reacted to his enthusiasm with surprise, but at least they didn't growl and sniff and demand for him to be thrown out.

Danny grabbed hold of that, and of everything Phoebe had said to him that morning, and stood before the table as though he owned it and everyone in the room. "Gentlemen, I trust you have made your decision."

"We have, Mr. Long," the MP at the head of the table said with a satisfied grin. "I won't waste any of your time by making long speeches. Of all the proposals this committee has received, yours was by far the most intriguing. The architectural plans you presented us with were top-notch. Your financial reckoning was sound and well thought out. Your history of development and other projects throughout the city is impressive. In short, sir, the committee felt as though we would be fools not to accept your proposal and grant this development deal to Long Property Ventures."

The other men around the table looked just as pleased as the speaker. They nodded and smiled, and one man even applauded. Danny let out a breath of relief. It felt as though the weight of the world had been lifted from his shoulders. What could be more encouraging than a vote of confidence from Parliament?

"Thank you, gentlemen," he said, unable to keep his smile inside. "Thank you a thousand times over. I won't disappoint you."

"We do have several business details we'd like to work out, if you wouldn't mind," another of the men at the table said.

"I will be conducting all the particulars of business for Mr. Long," Tuttle said, stepping up to the table and taking an empty seat as though he were every bit as superior as the men he was sitting down with. Danny had to admire his style. If Tuttle could do it, why couldn't he?

He did what he needed to do to assist Tuttle in the preliminary round of business negotiations, but the moment the decision was announced, Danny's thoughts were a hundred miles away. Not a hundred, he decided as he left the committee room and headed toward the stairs and the lobby, only about two or three. He had to find Phoebe so that he could tell her everything had worked out for the best after all. He would tell her he loved her, propose to her all over again if he had to, and pledge every last bit of himself to her in perpetuity. And he would gloat at how Cosgrove hadn't had the balls to step up and oppose him at the last minute after all.

"—really marrying her at the last minute?"

Danny caught the edge of a conversation as he made his way through the lobby. He wouldn't have noticed or cared, except that the two men conversing seemed so surprised.

"Who ever thought that old Cosgrove would marry at all?" one of them said.

Danny skidded to a stop, turning to the men.

"I bet Darlington arranged it before he kicked off," the first one said. "That would have been the sort of thing he'd do."

"The Darlingtons and the Cosgroves have been close for generations," the first one agreed.

"Excuse me, what?" Danny barged into their conversation.

The two men looked as alarmed by Danny's appearance as they were to be interrupted.

"Lord Cosgrove is getting married," the first man said.

"When?" Danny demanded. "To who?"

"Right now," the second man said. "Which is why it's so noteworthy."

"Who, man who?" Danny wanted to grab the man by his suit and shake him. He had a horrible feeling he knew the answer, a horrible feeling that Cosgrove had bested him after all, and in something that mattered far more to him than any land deal ever would.

"To Lady Darlington," the first man said. "You know he's—"

"Where is the wedding taking place?" Danny boomed over him, his heart shattering to pieces. He'd been such a fool to chase after a silly business deal instead of what really mattered. He should have stayed with Phoebe that morning and worked things out. He couldn't bear the thought that he might be too late to stop her from doing something she would regret for the rest of her life, and that he would regret too.

The two gentlemen were beyond startled. They gaped and cowered in the face of Danny's overwhelming energy. "St. Margaret's Church," the first one stammered. "Just across from Westminster."

It was all Danny needed to hear, all he was able to hear. He tore away from the men, sprinting for the door and out to the street. There was no telling how much time he had. He ran as fast as he could, dodging nobs and office boys alike. He didn't care who they were, and they didn't care who he was. All he knew was that if he didn't stop Phoebe from marrying Cosgrove, his life wouldn't be worth a damn.

CHAPTER 20

"No, no. Don't put those flowers there, put them over here," Phoebe's mother said, practically flapping her arms due to the level of her exuberance. "They need to be positioned just so. Everything needs to be perfect."

"Fine, Mama." Phoebe sighed, picked up the small vase of flowers that had been set on the front of the chancel in St. Margaret's, and started to carry them across to the first pew.

"Ladies, you look delightful." Lord Cosgrove stepped out of the small chamber to the side of the chancel, beaming as though it was his coronation day, not his wedding day. "You've made me the happiest man in England."

Phoebe rolled her eyes and stared warily at him. "It is all my mother's doing," she said, nodding to her mother, who skipped up to Lord Cosgrove's side like a woman half her age. At least it was cheering to see her mother in good spirits for the first time in years.

The vicar, who had been waiting impatiently by the altar as last-minute adjustments and fusses were made, cleared his throat. "Are we ready to begin?" he asked.

"Yes. Yes, indeed," Phoebe's mother said. "Phoebe. Come stand right here."

Phoebe still had the vase of flowers in her hand, but her mother's flapping had reached dangerous levels, so she held onto the flowers as she marched up to stand by Lord Cosgrove's side.

The vicar smiled tightly and opened his prayer book. "Dearly beloved," he began. "We are gathered here today—"

"No!"

Phoebe would have recognized Danny's bellowing shout anywhere in the world and in the dark. She, her mother, and Lord Cosgrove whipped around to see him charging into the chapel, his eyes wide with horror. His curly hair was tousled, and his face was red and sweating, as if he'd run all the way there from the moon. He continued to run up the aisle, barely bothering to skid to a stop as he reached the chancel.

"No, Phoebe, I won't let you do this," he panted. He grabbed the flowers from her hands and dumped them to the side. The crash of the vase made Phoebe jump and her mother shriek in alarm. Danny grabbed her hands.

"I won't let you marry him," he blustered on. "You don't love him, you love me. And I love you."

"Danny—"

"I know that it was wrong of me not to tell you about your inheritance," he charged over her, desperation in every aspect of his features. "I know I should have told you more about my own fortune as well. There are so many things that I should have done differently. If I could go back and change the way things unfolded between us, I would."

"Danny, I—"

"But I wouldn't have changed the way I fell in love with you, not for the world," he continued, squeezing her hands. "I wouldn't care if you really were a shop girl, just as I would hope you wouldn't care if I were nothing more than a pub owner."

"I don't care, but—"

"And it breaks my heart to think of the way you've been treated, and by the very people who should have come to your aid."

He glanced to her mother and Lord Cosgrove with a glare that was sharp enough to scold the entire aristocracy. Her mother and Lord Cosgrove, and the vicar, only stood there, mouths open in shock.

"But this is not the answer, love," Danny roared on. "You can't marry Cosgrove now, you just can't. I know you want to be accepted by the very people who rejected you and to take charge of your own life again. I know you're angry with me for being a bull-headed dolt, and too loud to boot. But marrying a man I know you despise, even if that gives you status and a title and legitimacy in the eyes of society, will only make you miserable."

"But I'm not—"

"It would make me miserable as well," Danny went on, shifting to draw her into his arms, plying her body against his. "I couldn't bear to see you in another man's arms, as another man's wife. I love you with my whole heart and my entire body. I would gladly sign over everything I have to you, hand you the reins of my entire business empire. I'll dress you in silks and furs and jewels and let you parade in front of all of the nobs we can find to show them how wonderful and valuable you are. Just say you won't marry this bit of excrement, say you'll—"

"Daniel Long, will you please shut up for one second," Phoebe bellowed, slapping a hand over his mouth.

Danny went rigid in her arms, his eyes wide and his mouth still open under her hand. She could feel his heart beating furiously against her chest as they pressed together, and his shoulders rose and fell with panting breaths.

"I'm not marrying Lord Cosgrove," she told him, hand still over his mouth, glaring at him. "I'm engaged to you."

"You are?" he mumbled behind her hand.

She wanted to laugh. "You were the one who asked me, or do you not remember?"

She dropped her hand so that he could say, "I

thought…after the tea party…you were angry…I assumed…."

Phoebe let out a frustrated sound and rolled her eyes, but through her anger and irritation with him, her heart swelled with affection. "Good God, man. If you think that one argument would drive us apart, if you think that we won't have even more arguments in what I sincerely hope is a long and interesting life together, then perhaps you are the one who isn't ready to be married."

"No, I am, I am," he insisted, as energetic and earnest as a child as he clutched her tighter. "But you were so furious."

"And I had every right to be," Phoebe laughed. "But I've never been fickle. Not like some of the ladies of my former acquaintance. Ladies whom I have no interest in spending so much as a second of my time with, nor in being accounted as one of them. That life is behind me, and good riddance."

"Phoebe," her mother hissed, scolding. "How could you?"

Danny continued to gape at Phoebe. He blinked. "But you're marrying Cosgrove. I heard them talking about it up in Whitehall just now."

Phoebe started. "They were talking about it in Whitehall?" It astounded her how swiftly gossip spread.

"I heard two gents talking about how Lord Cosgrove was marrying Lady Darlington," Danny said, confusion making him appear almost comical.

Phoebe pressed her lips together and stared flatly at

him. "For the last time, Danny. *I* am Lady Phoebe. *My mother* is Lady Darlington."

"I would be Lady Cosgrove already if you hadn't barged in with all your crass, flailing nonsense," Phoebe's mother snapped.

Danny looked as though he'd been hit in the head with a rotten cabbage. "You're marrying Cosgrove?" he asked incredulously.

"We've become quite close in the last few weeks," her mother said, taking Lord Cosgrove's arm and inching closer to him. "It seems in all my negotiating to convince dear Richard to marry Phoebe, I have fallen in love with him myself, and vice versa." She simpered up at Lord Cosgrove, who smiled tightly at her in return.

"I have agreed to let the two of them live at Credenhill Grange," Phoebe murmured so that only Danny could hear.

"You what?" Danny's confusion grew.

Phoebe sighed, glanced over her shoulder at her mother and Lord Cosgrove, then broke away from Danny to draw him over to the side of the room and well out of her mother's earshot.

"When Lord Cosgrove dropped his interest in your Earl's Court deal so swiftly, I suspected something wasn't right," she explained quickly. "The only way a man would agree to give up a business venture that stood to make him a great deal of money would be if he didn't actually have the ability to see the deal through."

Danny nodded as though following her line of logic.

"It dawned on me that he was relying on the income from Credenhill Grange to finance his development plans, but that if I didn't marry him—which he must have accepted I would never do—he wouldn't be able to complete his business."

"That...that makes perfect sense and is an astoundingly astute bit of reasoning." Danny grinned at her.

"Further," Phoebe went on, sending a glance to the altar and the three people who stood there, watching them, "it occurred to me that perhaps one of the reasons Lord Cosgrove was so eager to marry a woman with an estate to her name was because his own was in jeopardy."

"Is it?" Danny asked.

She leaned close and whispered, "Natalia says that he has been forced to sell his estate and that the sale just recently went through."

"So the man is homeless?" Danny's confusion began to clear.

"He has his London townhouse, but men like Lord Cosgrove need to lord over an estate," Phoebe explained. "So I offered to have him and Mama live at Credenhill Grange and to manage the place."

Danny's expression darkened. "You would be all right with an arsonist and a liar living on your family estate and marrying your mother?"

"If it gets my mother out of London and out of our business, then yes. A thousand times, yes," Phoebe said, staring pointedly at him. "Besides which, I have very few fond memories of Credenhill, and if I never visit the place again, it will be too soon."

Danny stared at her for a minute. Then his expression slowly spread into a grin. That grin burst into a full smile, and he laughed. "I swear to God, Phoebe Darlington, you are the most wonderful creature I have ever met in my life."

He swept her into his arms, spinning her in a mad circle before setting her on her feet and slanting his mouth over hers. He kissed her so thoroughly and with so much passion that Phoebe forgot she was in a church and that her mother, Lord Cosgrove, and the vicar were watching. It was glorious and giddy. Phoebe couldn't help but laugh, even as her cheeks burned with sheepishness, knowing they were being observed.

"I'm still angry with you," she gasped once Danny let her go. "You behaved frightfully."

"I know, I know," Danny said, warm and foolish, sliding his hands over her sides in a way that was entirely inappropriate for a church. "But you love me for it."

"I do," Phoebe admitted with a sardonic look.

Behind them, the vicar cleared his throat. "If you please, could we continue with this ceremony? I have a baptism at noon."

"He has a baptism at noon," Danny whispered, taking Phoebe's hand and walking to the altar with her. "Well?" he bellowed, gesturing to Phoebe's mother and Lord Cosgrove. "Get on with it."

"You are utterly impossible," Phoebe muttered,

shaking her head, as the vicar continued with the ceremony.

Not that Phoebe could pay attention to the ceremony or any of the congratulations and details once the marriage was complete. She and Danny ended up serving as witnesses when the documents were signed, but all she could think about was that it would be her turn soon, and what a wild adventure her life with Danny would be.

"Do you think that your mother will truly be content with a life in the country?" Danny asked as the two of them waved her mother and Lord Cosgrove off in the hired cab they'd managed to hail. A cab Danny paid for, of course.

"Oh, not in the least," Phoebe said, clutching his arm as they meandered down the street, looking for another cab that could take them home. As they were directly across from the Palace of Westminster, it didn't take long to hail one. "Mama will attempt to lord it over our old neighbors, but they all know how wretched my father was. They're likely to hear the entire story of how Mama came to rule over the estate again, and they'll shun her just as thoroughly as they have all along."

"Then how do you expect your plan for her happiness to be a success?" Danny said, helping her into the carriage that pulled to the curb for them.

"Lord Cosgrove is just as arrogant as she is," Phoebe reasoned. "The two of them will take solace in the fact that they are far superior to their neighbors in any case." Danny laughed, but she went on with, "They'll probably spend the season in London, at Lord Cosgrove's townhouse, leeching off the charity and influence of their lauded son-in-law." She sent him a mischievous grin.

"A son-in-law who will be the talk of the town, once it is revealed that he is richer than God and twice as good-looking," Danny said.

Phoebe laughed loud enough to compete with any pub crowd. It felt ridiculous to be so happy in such mad circumstances. But Danny was lively and wicked, and he truly was handsome by anyone's measure.

"I take it you were granted the Earl's Court deal?" she asked as the carriage hurried along, taking them home.

"Of course," Danny said with a proud grin. "It is impossible to think that the committee would have considered anyone else."

"Oh, yes, impossible." Phoebe sent him a sideways grin. "I'm sure Mr. Dandie will be pleased."

"Everyone will be pleased," Danny said, settling comfortably into his seat and drawing her into his arms as he did. "And I was thinking. What if we built a lovely townhouse of our own in the square I plan to develop? I would let you have final say on all of the architectural elements and the decorations."

A thrill of excitement shot through Phoebe at the idea. Perhaps it made her every bit as vain and concerned with presentation as her mother, but the idea of designing her own house—a house that all of the people who had once shunned her would marvel at and envy—filled her with joy.

"I think I would like that immensely," she said.

They spent the rest of the trip discussing design elements and plans, not just for their house, but for the terraced flats they would build for Mr. Dandie's friends. Danny was also brimming with ideas for rebuilding The Watchman and the buildings that surrounded it. Phoebe glanced across to the unfortunate building as the cab let them out at home. Demolition of the burned-out structure was already underway. Seeing the charred remains of what once was carted off bit by bit filled her with a solemn sense of satisfaction and renewal.

"Do you know," she said as she and Danny walked up the stairs to her flat, hand in hand, "I think that everything might just work out for the best after all."

Danny laughed, marching her right past the second floor and on up to the third floor and his flat. "Of course it will, love," he said, leaning in to kiss her cheek before finding the key to unlock his door. "Everything will be perfect, now that you're with me."

He opened the flat door, then grabbed Phoebe's hand and tugged her inside. She giggled as he whirled her into his arms, then shut the door with his foot and tossed his key onto the table beside the door. He missed, and the key clattered to the ground, but neither of them cared. Danny shrugged out of his jacket and threw that side as well before wrapping his arms around her and kissing her as though it were the secret to life.

"It's the middle of the afternoon," Phoebe managed to sigh between kisses that spun her head and turned her knees to jelly.

"There's no prescribed time for being wicked," he growled against her neck as he bent to kiss and nibble at her speeding pulse.

"Don't you have further business to attend to?" Phoebe giggled, working the buttons of his waistcoat free as he backed her toward his bedroom.

"That's what a man of business is for," Danny said, pausing his kisses long enough to fiddle with the buttons that ran down the front of her blouse. "Tuttle will take care of everything."

"I'm sure he will," Phoebe said nearly tripping as they crossed over the threshold into his bedroom.

He made quick work of the buttons on her blouse, then reached behind to unhook her skirt and tug at the fastenings of her petticoats. As soon as they came loose and sagged around her legs, he lifted her right out of the mass of fabric and laid her across his bed.

"Are you still angry with me?" he rumbled, shrugging out of his waistcoat and grasping at the buttons of his shirt. That came off within seconds as well, and he leaned over her, stealing another, long kiss.

"I think my feelings toward you are improving by the second," she answered, working loose the fastenings of his trousers.

He was already hot and hard as she pushed his trousers aside and slid her hands along his length. He made the most beautiful noise of surprise and pleasure and jerked under her touch as she tested his length and reached lower to cup his testicles. She still had so much to learn about the male body, about Danny's body, but everything she had experimented with so far had been a complete delight. She adored the way he could be powerful and masculine, but also vulnerable and at her mercy with just a simple touch.

"I adore you," he growled, pulling away from her long enough to remove his shoes and the rest of his clothes. Phoebe gasped and wriggled at the sight of his fully-naked body. The size and splendor of his erection had her aching to have him inside of her, but she had the feeling Danny was in a mood to drag things out as long as possible. "I am your servant, from now until the end of time," he said, climbing back over her for another lingering kiss.

Even though she still wore her corset, chemise, drawers, and stockings, she lifted her leg to cradle his hips. She wanted to feel her skin against his, to have him run his hands all over her body. He was intent on kissing her until she was breathless, though. His mouth against hers was downright wicked, and the way his staff pressed against the thin fabric of her drawers at the juncture of her thighs was scandalous. She didn't mind a little scandal, though. There would be loads of it as soon as their engagement was announced.

"No," he said, pulling up and balancing himself above her abruptly. "This won't do."

"What won't do?" Phoebe asked breathlessly.

"I want you naked," he said, starting on her corset's hooks. His hands were unsteady with passion, but he managed to work his way down from her breasts to her belly. "I want to see you flushed and giddy with pleasure in poses so obscene that even that bounder who writes the dirty stories wouldn't dare describe it in print."

Phoebe laughed and wriggled out of her corset, lifting her chemise over her head once he'd finished with the hooks. He tugged the drawstring of her drawers as she did, and between the two of them, she was every bit as naked as he was within moments.

"I should like very much to act out everything that so-called bounder wrote about us in his salacious stories," she said, opening her arms and legs to Danny as he surged back over her.

"Me too," he hummed before capturing her mouth in a searing kiss.

Everything about the way he kissed her, invading her with his tongue and teasing her with his teeth, ignited glittering sparks throughout Phoebe's body. The way he traced his hands gently along her sides one moment, then circled her breast and held her possessively, dropping his mouth to tease her nipple to a nub and to suckle her, was glorious. She wanted nothing more than to let him ravish her in whatever way he wanted. Every touch and every kiss ignited her, body and soul.

She was so consumed with joyous passion that when he paused, she whimpered in protest.

"I want you on top of me," he said, a wicked look in his eyes.

"On top of you?" Phoebe was both confused and thrilled by the idea.

Danny bit his lip, downright boyish mischief filling his eyes. He rolled off of her and onto his back, resting his head on the pillows. Phoebe's breath caught in her throat at the sight of him laid out that way, his sizeable penis standing straight up against his belly, like some sort of Greek satyr.

"Come here and ride me until we're both mad with pleasure, woman," he ordered her.

Excitement swirled through Phoebe as she crawled across the bed to him. It flashed to nervousness when she realized she had no idea what she was doing.

"Straddle me," he instructed her, his eyes dancing with mischief and lust.

Phoebe's heart beat in her throat and a giggle escaped from her as she followed directions, straddling his hips. "I must look ridiculous," she said, covering her face with her hands for a moment.

"Believe me, love. Ridiculous isn't the word. Not even close." His voice was deep and husky with desire.

He reached for her hips, pulling her forward a bit to the position he wanted her and caressing her backside. It felt wildly good to Phoebe, which made her bolder.

"What do I do next?" she asked with a grin.

"Take your hair down," he said.

Her eyes went wide at the simplicity of the request,

but she did as he'd asked, reaching up and pulling the pins from her hair. When she saw the heat that filled his eyes and the way his breath caught in his chest, she slowed her movements and teased him with what she hoped were lusty looks as she shook her hair loose down her back.

"God, you're pretty," he said, his voice a barely controlled growl.

"Now what do I do?" she asked.

"First, come here and give me a kiss." He crooked a finger at her.

Giggling again, Phoebe leaned forward and slanted her mouth over his. She was surprised at how empowering it felt to be the one kissing him, with him under her. She planted her hands on the pillows on either side of his head and thrust her tongue into his mouth as he'd done with her. He groaned with approval and caressed her backside, teasing his fingers deep between her legs. That gesture and the anticipation that came with it, made her impatient for more.

"What next?" she asked, stealing another kiss and grinding her hips against his. The heat and solidity of his member had her aching for union with him.

He must have felt the same way. "Take me in hand," he told her, voice deeper than ever, "and hold me upright."

With a shaky breath, Phoebe did as he instructed. Everything she needed to do next was suddenly clear to her, but she shivered with arousal all the same when he growled, "Now, fuck me."

Barely able to catch her breath, she positioned herself exactly as she needed to above him, then bore down, taking him deep inside of her. The sound she made as he slid deep within her, stretching her and causing glorious pleasure all through her, was wanton and shocking, but she loved it. His corresponding groan of satisfaction only heightened her enjoyment. Once she had him sheathed inside of her, however, she wasn't sure what to do.

"I'll help you," he panted, gripping her hips.

Without words, he taught her what to do, how to move on him while he jerked below her. They moved slowly at first, giving Phoebe time to learn the motions and how best to draw him in and out of her body. As soon as she got the hang of it and concentrated more on how she felt instead of what she was doing, her body answered with pleasure that coiled tighter and tighter inside of her.

"That's it, love," Danny rumbled, helping her move and thrusting himself. "That's definitely it."

He was watching her, drinking in the sight of her body as she strove for completion, and he was deriving as much pleasure from that as he was from being inside of her. Wickeder than ever, she smiled, arching back in an attempt to give him even more to gaze at. He made a sound that was as pleading as it was ravenous and jerked harder into her. Phoebe matched his movements, feeling the tell-tale signs of her body rushing toward completion. Her heart thundered within her as she watched him completely transported by everything she was doing. She was the one who had him exactly where she wanted him.

That feeling of power carried her over the edge. She burst into ecstasy as Danny bucked beneath her, pleasure throbbing through her so intensely that she threw her head back and cried out with it. Moments later, she felt Danny tense and surge, crying out himself as his seed spilled into her. It was shattering in its completeness, and the joy she felt as the intensity of their orgasms gave way to deep contentment was the stuff dreams were made of.

"That was brilliant," she panted as she settled onto the bed beside him.

"That was only the beginning, love," he laughed, twisting so that he could close his arms around her and kiss her with sated passion.

They were too exhausted and their bodies too over-heated to do more than lie in each other's arms, but as far as Phoebe was concerned, that was all she needed.

"If anyone attempts to dismiss me for marrying a simple pub owner," she said, "I will simply tell them that you are capable of all that. Then they will be ragingly jealous."

Danny laughed, nuzzling her neck. "I'll give them even more to be jealous about," he promised.

"I'm sure you will," Phoebe giggled, resting her head against his shoulder. "I'm sure you will for the rest of our lives."

EPILOGUE

$\mathcal{I}$t was the wedding of the season, and Lenore Garrett was thrilled to have an important role in it. Phoebe had asked her, along with Natalia Townsend and two charming girls named Hilda and Imogen from Harrods, to be her bridesmaid. That meant that not only was she close to the center of attention during the ceremony itself, when every one of the high and mighty aristocratic ladies who had shunned Phoebe in her hour of need flocked to St. Paul's Cathedral to see her marry a man who had recently been revealed as one of the wealthiest men in London, it meant she was one of the privileged few invited to the raucous reception, held at an ordinary music hall in Fitzrovia.

"I cannot imagine how the society pages of *The Times* will report on this," Freddy shouted to her over the din of the band playing and the jolly cries of Danny's long-term patrons from his pub.

"I don't think they have the vocabulary to describe it," Lenore called back to him, laughing as one of The Watchman's barmaids let out a screech when Freddy's friend, Lord Landsbury, a marquess, spun her onto the dance floor. "I don't think London is used to seeing this sort of social mingling."

"It's a horrific scandal, to be sure," Reese laughed from Freddy's other side. He followed that by grasping Freddy's hand and inching toward the dance floor. "Come on," he told Freddy with a shockingly intimate look. "This is one night when not a soul in attendance will care who dances with whom."

Freddy flushed under the heat of Reese's stare. He glanced to Lenore as if for approval.

"Go ahead," Lenore said with a casual shrug.

She grinned after Reese and Freddy as they dodged their way into the thick of the dancing crowd. They really were sweet together. She fancied herself quite the modern woman for thinking as much. But after nearly a year of being engaged to Freddy for the sole purpose of being allowed to stay in England—for reasons she had yet to whisper to a single one of her new, dear friends—she had seen how devoted the two men were to each other. It would be a blessing indeed if she found a man who loved her as much as Reese and Freddy loved each other.

"Miss Garrett, you look lovely this evening."

Lenore dragged her gaze away from Reese and Freddy to find the enigmatic, not to mention surprisingly handsome, Mr. Phineas Mercer approaching her.

He adjusted his spectacles as he took in the sight of her in a way that Lenore found as suggestive as it was charming.

"Mr. Mercer. How good to see you again." She smiled and extended her hand to him as any man would have done with another man. "You're looking quite well yourself."

And he most certainly was. In the few encounters Lenore had had with the man, she had come to believe that the reports of his ordinariness and unimpressive looks were entirely false. Yes, Mr. Mercer held himself in such a way that he didn't draw attention, his clothes were understated, and his spectacles were likely a deterrent to some of the vainer ladies of society. But, in fact, he had broad shoulders and a lean waist, his face was made up of strong, pleasing lines, his blue eyes were sharp, and his sandy hair made Lenore contemplate what it would be like to run her fingers through it.

"Thank you." Mr. Mercer bowed, then took up a position by Lenore's side, watching the dancers. "It was quite an unusual wedding," he said, opening a conversation.

Lenore felt in an instant that he was fishing for something. "It was," she agreed. "I don't think London society was prepared for it, but the whole thing reminded me of some of the shindigs we had back home when people married."

"Shindigs?" Mr. Mercer arched an eyebrow at her.

"As you will remember, Mr. Mercer, I'm from the

Wild West." Lenore grinned at him, eyes sparkling, she was sure.

Mr. Mercer tried to hide his enjoyment of her behind a staid smile. His eyes told a different story, however. He liked her.

He nodded to Freddy and Reese. "You don't mind the fact that your betrothed is dancing exuberantly with Lord Howsden?"

Lenore's grin turned wickedly knowing as she glanced to him. "Not at all."

The faintest bit of surprise registered in Mr. Mercer's expression. "Curious. And have you and Lord Harrington set a date for your own nuptials?"

"We have not," Lenore replied, her grin widening.

She had a feeling she knew precisely what Mr. Mercer was actually asking her. They'd enjoyed the brief time they'd spent together months ago while helping Phoebe to plot a way to expose Lord Cosgrove's villainy where Danny Long was concerned. Lenore had considered it a crying shame that their paths hadn't crossed much since then. She couldn't seem to get the mysterious man out of her head. He captivated her.

She realized with a start that she'd been studying him in silence for too long, and that a slow grin had spread across his expressive lips.

"I have something for you, Miss Garrett," he said once her focus was back on the moment.

"Oh?" She smiled. "I love unexpected gifts."

"I hope you will like this one," he said, reaching into

his jacket. He took out a small, crisp newspaper printed on pink-tinged paper. Lenore's mouth dropped. She knew exactly what the journal was, *Nocturne*. "Hot off the presses, as they say," Mr. Mercer said, handing it to her.

"Wherever did you get your hands on this?" she asked with a giddy giggle.

Mr. Mercer shrugged. "I have connections."

"I bet you do," Lenore said.

She thumbed through the first few pages, wondering what scandalous and juicy stories the latest issue of the erotic journal held. Before she could say anything, though, Mr. Mercer bowed abruptly and stepped away.

"Good evening, Miss Garrett. I hope we meet again soon," he said.

"You're not staying?" she called after him as he walked away. She'd been hoping he would ask her to dance.

"I have duties elsewhere," he said with that cryptic grin of his, nodded, then walked off.

Lenore watched him go, feeling as though she'd let something precious get away, then glanced at the copy of *Nocturne*.

As soon as she read the title of the first story, her heart caught in her chest. "Confessions of an American Heiress from the Wild West." Her mouth dropped as she read the first paragraph of the story. It leapt right into what purported to be a first-hand narrative of the scandalous adventures of a rancher's daughter let loose in London.

By the time she reached the second paragraph, Lenore's cheeks were burning.

"Oh, dear," she giggled, unsure whether to be scandalized or delighted. It seemed as though she was the latest victim of the mysterious erotica author's fantasies.

I HOPE YOU'VE ENJOYED PHOEBE AND DANNY'S story! I've actually had this one in mind for a long, long time, and it was so much fun to finally get to write it. Society and the concept of wealth was changing fast by the end of the nineteenth century. Old money and the families that had controlled it were dying out at a rate that alarmed the British upper classes. I'm sure you've heard plenty of stories of the American dollar princesses that swooped in to shore up the fortunes of great families (like the Churchills). And hint, hint, you'll get to hear more about dollar princesses and their aims when Lenore and Phineas have their day in *Scandal Meets Its Match*, coming soon!

But the other side of the story is Danny's side. Men who were born into middle-class circumstances were the ones who were rising to the top as the new brand of aristocracy, even though they didn't have titles. Yes, some were granted titles after the fact for their contributions, like the Rothschilds. But not everyone. I have a hard time believing Danny would accept a title if one were offered to him.

The other aspect of this story that was fun to write about was the development of Earl's Court. Whenever I visit London, I love to stay in Earl's Court. Not only is it convenient to two Tube stations, the architecture is just lovely. So me being me, I started researching the area, and I was surprised and delighted to find out that it was built up at exactly the time I've been writing about. London was in the midst of a decades-long housing crisis by the end of the nineteenth century as more and more people flocked into the city for factory, business, and commercial jobs. There was no place to put them at first, so the push to build hard and build fast was a huge one. Parliament was, indeed, responsible for handing out contracts to development companies, and more than a few men made huge fortunes on the developments.

I also just had to throw in a little shout out to my M/M series, The Brotherhood, in this book as well. Because it is also historically accurate that there were entire neighborhoods of London that were well known as being safe spots and enclaves for the LGBTQ community. Most of them were in areas like Marylebone and closer to the East End, but I took the liberty of having Danny's future development in Earl's Court be one of those secret-but-not-so-secret areas.

. . .

As I mentioned earlier, if you're curious about Lenore Garrett and Phineas Mercer, about Lenore's true reasons for coming all the way to England from America's Wild West, and about Phineas's super-secret, naughty, behind the scenes activities, be sure to read *Scandal Meets Its Match*, coming next month! Keep clicking to get started reading Chapter One now!

If you enjoyed this book and would like to hear more from me, please sign up for my newsletter! When you sign up, you'll get a free, full-length novella, *A Passionate Deception*. Victorian identity theft has never been so exciting in this story of hope, tricks, and starting over. Part of my *West Meets East* series, *A Passionate Deception* can be read as a stand-alone. Pick up your free copy today by signing up to receive my newsletter (which I only send out when I have a new release)!

Sign up here: http://eepurl.com/cbaVMH

Are you on social media? I am! Come and join the fun on Facebook: http://www.facebook.com/merryfarmerreaders

I'm also a huge fan of Instagram and post lots of original content there: https://www.instagram.com/merryfarmer/

. . .

AND NOW, GET STARTED ON SCANDAL MEETS ITS MATCH…

Chapter One

London – October, 1887

Lenore Garrett was perfectly happy with the way her life had turned out, though she was certain that almost every one of her friends back home in Haskell, Wyoming would balk and make faces at her if they knew the truth of her situation in life. What they didn't know wouldn't hurt them. Literally. And if they all believed that she had dashed off to foreign shores as one of dozens of American Dollar Princesses, intent on marrying a titled gentleman so that she could lord it over folks back home, then that's what they could believe.

Lenore knew better.

She'd traveled to England a year before with her father, who had made the trip for business purposes. Lenore had begged him to let her tag along. Indeed, her life had depended on it in very real ways. Her dear papa always had been indulgent, so of course he had allowed her to make the trip with him. He might not have been so quick to bring her to London if he'd known she had no intention whatsoever of returning to America. Ever. Returning to America, let alone Haskell, would be a death sentence.

"Do you need a drink of something?" Freddy—that is, Lord Frederick Herrington, Earl of Herrington, her fiancé—asked, leaning closer to her as they stood in the crowded theater lobby.

"Oh. What?" Lenore blinked her way out of her pensive thoughts and turned to Freddy, fanning herself furiously to cool her suddenly overheated face. "Do theaters serve refreshments before the show has started?"

Freddy shrugged, a genial smile on his handsome face as he glanced around the lobby for the answer to her question. "Probably not," he said. "But you look a bit piqued, so I thought I'd ask."

"Dear Freddy." Lenore grinned, resting her free hand in the crook of his arm. "You really are a gem." She raised her fan to hide her face from casual onlookers and proceeded to say, "Reese is a lucky man indeed."

"I most certainly am," Lord Reese Howsden said, leaning into Freddy's other side so that the three of them formed a secretive cluster. He winked for good measure.

Lenore knew full well he was winking at Freddy, even though, to the outside observer, it would look as though he were teasing Lenore with the wink. Lenore knew full well that Reese and Freddy were lovers, and that they were passionately devoted to each other in a union that was stronger than most marriages she knew. They'd even adopted a baby girl, Rose, from a tenant on Reese's country property to raise together, along with Reese's son, Harry, from his long-deceased wife, though to the rest of the world it seemed like nothing more than Reese's generosity at taking in a foundling child to keep his son company. Lenore knew the truth. Indeed, she considered herself a co-conspirator in her friends' love story.

And if she were honest—which she hadn't been, not as she should—the false engagement she had entered into with Freddy did far more to protect her than it ever would to protect Freddy and Reese.

"You do look a bit anxious, though," Reese picked up where Freddy had left off, frowning gently at Lenore. "Is the crowd?"

"I've never seen a crowd so large or so boisterous at an opening night for an untested play," Freddy added, glancing out over the packed lobby.

"All of London has been buzzing about this young upstart, Everett Jewel," Reese said with a slight shrug, nodding to the poster hung on one of the far walls. It depicted a dazzlingly handsome man, Mr. Jewel, dressed as the character he would be portraying that evening. "They say he's the greatest talent since Edmund Kean."

"Well, he's better looking than Kean at any rate," Freddy added with a laugh. "Much better looking."

"Don't get any ideas, love," Reese teased him, chuckling himself.

"It's hard not to with a figure like that," Freddy murmured, swaying closer to Reese.

"Are you trying to make me jealous?" Reese all but whispered in return.

"Stop," Lenore laughed loudly, drawing attention from some of the expectant theater-goers near them. "The two of you will land in hot soup if you don't behave with a little more decorum."

"Land in the soup?" Reese snorted. "Is that an Americanism?"

"No one would dare to suggest I am guilty of any impropriety when I have such a dazzling and clever fiancée," Freddy said, inching closer to Lenore and hugging her arm to his side.

Lenore chuckled and smacked him with her fan. She would never be in love with Freddy, for obvious reasons, but he was the best friend she ever could have hoped for. Reese as well. The three of them made the perfect team. The antics they got up to—with or without involving the children—were almost enough to content her with not finding real love.

Almost.

"Are you certain you're still happy with our arrangement?" Freddy asked, as if sensing her thoughts. Or perhaps he'd read her expression, which had fallen as her attention was snagged by a particularly amorous couple at the far end of the lobby. She knew Lady Agnes Hamilton vaguely. The way the woman smiled adoringly at Lord Granger, her color high and her eyes bright, left

Lenore with a wistful feeling in her chest that she couldn't avoid.

"I am perfectly happy," Lenore said, standing straighter and insisting inwardly that she wasn't saying that to convince herself. "I have a delightful life here in England. I have wonderful friends. And I get to attend opening nights of plays that all of London will be talking about tomorrow."

"True," Freddy said, tilting his head to the side, then leaning closer to go on with, "But I've come to know you well enough in this last year to know that you would be much happier if you could end the evening in bed with a bloke who fancies you instead of curled up with yet another issue of *Nocturne* and the unmentionable item you failed to hide fast enough when I knocked on your boudoir door to see if you were ready earlier."

Lenore's already flushed face went beet red at Freddy's mention of the artifact in question. "You're not supposed to even know about such things," she hissed, "let alone mentioning them in public."

"Darling," he said with a smirk. "I not only know about those things, Reese and I have an entire set for when we're in particularly high spirits."

Lenore laughed so hard she snorted, drawing far more attention than she needed to. She found herself feigning a coughing fit just so that the middle-aged matron who frowned at her would glance away instead of attempting to listen in on the conversation.

"I find *Nocturne* to be quite enough on its own at the

moment," she whispered to Freddy. "The stories in that particular periodical are educational as well as entertaining." She assumed a superior attitude and punctuated her statement with a nod.

"That publication is pure smut," Reese said, leaning in so that the three of them formed a triumvirate again. "Which is why everyone adores it, of course."

Lenore and Freddy both laughed like naughty schoolchildren who had been caught with the journal in question. In fact, *Nocturne* had been captivating London audiences for over a year with its highly erotic content. Mostly because every scandalous story contained in its pages was clearly about someone in society who everyone knew, based on their behavior at various parties and events throughout the season. The new season had yet to officially begin, but London was buzzing with enough activity that high and low both were waiting with baited breath for the latest edition, which was weeks overdue, as far as everyone was concerned.

In more ways than one, Lenore considered herself lucky to have avoided inclusion in *Nocturne*. She was exactly the sort who its author—whoever that may have been—included in its pages. She was young, beautiful, wealthy, and American. And she wasn't particularly shy about making her presence known at social events. But it was all the things that society didn't know about her, all the things that even Freddy and Reese didn't know about her, that she dreaded the author of *Nocturne* getting wind of. As flattering to her saucy sense of vanity as it might have been to be included in *Nocturne's* pages, she had too many things to hide.

A burst of shrill laughter shook Lenore's out of her thoughts, and she glanced across the room to see Lady Agnes nearly hyperventilating as she clung to Lord Granger's arm. The circle of waiting theater patrons near the pair took a step back, affording the couple a bit of space. Lady Agnes seemed to be dancing on her spot and fanned herself furiously as her laughter continued unabated. Lenore frowned. Whatever Lady Agnes was up to, it was more than simply flirting. If she had been a betting man, like her father, she would have said something was wrong with the poor woman.

No sooner had that thought struck her than Lenore spotted a shadowy figure beyond Lady Agnes, near the theater door, staring straight at her. Her heart leapt in her chest, and she suddenly felt every bit as agitated as Lady Agnes.

"Is that Mr. Mercer staring at you as though he'd like to take a bite out of you?" Freddy asked with a teasing grin.

"I believe it is," Lenore said with feigned casualness, fanning herself as she made eye-contact with Mr. Phineas Mercer.

"Have you two spoken since that coup you pulled to get old what's his name to confess to burning down Danny Long's pub?" Freddy asked on.

"Only in passing, at parties and the like," Lenore said, cursing herself for sounding so breathless. "We had quite a conversation at Lady Phoebe and Mr. Long's wedding reception."

"You should go over and say hello to him." Freddy let go of her arm and nudged her into motion. "I'm sure he'd love the chance to be reacquainted."

Lenore glanced over her shoulder at Freddy with a flat stare that said she knew exactly what he was up to. Knowing didn't stop her from heading toward Phineas, though. Freddy leaned in to say something to Reese, no doubt at Lenore's expense, as she faced forward, setting her sights on Phineas.

WANT TO READ MORE?
PICK UP SCANDAL MEETS ITS MATCH TODAY!

Click here for a complete list of other works by Merry Farmer.

ABOUT THE AUTHOR

I hope you have enjoyed *The Road to Scandal is Paved with Wicked Intentions*. If you'd like to be the first to learn about when new books in the series come out and more, please sign up for my newsletter here: http://eepurl.com/cbaVMH And remember, Read it, Review it, Share it! For a complete list of works by Merry Farmer with links, please visit http://wp.me/P5ttjb-14F.

Merry Farmer is an award-winning novelist who lives in suburban Philadelphia with her cats, Torpedo, her grumpy old man, and Justine, her hyperactive new baby. She has been writing since she was ten years old and real-ized one day that she didn't have to wait for the teacher to assign a creative writing project to write something. It was the best day of her life. She then went on to earn not one but two degrees in History so that she would always have something to write about. Her books have reached the Top 100 at Amazon, iBooks, and Barnes & Noble, and have been named finalists in the prestigious RONE and Rom Com Reader's Crown awards.

ACKNOWLEDGMENTS

I owe a huge debt of gratitude to my awesome beta-readers, Caroline Lee and Jolene Stewart, for their suggestions and advice. And double thanks to Julie Tague, for being a truly excellent editor and assistant!

Click here for a complete list of other works by Merry Farmer.

Made in the USA
Columbia, SC
08 May 2021